SHADOWGHAST

THOMAS TAYLOR
ILLUSTRATED BY TOM BOOTH

WALKER BOOKS

Text and map copyright © 2021 by Thomas Taylor
Illustrations copyright © 2021 by Tom Booth

First US edition 2021

Library of Congress Catalog Card Number pending
ISBN 978-1-5362-0860-3

21 22 23 24 25 26 LSC 10 9 8 7 6 5 4 3 2 1

Printed in Crawfordsville, IN, USA

This book was typeset in Bell MT.
The illustrations were created digitally.

Walker Books US
a division of
Candlewick Press
99 Dover Street
Somerville, Massachusetts 02144

www.walkerbooksus.com

A JUNIOR LIBRARY GUILD SELECTION

FOR BENJY

TT

MAP
OF
EERIE-ON-SEA

Harbor Wall

S E A   M I S T

Seegol's Diner

Theater at the End of the Pier

The Wreck of the LEVIATHAN

THE PIER

M A W   R O C K S

CONTENTS

CHAPTER 1

ALL HALLOWS' EVE

o you remember your first Ghastly Night?

The first time you saw Eerie-on-Sea's special Halloween show?

The first time you gathered on the pier with your friends and family and huddled in the cold night air—and the glow of the manglewick candles—as you waited for the magic to begin?

Perhaps you were carried there on your dad's shoulders, caramel apple in one hand, sparkler in the other? Or perhaps you peeked from snug inside your mum's coat as the puppet master lit the lantern.

Remember how you blinked in the beam of eerie light?

Remember how the strange fumes tickled your nose?

Remember how you gasped in wonder as the showman's hands conjured puppets of shadow—forms and phantasmagoria that crept and capered and danced above you in the smoky autumn air?

And did you see it?

Did you catch a glimpse of that *extra* shadow—one not made by the skillful showman's fingers?

A shadow not cast by anything at all?

A crooked figure, cavorting in dark delight at the edge of the lantern's beam, never—when you turned to look—quite where you thought it was, but always there, hunting, tormenting, *snatching* the showman's shadow puppets one by one till the show was ended.

And the smoke curled away to nothing.

And all the shadows were gone.

And no sound remained but the hiss of the lantern and the creak of the pier and the churn of the endless sea.

Well? *Do* you remember?

Did you ever see the Shadowghast?

But what am I saying?

Of course you didn't!

You've probably never even heard of Ghastly Night, or manglewick candles, or any of it.

Unless, that is, you've been to Eerie-on-Sea before, and asked too many questions. But even then, I'm sure you'd have forgotten this strange tradition of ours, falling as it does on the night the rest of the world knows as Halloween. Like most people at this time of year, you're probably too busy carving pumpkins or planning your trick-or-treat costume to pay much attention to the funny old ways of a little seaside town. Too busy make-believing in goblins and ghosts to worry about the one legend of a bad spirit that might actually be true.

And that's fine.

For you.

But if you lived in Eerie, you'd see it differently. If you stayed behind when the summer tourists left, and the candy-colored signs of seaside fun faded into the dark of winter, you'd know. You, too, would hurry a little faster through the blustery streets as the days grew shorter and the shadows long. And when the end of October finally arrived, you'd put up a manglewick candle for protection, too.

Just in case.

Just in case this is the year that Ghastly Night is forgotten and no showman lights a lantern on the pier to conjure shadow puppets in offering to the dark. For if that should ever happen, so folks say, the Shadowghast—enraged by the insult—would hunt instead for the shadows of the living.

But I see you're smiling.

You're still thinking the Shadowghast is nothing more than a silly superstition.

No more than a trick of the light.

Only, remember this: at the heart of every legend is a spark of truth. And when the sunlight dies and you're running from the shadows through the deepening streets of Eerie-on-Sea, a spark—no matter how small—is sometimes all you need.

Unless that trick of the light is actually a trick of the dark.

CHAPTER 2

BIRTHDAY BREAKFAST

S ome words just seem to belong together, don't they?
Like *magic* and *lantern*, or *strange* and *shadow*, or *fireside*
and *story*. But right now, in the light of morning and the
warmth of the hotel dining room, no words seem to go together
quite so well as *hot* and *buttered* and *toast*.

And I should know. When it comes to breakfast, I, Herbert
Lemon—Lost-and-Founder at the Grand Nautilus Hotel—am
something of an expert. Which is why I'm concealed behind this
giant potted fern, pressing my nose against the glass panels in
the dining room wall as the kitchen staff load trays of delicious
things onto the sideboard, experting as hard as I can.

Today is a special day, and a breakfast to end all breakfasts is spreading out before my eyes, dancing up my nostrils, and making my gums go tingly.

Don't believe me? Well, come and press your nose to the window next to mine and take a look for yourself at the heaps of sizzled sausages, at the stacks of bacon strips, at the mounds of crispy, hot hash browns. At the eggs, fried white with yolks ready to run, or scrambled to light and peppery perfection; at the honey-glazed button mushrooms, seared tomatoes, and piping-hot baked beans; at the toast, fried or hot and buttered (yes!); at the baskets of just-baked, golden-flaked continental pastries; at the waffles and maple syrup; at the breakfast doughnuts, sparkling with sugar and filled with Chef's special raspberry jam.

And in the center of it all, towering above the silverware,

fine bone china, and antique knives and forks, stands an enormous cut-glass bowl filled to the creamy brim with a festive and magnificent sherry trifle, topped with a single glacé cherry.

No wonder my window is getting fogged up! I bet yours is, too.

Because, you see, today is Lady Kraken's birthday. And Lady Kraken, the owner of the Grand Nautilus Hotel, has long since decreed that on her birthday a special breakfast will be served, and all—*all*—the hotel staff are invited.

The lady herself won't be present, of course. She never is these days, not now that she's become such a recluse. But once her own breakfast—a single hard-boiled egg and a thimble of ground cumin—has been carried up to the sixth floor beneath a gleaming silver dome and served in her private chambers with a small cup of black coffee, the rest of us can dig in.

At least, that's the theory. But there's a complication . . .

"Hurry along!" come the peevish tones of Mr. Mollusc as he claps his hands in clammy command. "Let's get this over with. The sooner you all get back to work the better."

And I duck down below the glass panel as he strides across the dining room, twitching his mustache in anticipation at the bacon and pastries. You see, while it's Lady Kraken who is giving us all breakfast this morning, it's Mr. Mollusc, the hotel manager, who decides who eats it first.

And last.

"Are you worried you won't get any?" asks a female voice behind me, and I jump. A hotel guest must have found me hiding in the fern! I should turn around to see if she needs something, but I can't tear my eyes away from the dining room, where the breakfast situation is developing in alarming ways.

Mr. Mollusc has seated himself at the best table and is waving the waiters over to pile sausages and eggs on his plate. On the far side of the restaurant, the chambermaids, who will be next, are already beginning to gather in a hungry line.

"Well, I didn't get any last year!" I explain to the person behind me. "Or the year before that. Me not getting any of Lady Kraken's birthday breakfast has almost become part of the tradition."

"Oh," says the voice. "That's sad."

"Well, I *might* get a croissant," I admit as I see a waiter lay three of the buttery pastries at the manager's elbow. "If there are any left. But only once it's been lying around a day or two to get all stale and chewy."

"This year will be different, Herbie," says the voice. And it's a lovely voice, too, like dark honey, and it makes the nape of my neck go all ticklish. "I promise."

I feel a hand straighten my cap gently, then pat me on the shoulder.

And I go still.

The breakfast smells have stepped aside, making way for a wisp of perfume, though it's gone before I can get a good sniff. I'm left wanting to smell that perfume again. I finally turn around to see who was speaking, but there's nothing there now except the fronds of the fern I thought I was hiding behind. I get a bit tangled in the pesky plant before I can step back out into the lobby to see who it was.

There are people at the reception desk, checking into the hotel. A stout red-faced man with a homburg hat is being handed several room keys by Amber Griss, the hotel receptionist, while two tall men dressed head-to-toe in black stand behind him, laden with boxes and cases. None of these seems like the lovely-voice-and-perfume type, but beyond them is a fourth figure.

A woman is standing beside the brass elevator, her back to

me. She is tall and willowy, with raven hair, and wears a black embroidered coat that catches the light in odd ways. I find myself wishing the woman would turn around, but she doesn't.

Then something strange happens.

The clouds over Eerie-on-Sea part, and a ray of golden sunlight streams through one of the tall hotel windows, and over the group.

And I see . . .

something!

Something wrong with the scene, with the way the light falls, or the way the shadows are cast, or . . .

I rub my eyes and blink as I try to get a fix on the strange effect, but just then the elevator arrives and the woman with the raven hair steps into it. The men with the luggage crowd in behind her. The elevator door closes, and they are gone.

I rub my eyes again. Maybe I'm going a bit bonkers due to lack of breakfast.

But I can't help wondering about the woman with the raven hair.

Who is she? What did she mean?

And, I ask out loud, "How does she know my name?"

CHAPTER 3

MR. MUMMERY

First of the oddballs already arrived, then?" I say to Amber
Griss at the reception desk.

Amber gives me a warning tut.

"Don't let Mr. Mollusc hear you talk about our guests that
way, Herbie."

She doesn't add "even though it's true," but she doesn't need
to. We both know that Lady Kraken's birthday, falling as it does
near the end of October, marks the beginning of the winter
season. We won't see a shovel-and-pail tourist for months now.
But what we will see, as the town closes up and the weather
closes in, is . . . well, we'll just have to wait to find out, won't
we? But one thing's for sure: in Eerie-on-Sea, in the winter,

we're bound to see *something*. Whether we want to or not.

"Who are they?" I ask, trying to catch a name in the register that Amber is writing in. "Those new guests? They had some weird-looking luggage."

"They're a theater troupe of some kind." Amber closes the book quickly and clicks her pen.

"But have they stayed here before?" I'm still wondering how the woman with the raven hair knew my name.

"I don't recognize them," Amber replies. "All I know is that they've been invited to town to put on this year's Ghastly Night show."

"Really?" I say.

"It's Lady Kraken's idea," Amber explains. "She thinks it's time we celebrated the thing properly again, in the theater on the pier, like in the old days . . ."

Then Amber trails off, her spectacles flashing in warning as she spots something over my shoulder.

I do a gulp.

I know what's coming.

My mind races as I try to think of a way to make myself look busy, but since I'm leaning on the reception desk with my hands in my pockets and my Lost-and-Founder's cap at a jaunty angle, I don't have much to work with.

"Herbert Lemon!" comes the jabby voice of Mr. Mollusc

behind me. "What precisely are you doing? Or rather *not* doing. Just because you don't have any proper work to do doesn't mean you should keep Miss Griss from doing hers."

I turn around and slowly straighten my cap. The hotel manager is standing over me, his mustache bristling with annoyance. There's a blob of egg yolk on his tie.

"I was *sort of* doing work, sir," I reply. "I was just offering to cover Reception while Amber . . . Miss Griss, I mean . . . goes in for the yummy birthday breakfast. I wouldn't want her to miss out, sir. Imagine not getting any breakfast at all, sir! That would be sad, wouldn't it, sir?"

And I give him my most hardworking and deserving face, full beam.

"Yes, well . . ." says Mr. Mollusc, ignoring the face completely. "You should indeed go in for the breakfast now, Miss Griss. There is still a little left, though there won't be for long—the laundry workers are in next, and then the kitchen staff will polish off the rest, I expect. I suggest you make haste, Miss Griss. The bacon is already finished."

"!" I blurt out, because I can't help myself. *Bacon* and *finished* are two words that never go well together. "Sir . . . !"

Mollusc ignores me as he waves Amber away.

"I will watch the reception desk myself," he declares as if doing everyone an enormous favor. Then he sinks into Amber's chair and finally looks me in the eye. "I suggest you go watch yours, boy."

"But . . . !"

"No buts!" Mr. Mollusc shuts me down. "And no sneaking out the cellar window, either. Oh, yes, Mr. Lemon, I know all about that. I'm tempted to move the hotel garbage cans in front of that window to stop you and that annoying friend of yours from climbing in and out. This is a respectable hotel, not a school for burglars. Now, go!"

And just like that, I'm dismissed. I trudge back to my cubbyhole, my feet heavy, my tummy a birthday-breakfast–free zone once again.

So much for this year being different!

✿⚙✿

If you've been to the Grand Nautilus Hotel before, you'll know all about my cubbyhole. It's in the hotel lobby, across the polished marble floor from Reception. It's a little arched opening in the wall, with a flip-up desk so that I can get in and out. The cubbyhole is the only part of the Lost-and-Foundery the guests ever see, so it probably doesn't look like much. But if you've stayed here, and if you lost something while you did, you probably found yourself at my desk at least once, ringing the bell, waiting for yours truly to come to help. And I bet, if you did report something missing, there's a good chance I found it for you, too. Because—whatever you may have heard old Mollusc say—I'm actually quite good at my job.

I flip up the desk and flop down in my chair.

There is a folded piece of paper waiting for me, with a big *H L* for Herbert Lemon scrawled on it. A message? I open it up and read what's there:

Herbie, come quick! It's an emergency!! Lost-and-Foundering urgently required!!! Bring Clermit!!!!

Violet x

I sigh. Not this again!

Violet—my very best friend in Eerie-on-Sea—did not have a good summer. She arrived last year in the depths of winter and promptly propelled me into two—*two!*—epic adventures that would make your niblets go knobbly if you heard about them. Adventures that left her expecting life in Eerie-on-Sea to be nonstop mystery and excitement forever. But the long ice-cream months of May to September—with their tourists and deck chairs and sandy swimming trunks—were a disappointment to Violet. She's been itching to find another Eerie adventure for weeks now, and every note she sends claiming to have spotted one has more exclamation marks on it than the last.

But I'm not in the mood for this right now. I glance again at the door of the elevator and get a memory rush of the mysterious raven-haired woman's intoxicating perfume. I'll go to see Violet later.

My eye falls on a white pearlescent shell on a shelf nearby.

"Hello, Clermit," I say to the shell as I lift it down and blow a few loose grains of sand from out of the brass-rimmed keyhole in its side.

It may seem funny that a shell should have a name (and a keyhole!), but *this* shell is special. Not only does it have some nifty clockwork inside, but, you see, I once made this shell a promise.

Clermit—which is short for "clockwork hermit crab"—is one of the lost things in my Lost-and-Foundery. I need to take care of him until I can find his rightful owner. I've been carefully cleaning him over the summer, but I can't quite bring myself to wind his winder-upper just yet. Last time I did, it led to one of those epic adventures I mentioned.

Violet has been begging me to wind Clermit again for *months*.

I pick up a fine screwdriver and carefully coax out a few more grains of sand from inside the clockwork hermit crab's fabulously complicated mechanism. I can't help wondering what the woman with the raven hair would say if she came along and saw me fixing such a beautiful and complicated little gadget . . .

I put Clermit down and sigh.

I don't seem to be able to concentrate on anything today.

I look at the bell on my desk.

I find myself fantasizing that the raven-haired woman is about to ring it and ask for my help. I'd like that. And I'd jump straight to it, too, and be amazing, and help her out, and Mr. Mollusc would grind his teeth because she would smile and say, for all to hear, "Oh, Herbie, you are the greatest Lost-and-Founder I have ever met" and "This year will be different, Herbie, I promise you that," and I like this daydream so much that I can almost see her slender hand reaching out and ringing my bell with a bright and cheery . . .

TING!

My bell rings sharply, and I slide off my elbow, blinking at it in surprise.

There is indeed a hand there, but it's far from slender.

TING! goes the bell again as a podgy red finger hits the *ting*-er once more with a short, bad-tempered poke.

"Are you open?" says a voice. "It says on the sign that you are open."

I look up. Instead of the mysterious raven-haired woman, the stout man with the homburg hat is glaring at me. It's such a shock to see him there that my cap slips over my eyes.

"This year will be different!" I blurt out before I can stop myself. I push the cap back onto my head. "I mean, yes, I'm open. Herbert Lemon, Lost-and-Founder, at your service."

"Hmm," says the man. "Not much to look at, are you?"

I'm not quite sure how to answer that, so instead I take a

moment to do a bit of looking of my own. The man is even more red-faced than I realized, and he wears a dark-gray suit that stretches across his belly thanks only to three waistcoat buttons under enormous strain. He looks nothing like an actor in town to put on a show. He looks more like a banker, here to close down the show and throw everyone out for not paying rent.

"I try my best," I say eventually. "I could stand up, if that would help."

"It would," says the man briskly. "I have been sent to summon you. I . . ."

But before he can say more, Mr. Mollusc slides into view beside him.

"Excuse me, sir, but is the boy bothering you?" says the hotel manager.

"No, not yet," the man in the hat replies.

"Are you sure?" Mollusc is clearly disappointed. "He's good at hiding it."

"Yes, he seems the type." The man narrows his eyes at me as if his worst suspicions have just been confirmed. Then he turns. "And you are?"

"Mr. Mollusc. I run this hotel."

"Ah," puffs the man in the hat, brightening a little. "And I am Mr. Mummery, theatrical agent. How do you do, Mr. Mollusc?"

"And how do *you* do, Mr. Mummery," replies the manager, and

Mollusc and Mummery shake hands and nod at each other, and I have a bad feeling that I'm watching the birth of a horrible double act. Sure enough, once the greeting is over, the two men turn and fix me with exactly the same expression of doubt and disdain.

"Um," I say, because I think it's about time I said something. I raise an eyebrow at Mr. Mummery. "Did you say I was being summoned?"

"Indeed," Mummery replies. "Against my better judgment, I must say. You are to come with me to the sixth floor, Herbert Lemon, to Lady Kraken's private rooms. It is time for your interview. Everybody is waiting."

"Interview?" I can feel the cap slipping over my eyes again. "But . . . how . . . ? *What . . . ?*"

"There's no need to look so alarmed," says Mr. Mummery. "I'm sure you've prepared thoroughly. Now, come along."

"Is the boy . . . ?" Mr. Mollusc gasps, a look of desperate hope in his face. "Is the boy in some kind of *trouble?*"

"That"—Mr. Mummery glances down his stubby red nose at me—"remains to be seen."

And with this he sets off at a brisk walk toward the great brass elevator of the Grand Nautilus Hotel, clearly expecting me to follow.

And what else can I do?

Under the gaze of a triumphant Mr. Mollusc, I scuttle after him.

CHAPTER 4

SMOKE AND MIRRORS

I'm in a daze as I get into the elevator. I'm still in a daze as I get out of it. What's happening? *What* interview? I haven't done anything!

Or have I?

At least, I tell myself, Lady Kraken will be there. My employer may be as loopy as a bowl of spaghetti, but she won't let anything happen to me.

Or will she?

Oh, bladderwracks!

As I follow my mysterious companion down the coral-pink and sea-blue corridor that ends at the door to the Jules Verne Suite, I finally find enough of a straight line in my brain to speak to him.

"I *haven't* prepared," I say. "I don't know what any of this is about!"

"You haven't?" Mr. Mummery stops and turns. "You *don't*? But you are Herbert Lemon, are you not? Lost-and-Founder at the Grand Nautilus Hotel?"

"Well, yes, but—"

"You are the boy who washed up on the beach at Eerie-on-Sea in a crate of lemons? The shipwrecked boy who has no memory of his past?"

I nod, wide-eyed.

"Then there is no mistake," Mr. Mummery replies. "You are the claimant."

"Claimant? But I haven't claimed anything?"

"Maybe not," Mr. Mummery sniffs impatiently, as if that is merely an inconvenient detail, "but you have been sought for many years. My employer has corresponded with your employer these last few weeks, and now, finally, we are here to cross-examine you in person. Kindly try to be a little more convincing, or our journey will have been wasted."

And with this he turns and continues down the corridor.

"Who . . . ?" I ask as I run to catch up. "*Who* is your employer?"

"As for that," Mr. Mummery responds, with a tone that suggests he's tired of my questions, "you are about to meet her. I suggest you straighten your cap and stop twitching, boy."

And with this he pulls the cord beside the great doors to Lady Kraken's private suite, causing the *ding* of a distant bell. A moment later, on the panel beside the door, a light bulb flickers on, illuminating tiny curly letters that say:

COME IN.

The doors swing open, and I am faced with the gloom beyond.

Mr. Mummery propels me inside.

⚙️

The first thing I see is the large circular table that Lady Kraken keeps in the dead center of her sitting room. It is usually covered in a layer of dust, like much of its owner's possessions, but today there is a patterned tablecloth over it. And on the cloth there are teacups, an ornate teapot, and a plate of untouched golden pastries, just like the ones Chef makes. Despite everything, my tummy manages a *blurble* of hunger at the sight of them.

"Ah, there you are, Mr. Lemon," says a creaky old voice, and Lady Kraken—the owner of the Grand Nautilus Hotel—trundles her antique electric wheelchair into the lamplight. "What have you got to say for yourself, eh?"

"Um . . ." I flap my mouth open and closed until I find an answer. "Happy birthday, Lady Kraken?"

"Good lad." The old lady bobs her wrinkly head. "I trust

you enjoyed the special breakfast? The fancies? The trifle? I'm a hundred and something today!"

And she creases her wizened face into a turtle smile.

I'm about to exclaim, "What breakfast?" but there's something in Lady K's face that I've never seen before. And a similar something in her voice. And though I don't know what that something is, it leaves me with a sudden sense that everything has changed.

"Come closer, Herbie," Lady Kraken continues. "No need to fiddle with your buttons, boy. There is someone here to see you."

And so I come forward. Then I turn.

The woman with the raven hair is sitting in a high-backed armchair across from Lady Kraken. She's still wearing her coat, which is in iridescent raven shades itself and embroidered in complex ways that make it hard to look at. Her face, which is proud and pale, reminds me of a fairy-tale queen, and her dark eyes shine bright. She doesn't take them off me as she gets to her feet.

"The Lemon boy," says Mr. Mummery, indicating yours truly, as if there can be any doubt. "Would you like me to conduct the questioning, Caliastra?"

"No," the woman replies. "Wait for me downstairs, and take Rictus and Tristo with you. I can handle this from here."

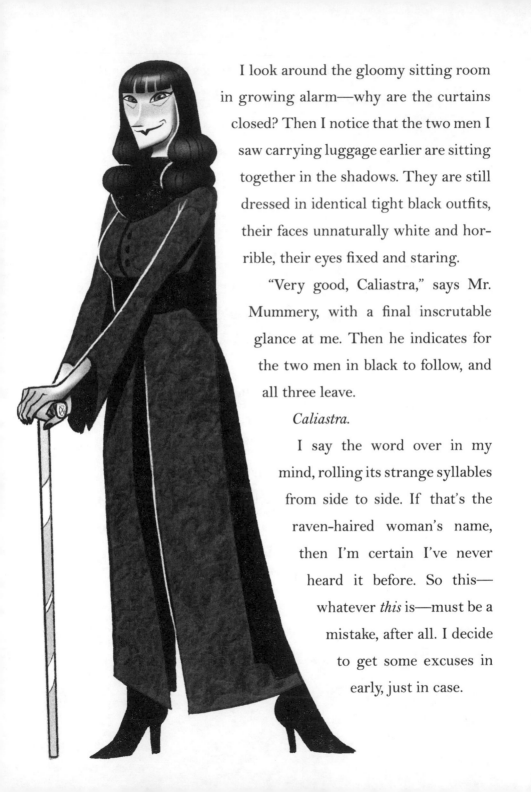

I look around the gloomy sitting room in growing alarm—why are the curtains closed? Then I notice that the two men I saw carrying luggage earlier are sitting together in the shadows. They are still dressed in identical tight black outfits, their faces unnaturally white and horrible, their eyes fixed and staring.

"Very good, Caliastra," says Mr. Mummery, with a final inscrutable glance at me. Then he indicates for the two men in black to follow, and all three leave.

Caliastra.

I say the word over in my mind, rolling its strange syllables from side to side. If that's the raven-haired woman's name, then I'm certain I've never heard it before. So this— whatever *this* is—must be a mistake, after all. I decide to get some excuses in early, just in case.

"Can I just say, I'm *really* sorry?" I begin, backing away. "I didn't mean to do it. And I won't *ever* do it again. And I'll tidy up the mess and/or apologize, as required. Also, it wasn't really me. I wasn't even there!"

And I trip backward into an empty chair, sending up a cloud of dust.

"But my dear boy!" cries the woman called Caliastra. "You aren't in any trouble." And she smiles a dazzling smile that is every bit as wonderful as the one I imagined downstairs. "Maybe this is too sudden," she continues, turning to Lady Kraken. "Maybe I should have waited a day or two before presenting myself to him? But I've waited so long already."

"Maybe." Lady Kraken shrugs in response, making the wicker back of her wheelchair creak like a haunted house. "But I find the best way with dunderbrains is to just get it out and tell 'em straight."

Caliastra nods. She tugs flat the front of her coat and brushes imaginary crumbs from its immaculate black surface as she rises. I do the same thing when I'm nervous and want to make a good impression. I take the chance to get a good look at her then—at her strong features, her long nose and high cheeks. It's the face of someone who is used to commanding people. So why would someone like that care what a scrappy-haired and slightly crumpled Lost-and-Founder like me thinks?

"Herbie," she says. "May I call you Herbie?"

I nod, holding my cap in place.

"I am Caliastra," the woman continues. "But that is not my real name. It is my stage name. Perhaps you have heard of it?"

I haven't. I try to look polite, but I think I'm probably blinking too much for that.

"No matter." Caliastra seems genuinely unconcerned by this. "That is the name I am known by in London, Paris, New York—wherever I perform my act. I'm pleased to say I enjoy some success with my little magic show, even if my fame hasn't yet reached the basement of the Grand Nautilus Hotel."

"Magic?" I gasp. "You're a . . . a . . . ?"

A change comes over Caliastra as I struggle to get the word out. She fixes me with a crafty eye. Then she holds out one hand, palm outward, pale fingers splayed. She flips her hand over, then back again, so that I can see that both sides are empty. She allows her sleeve to fall away, revealing a bare wrist.

Then she snaps her fingers.

A playing card appears from nowhere—the queen of hearts—held between her slender fingers. She snaps again and now the card is flying, spinning furiously. It makes a neat circular flight around the room—once, twice—before returning to Caliastra's hand, which hasn't moved at all. She plucks the card from the air and snaps one more time, and there is a flash of explosive light.

I blink as a sulphurous smell assaults my nose.

When I can look again, the card . . .

is gone!

Caliastra presents her hand for inspection, and it's as empty as before. Then she raises an eyebrow at my Lost-and-Founder's cap.

Really?

I reach up, disbelieving, and take off my cap.

There's something inside.

It's a playing card.

"Goodness me!" croaks Lady Kraken.

"The queen of hearts," I whisper as I stare at the card in my hand. Then I look up at the raven-haired woman with the dazzling smile. "You're a magician!"

"I am," Caliastra replies. Then she gives an elaborate bow. "But just as *Caliastra* is not my real name, so, too, is *Herbert Lemon*—Herbie—not yours."

I can't speak. I try to put my cap back on my head and miss.

"But I know your real name, Herbie," she says. "I know who you really are because . . ."

Caliastra stops, her words stumbling over a choke of emotion. She takes a moment to compose herself before continuing.

"Do you have any memory of your life before, Herbie? Do you have any memories of your mother?"

CHAPTER 5

CALIASTRA

M y mother."

I say the word blandly, forgetting even to add a question mark, as if the word *mother*—which goes so well with almost any word in the dictionary—doesn't have anything to do with me, even though my mind is exploding and my vision tunnels in on the woman standing in front of me with a look on her face that I can't describe.

"Yes," that woman says in a whisper.

"What?" Lady Kraken gasps. *"What!"*

I start to shake.

"I mean, yes, *I knew her,*" Caliastra adds hastily. "I . . . I *knew* your mother, Herbie. Because we . . . were very close.

Yes, as close as can be. She was my . . . sister."

My world spins a little less dizzyingly as a different realization dawns. But it's still an extraordinary one.

"That means . . ." I start to reply.

"Yes, Herbie," Caliastra says, glancing at Lady Kraken as if for assurance. Lady Kraken's eyes are nothing but slits of suspicion now. "That would make me your aunt." Then she hits me with that smile again. "I've tracked you down, at long last, my boy. I'm here to take you home."

"Let's not get too far ahead of ourselves, shall we?" Lady Kraken cuts across my silence. And that's when I recognize the "something" in my employer's voice, the something I noticed earlier. Lady Kraken has ruled this hotel for years, and her word holds sway over everyone within it, all the way down to me. But now, suddenly, there is someone with a claim on me that supersedes hers.

If, that is, the claim is true.

"Herbert Lemon has been my Lost-and-Founder since the day he washed up in Eerie," Lady Kraken declares. "No matter that he is the most dunderous of dunderbrains, and a ninnyhammer, to boot, he is my responsibility and not to be claimed by just anyone. At least," Lady K adds, as if conceding the point, "not without proof."

"Of course," says the magician, sitting back down in her

chair and crossing her legs. "And I wouldn't dream of coming here and telling you this without some way to back it up. If we were in a story right now, I suppose this would be the moment I would mention his strawberry birthmark."

"I have a strawberry birthmark?" I cry. I scan my body with my mind's eye, trying to remember if I've seen such a thing in the bathroom mirror. I'm pretty sure I haven't. Unless it's tucked away somewhere I never think to look. I feel my face going as red as a whole *basket* of strawberries.

"No!" Caliastra says with a bright chuckle. "But you do have a *V*-shaped scar on your left forearm. Don't you, Herbie?"

I stare at Lady Kraken. She bobs her head at me. Then both our eyes swivel down to look at my left arm, which is covered by the sleeve of my uniform. Lady K twists her lamp so that light falls on it. I pull the sleeve back.

There, on my arm, is a little white *V* of scarred skin.

"Or maybe it's an *L*," Lady Kraken says. "*L* for Lemon."

But she suddenly sounds less sure.

"How did you know about that?" I ask Caliastra. "I've always wondered how I got it."

"It happened many years ago," the magician replies, suddenly serious. "A silly accident." Then she looks into my eyes. "Your mother said it would scar you for life. And she was right."

"Have you ever shown this mark to anyone, boy?" Lady

Kraken demands. "Think, now. This is important."

I shake my head.

"Pah! This is hardly proof of anything." Lady K swings around to confront Caliastra with a whir of electrical motors. "You could have found out about the scar from someone at the hotel. Is this really the best proof you have? From your correspondence, I was expecting a birth certificate, at least."

"Sadly, I don't have that," Caliastra admits, holding up her open hands. I wonder for a moment if she is going to do another magic trick, but this time it seems the empty hands are purely metaphorical. She turns to me.

"Herbie, what do you remember of the day you arrived in Eerie-on-Sea?"

I call up the vague recollections I have of clinging to a crate as the waves tossed me around, all those years ago. If you've been to Eerie-on-Sea before, it's possible that you've heard the story of the shipwrecked boy yourself—of the boy who washed up on the beach in a crate of lemons, with no memory of where he came from. I'm a bit of a local legend myself, I suppose. But what I remember of the event is such a wispy, overused memory that I could add any detail I like at this point and probably believe it was true.

"The only thing I know for sure," I reply, "is that I was alone. I was the only survivor of a shipwreck."

"No, Herbie." Caliastra's eyes flash. "*Not* the only survivor. There were others."

"There were?"

"A few, yes," the magician continues. "Some people were pulled out of the sea by rescue ships before they could be eaten by . . . before they were lost, I mean. And some managed to swim to a lifeboat. Like me."

"You!" My cap nearly flies off my head. "You were on the ship? The same ship as me?"

Caliastra's face becomes resolute, as if she is mastering her emotions.

"I will never forget that night," she says, "the screech of the iceberg as it peeled back the hull, the sound of the water flooding the corridors, the *screams* . . . but I should spare you the details. It's proof of our connection that you need right now, not horror stories. Herbie, what can I tell you to prove that I am who I say I am?"

And straightaway I know the answer to that. It may be that I have no memory of my life before Eerie-on-Sea, but—against all the odds—I have been able to find out *something* about it: I know the name of the ship I was on, the ship that struck an iceberg and was wrecked.

I found this out with Violet, on our last big adventure together, around the time I got Clermit. But right now, the most important thing about it is this: as far as I'm aware, only two other people in the world know the name of the ship, and Violet would *never* tell.

And the other person? Well, he's dead.

So I see no way that a complete stranger could ever know that I was aboard a cruise ship called SS *Fabulous*.

"The name of the ship," I say. "Tell me the name of the ship."

Caliastra nods.

"Well?" asks Lady Kraken.

"First let me set the scene," Caliastra replies as Lady Kraken's eyes begin to narrow again. "Earlier in my career I took a few tours on cruise ships, as part of the onboard show. Lots of performers do that when they're starting out, and all the best luxury liners had a magician back then. Your father was a pianist and—no, don't get up! I will tell you all about him later, Herbie, I promise, but the main thing to know is that you come from a family of entertainers."

"And his mother?" Lady Kraken demands.

"I'm sorry?"

"You said his father was a pianist. What about his mother?"

"Oh, she was part of the show, too." Caliastra waves the question away. Then she turns back to me. "Herbie, your parents needed work, and I got them places in my cruise ship show. And not a day has gone by that I haven't regretted it."

"The name?" says Lady Kraken. "None of this is proof of anything. Tell us the name of the ship."

Caliastra glances between us both and lets the crafty look come back over her face again. She gets to her feet, lifts the plate of freshly baked pastries from the table, and offers it to me.

"Breakfast, Herbie?" she says. "These are your favorites, aren't they?"

Automatically I take the topmost croissant and feel its buttery perfection between my fingers. On any other occasion I would probably cram the whole thing in my mouth and spend the next three minutes blissfully chomping. But not today. My nostrils fill with Caliastra's perfume as she smiles down at me. The strange pattern on her coat seems to swirl. And suddenly I can't stand it.

What if she says the right name?

What if she *doesn't*?

"I have to go!" I blurt out, jumping up and backing away from the table, from Lady K, from this whole impossible situation. I run for the door.

"Herbie!" Caliastra cries out. "Wait!"

But I don't want to wait. I fling the door open and almost fall back into the room at the sight of Mr. Mummery standing there. He is straightening quickly. Was he listening at the door? Then I notice the other two men—Rictus and Tristo—behind him.

I see immediately why their faces were so disturbing earlier, in the half-light of the sitting room. Both men are wearing heavy black-and-white face paint—one with a leering grin, the other with a terrible frown. They step forward, as if startled at my sudden appearance, and raise their hands to grab hold of me.

"Leave him!" Caliastra commands from inside the room.

I don't hang around to see if they obey. I'm off down the corridor like a firework up a drainpipe, the croissant still clutched in one hand. I ignore the elevator and fly down the stairs, three at a time.

"Herbie!" I hear the magician cry, far behind me. "Herbie, I'm sorry!"

CHAPTER 6

VIOLET

I don't stop running till I'm out through the great revolving doors of the hotel, and the cold air of autumn has slapped me in the face. I stumble across the cobblestones to the seawall and lean against it, gasping for breath, trying to get my thoughts straight.

Has it finally happened?

The one thing left that could still have the power to make me doubt *everything* else?

I've been Herbert Lemon, Lost-and-Founder at the Grand Nautilus Hotel, for as long as I can remember. It's who I am. But deep down I've never been able to quite forget that it isn't my real name, that it's not who I *really* am. The name *Herbie* was given to me because I had no memory of any other. Dr. Thalassi, the town's medical man, used to say that in time my memories would return one day. They never have, and the doc doesn't mention it anymore. I'd almost given up on finding the truth. But now, has that truth come to find *me*?

Below me the ocean crashes gray and white on either side of the pier. The seagulls wheel through the sky above and cry their pterodactyl cries. One of them swoops for the croissant in my hand, but I swipe the bird away. Then I set off at a run down Spindrift Alley and into the ancient, twisting streets of Eerie-on-Sea.

I need somewhere to hide for a bit and *think*. And I know just the place.

⚙

There's a rule of Lost-and-Foundering that says *A problem shared isn't a problem at all. It's an adventure.*

I sometimes wonder if my friend Violet wrote this rule and sneaked it in with the rest. I'm wondering this again as I reach Dolphin Square, high on Eerie Rock, and approach Violet's home. The wind is raw and loaded with dead leaves, and the only people I see are hurrying across the square, heads down, looking as cold as I feel. It turns out it's easy to forget to put on a coat and scarf when you are running away from . . .

From *what*?

"A long-lost aunt?" I say aloud to the dolphin statue in the middle of the square. "Or the possibility that she's . . . *something else?*"

"You can run from the truth all you like, Herbert Lemon," says a lazy voice from somewhere, "but you can never hide from it."

I look around. There is no one there—just the whistling of the wind and the rattle of window shutters—but then I notice, up on the weathered green head of the bronze dolphin, a white cat with ice-blue eyes, sitting, licking one paw, and pretending to ignore me.

It's Erwin, the bookshop cat.

"Is that supposed to be helpful?" I ask him.

But, of course, Erwin says nothing.

The bookshop itself is close by, its wide bay window dark and mysterious with a hint of warm light inside. I call it the "bookshop," but the painted letters across the glass describe it slightly differently:

THE EERIE BOOK DISPENSARY

Have you ever been to the book dispensary in Eerie-on-Sea? I think you'd know if you had. Surely, no one could forget the grotesque mermonkey that squats in the window and leers horribly at everyone who pauses before it.

"Herbie!" comes a cry as the door of the shop is flung open with the ding of a bell. A head appears, beneath a mass of wild black curls, and a pair of brown eyes flash at me. "There you are! Have you only just gotten my note? What kind of Lost-and-Founder are you if I can't find you when *I've* lost something?"

"Er . . ." I say. "Hello, Violet."

As is often the case with my friend Violet Parma, I already feel as if she's two pages ahead of me.

"You said something about an emergency?" I suddenly feel a bit bad for ignoring Vi's note.

"Yes!" Violet says, beckoning impatiently. "At least, maybe. I . . . I don't know. But don't just stand there looking surprised, Herbie. Come *in!*"

And so, I come in.

Inside the bookshop, I'm surprised to see no cheery blaze in the great marble fireplace. It's still warmer in here than outside, though, so I flop gratefully into one of the big tatty armchairs. Gazing up, I see the countless spines of books around me, rising, shelf over shelf, up every wall to the ceiling. And beyond that ceiling—colored midnight blue and painted with constellations of tiny glittering stars—I can almost sense the mass of books upstairs, as they continue, volume upon volume, story after story, right to the top of Eerie-on-Sea's strangest bookshop.

In the window the mermonkey sits, its hairy back to me now, coiled on its iridescent fish tail before an antique black type-writer. It holds out a battered top hat for an offering from all those who would consult it.

Outside of my Lost-and-Foundery—and perhaps Mr. Seegol's fish and chip diner on the pier—the main room of the Eerie bookshop, beside the fire, is my favorite place in Eerie-on-Sea. And just the hideout I need to get my thoughts about Caliastra together. But today something doesn't seem quite right. The books, now that I look at them again, are jumbled and untidy on their shelves, as if someone had been rifling through them and didn't much care about the mess they made.

"There's no time to sit, Herbie," Violet declares, grabbing her coat. "We need to get out there and look. The trail is already growing cold."

"Look?" I blink. *"Trail?"*

"I've written down everything that might be important." Violet rummages in her pocket and pulls out a well-thumbed notebook. Then she nods at the crumpled croissant in my hand. "You can eat your breakfast on the way."

It's only then that Violet seems to notice that I'm not her normal, dependable Herbie today.

"Hey, wait. Are you all right?" Violet shoves the notebook

back in her pocket and peers at my face. "You look as if you've seen a ghost."

"Well, I've seen a *guest*," I reply, "who might be a ghost. At least, in a way."

And I tell Violet about the extraordinary woman with the raven hair who has just checked into the hotel. And about her even more extraordinary claims about me.

"Your aunt?" Vi stares at me in astonishment as I stammer to the end of my account. "But that's . . . wonderful, Herbie. I think. Isn't it?"

I do an enormous shrug.

"It *is* wonderful," I agree, "but . . ."

"But you're wondering if she's really who she says she is." Violet nods, seeing right through me, as ever. "So, did she know the name? The name of the ship?"

"I, um, I sort of left before she could answer," I reply. "But she had the chance to tell me and didn't. Actually, she seemed to be stalling. And Lady K didn't look too impressed. So, I suppose she doesn't know it, after all, and everything she says is a load of old nonsense."

"And yet, you're not quite sure it *is* nonsense, are you?"

Violet is peering into my eyes now. Sometimes I think she can read me like a book.

"Caliastra," Violet says then, testing the name out just as I did when I first heard it. "I think I've heard of her. Isn't there a famous magician named Caliastra? On television?"

"Television?"

"We can look her up," Violet says. "But right now all I know is this: if *I'd* been on an ocean liner that had struck an iceberg and sunk far out in the ocean, and I had somehow managed to survive, I think I'd remember the ship's *name*, at least."

"I forgot it, though, didn't I?" I reply. "When they found me washed up, I couldn't remember a thing."

Violet has no answer to that. She flops down in the other armchair and looks at me some more from inside her hair.

"It probably *is* all rubbish, anyway," I declare then, almost convincing myself. "But at least I got a croissant out of it."

And I tear the battered pastry into two halves and give one to Violet.

"Why would someone play such a sick joke on me?" I manage to say between chews, as golden flakes rain down the front of my uniform. "I almost wonder if old Mollusc is in on it somehow. Maybe this is part of some plan to get rid of me, once and for all. He's tried every other way . . ."

But I see that Violet isn't eating. She's staring into her half of the croissant, her eyes big and round.

"What?" I ask.

But Violet doesn't reply. Instead she reaches into the heart of the pastry and pulls something out of it, something that was concealed inside. She holds it up to catch the light.

It's a metal tube.

"One end looks as if it will screw off," says Vi, shaking the tube and making a dull rattle sound. "Herbie, I think there's something inside!"

CHAPTER 7

THE MERMONKEY BLINKS

I have to wipe my buttery fingers on a napkin before I can get a grip on the metal tube. Then I twist off the end and tip the tube into my palm. A rolled-up slip of paper slides out.

"What is it?" demands Violet.

I remember how when I asked Caliastra, "What is the name of the ship?" she offered me the plate of pastries in response. I also remember the crafty look in her eyes.

"I think," I say slowly, "that this is the payoff to a magic trick I didn't even know was happening."

And I unroll the slip.

The paper is crinkly, as if it has once spent time in the sea. It's printed on one side with a date and time of departure and a list of distant, exotic ports I've barely heard of. At the top is a drawing of an enormous ocean liner with four funnels, and above the drawing—in grand letters—is the name of a ship:

On the other side some details have been stamped on with green ink. Even though they are sea-faded and smudged, it is still possible to read the words:

ISSUED TO: PERFORMER KNOWN AS "CALIASTRA," MAGICIAN

NONTRANSFERABLE

2ND CLASS ACCOMMODATION

"It's a ticket!" I cry, handing it over to Violet. "She must have put this in the croissant before I even got to Lady K's room. It's the proof I asked for. She *was* on the ship with me."

"But how did she know what you would ask," Violet replies, turning the ticket over in her hands, "before you even asked it?"

I'm not sure what to say to that. Until I am.

"She's a magician, isn't she?" I shrug. "Maybe she used magic."

Violet snorts, unimpressed.

"Lucky guess, more like it. Besides, if this is the only proof she has, what else would she hide in the croissant? 'Magic,' my foot, Herbie! I'd like to meet this magician of yours for myself. She wouldn't get any tricks past me!"

And that's when there's a sharp tapping on the shop window. We both look up in surprise.

Caliastra is peering in at us through the glass of the shop door, her raven hair whipping in the wind. She smiles a half smile of apology.

"Is that her?" says Violet with a gasp.

But I don't need to answer that, do I? Instead I get up and let the magician in.

"I owe you an apology," Caliastra says as she steps into the shop in a gust of cold wind. She is still dressed in her strange black coat, and she carries a honey-colored walking cane of twisted glass. "I've handled this badly from the start. I don't want you to feel you have to run away from me, Herbie. I *never* want that. I'm really, really sorry I gave you such a shock."

"But how did you know I would be here?" I say, amazed.

Caliastra's face slips into a conspiratorial expression that makes me feel as though we're both in on some secret together. She leans in toward me, and I find myself leaning in, too.

"I'd like to be able to wave my hands mysteriously and say, 'By magic, Herbie. By magic!' But, well, that wouldn't be true," Caliastra confesses. "I followed you. Plain and simple."

Then she straightens and looks around the shop.

"Of course, I've heard of the Eerie Book Dispensary, and I hoped to visit it during my stay in town. So, let's just say I've come here earlier than expected."

Her dark eyes fall on Violet.

"Oh," she says, "who's your friend?"

I do a quick introduction, and Violet and Caliastra shake hands.

"Violet works here," I explain. "She's Jenny's assistant."

"Jenny?"

"Jenny Hanniver," says Violet. "She's the owner of this place. I help her customers consult the mermonkey."

"Ah, yes!" Caliastra beams a bright smile and turns to the hairy creature hunched in the window. "The famous mermonkey of Eerie-on-Sea."

"It's the mermonkey who chooses your book for you,"

explains Violet. "Probably not the book you want, or the book you were expecting, but . . ."

"But quite possibly the book you need," Caliastra finishes for her, nodding. And she walks over to the window bay to admire the mermonkey up close.

"Magnificent, isn't it?" she says, gesturing with her glass cane. "But quite a brute. I imagine the mechanism must be a wonder to behold . . ."

And she reaches out as if to pull open the mermonkey's waistcoat.

"No!" Violet cries, making Caliastra snatch her hand back. "I mean, Jenny prefers it if customers don't touch," Violet continues, smiling widely in apology. "Sorry. Would you, um, would you like to try the mermonkey for yourself?"

Caliastra arches one eyebrow at Violet. Then she turns back to consider the mermonkey, tapping the top of her glass cane— which is formed into the shape of an owl—on her perfect teeth. The mermonkey grins back at her, its own teeth like filthy yellow dominoes. A fat bluebottle fly buzzes around it and comes to land on its hat. The fly's metallic backside is as iridescent as the mermonkey's tail or Caliastra's embroidered coat. The magician looks entirely at ease before the hideous fish-tailed monkey, as if she and it belong to the same world of mystery and secrets. Then Caliastra smiles.

"I believe I will," she says finally. "I presume I put a coin in its hat?"

Violet nods.

Caliastra removes her gloves and slides a change purse from her coat pocket. She pulls out a coin and drops it in the hat.

Nothing happens.

She drops in another, which clinks against the first.

Still nothing happens.

"I see!" says Caliastra, putting her hands on her hips. "It knows its own worth, clearly."

"Sometimes it's a little, um, slow," Violet says, with an embarrassed shrug.

Caliastra glances at me and winks. Then she tips up her change purse entirely and a shower of loose change tinkles out of sight into the shadow of the mermonkey's hat.

The creature's arm sags under the weight.

Then the mermonkey judders.

The arm lifts—slowly—slowly—with a *tick-tick-tick*ing of grinding gears till it plops the heavy hat onto its own head. The coins fall in a hectic rattle down into the creature's mechanical insides, and its light-bulb eyes flash on.

The mermonkey begins to scream.

"Noisy!" Caliastra mouths to us, holding her hands over her ears to block out the terrible sound. Clockwork grinds, gears rattle, and puffs of steam—or is it smoke?—curl around the infernal machine. The comforting smell of the old bookshop—a mix of hot chocolate, wood fire, and aging paper—is smothered by the stink of antique electrics and singed fur as the mechanical creature reaches one bony fist toward the typewriter, extends its index finger to type, and . . .

Stops.

A sudden fizzing, clicking silence falls over the shop.

The mermonkey's finger remains poised over the keyboard, but instead of stabbing out the code it types to dispense its books, the creature does nothing.

Well, not *quite* nothing.

The mermonkey's eyes flicker, as if it is blinking at Caliastra.

Then it tips its head to one side. If I didn't know better, I'd say it was carefully considering what to do next.

Outside, I notice that Erwin—the bookshop cat—is watching us closely through the window.

"What happens now?" Caliastra whispers.

"I don't know," Violet whispers back. "It's never done this before."

"Maybe it needs a little encouragement," Caliastra suggests, and she raises her glass cane.

"Prestocadabra!" she cries.

And before anyone can say or do anything, she twirls the cane and then taps its tip firmly onto the mermonkey's forehead.

CHAPTER 8

THE SUBTLE MASK

The mermonkey gives another mechanical shriek, and its eyes blaze with light. Its crooked hand crashes down onto the keyboard, and with a *KLACK!* and a *KLICK!* and a *KLICKETY-KLACK!* it bashes out its book prescription. Then it yanks its hand back as if the keys are too hot to touch and returns the hat to the "Try me?" position faster than I've ever seen.

Its eyes wink out, and the mermonkey falls still.

There's a *TING* from the typewriter, and a card flies out. It flutters to Caliastra's feet.

The magician plants the tip of her cane onto the card. With

a lightning-fast motion, she sweeps the card up off the floor and snatches it from the air.

On one side of it we can see the familiar drawing of the mermonkey. On the other is the code—the code that will lead to the book the mechanical creature has dispensed for the lady with the raven hair.

Caliastra hands the card to Violet.

"Your mermonkey has, it would appear, chosen me a book. Though, I'm not sure how to claim it."

"This code," Violet explains, holding up the card so we can all see the line of numbers and letters on it, "leads you first to the *floor* of the shop your book is on. Then it leads to the *room* it's in, then to the *wall* in that room, then to the *shelf* on that wall, and finally to the *book* itself. Would you like me to show you . . . ?"

"Oh, I think I can trust you to handle it for me, thank you," says Caliastra, in a tone that suggests she has better things to do. Violet is left with little choice but to set off into the heart of the Eerie Book Dispensary, in search of Caliastra's book.

And now, for the first time, I'm alone with the magician—the magician who claims she's my long-lost family.

"May I . . . ?" I blurt out. "May I ask you something?"

"You may, Herbie." Caliastra smiles kindly. "You must have

so many questions. I will do all I can to tell you whatever you wish to know."

"Are you . . . ?" I'm still blurting. "I mean, is it true . . . ? That you . . . ?"

"Yes, Herbie?"

". . . that you've been on *television*?"

Caliastra raises her eyebrows in surprise. Then she throws her head back and laughs.

"Yes, Herbie, it is true. I've come a long way since my cruise ship days. But I still sometimes tour provincial theaters," Caliastra explains, "like yours here in Eerie. Indeed, my ulterior motive for visiting Eerie-on-Sea is to give a special shadow puppet show for this year's Ghastly Night celebrations. Perhaps you've heard?"

At that moment, Violet returns with a book in her hands.

"Did you say . . ." she asks, "the Ghastly Night show?"

"I did."

Violet's face is alight with interest. Ever since she first heard of Ghastly Night she's been obsessed with it. Apparently, Eerie-on-Sea is the only place in the world where it's celebrated, though I find that hard to believe. But that's what Violet says, and she knows more about the outside world than I do.

"How do you know about it?" Violet asks. "I thought it was just a funny old Eerie tradition."

"It is," Caliastra says. "But the legend of Ghastly Night, and the terrible Shadowghast, is often discussed among members of the Magic Circle. There is, after all, a magic trick at the heart of it, in the form of a shadow puppet show like no other. I have studied the old story, and I believe I have discovered the secret of that trick. It is a great honor to be invited to perform it myself, here, in Eerie-on-Sea."

"But I thought . . ." I start to say. "I thought you came here because of me."

Caliastra lays one slender hand on my shoulder.

"Herbie, I did come here for you," she says. "But I may never have found you if I wasn't already studying the lore of Ghastly Night. It was as I researched the legend of the Shadowghast that I first heard about Eerie-on-Sea's famous castaway and began to wonder. I've been looking for my lost nephew for years and had all but given up hope. When my contact in Eerie-on-Sea told me about the boy who washed up in a crate of lemons, I knew at once I had found more than some old magic trick here. That's why I wrote to Lady Kraken and, eventually, why she invited me here. Ghastly Night is just an excuse. You, dear Herbie, are the *reason*."

I nod. I can't think what to say.

"What contact in Eerie-on-Sea?" Violet asks.

"Ah!" Caliastra's eyes light up as she finally notices what's in Violet's hands. "Is that my book?"

"Oh." Vi looks as if she had already forgotten about it. "Yes. This is the book the mermonkey chose for you. Here . . ."

And she hands a thick, grubby yellow hardback book over to the magician. On the cover is a drawing of two masks—one with an exaggerated happy face, and the other with a sad frown—the kind of tragedy and comedy faces you sometimes see at a theater.

"*The Subtle Mask*," Caliastra reads the title aloud, "by Questin D'Arkness. Interesting choice. A bit long-winded, though. These Victorian writers did like an endless sentence, didn't they?"

And she hands to book back to Violet.

"But"—Violet looks confused—"it's yours."

"I've already read it," Caliastra replies. "And besides, I know precisely why that particular book has been dispensed to me."

"You do?" Violet and I both say at exactly the same time.

"Oh, yes." The magician nods. "Even the name of the author is significant."

When we don't respond, Caliastra continues.

"Questin D'Arkness?" She gives a bright chuckle. "No one is really named *Questin D'Arkness*, Herbie. It's a pen name, just as *Caliastra* is a name for the stage. The author was really one Pumphrey Doolittle, but you can't write Gothic horror stories and be taken seriously with a name like Pumphrey Doolittle, now, can you?"

"I guess not," I reply.

"*The Subtle Mask*," the magician explains, "is the story of an actor who sells his soul to the devil in exchange for supernatural talent and the fame and fortune that comes with it. By the end of the novel, he has lost himself entirely in fiction and lies, and the devil claims his soul. It's a reminder to me, Herbie, to be more honest with you. No more tricks or stage effects; no more clues hidden in breakfast pastries. I should have just given you that ticket instead of playing games. And I am very sorry."

"Oh," I manage to say.

"And I want you to promise me something in return," Caliastra continues. "I want you to feel you can always come to me, Herbie. For anything. No more running away. Agreed? We are family, after all."

I nod.

"Don't look so alarmed." Caliastra smiles, giving my nose an affectionate tweak. "This should be a happy time. I know—come watch me rehearse later today. You can both come, if you like. We'll be in the theater on the pier, preparing for the greatest show Eerie-on-Sea has ever seen. It will be good for you to see all the props and mechanisms, Herbie. You have a lot to learn; although, something tells me that you will be perfect for the job."

"Job?"

"Of course," Caliastra replies. "For some time now, I've needed help with the more subtle tricks and contraptions. From what I've seen already, you will be just the assistant I need."

Violet gasps.

"Does that mean you're staying in Eerie-on-Sea?" she says. "For good?"

"Staying?" Caliastra cries, with the face of someone who has just heard something preposterous. "Of course I'm not staying. I'm performing in Copenhagen in ten days' time, then on to Oslo, Helsinki, and St. Petersburg. No, when I leave Eerie, after the Ghastly Night show, my nephew will leave with me. To start his new life as a magician's assistant."

Then she turns to me with her radiant smile.

"Your long wait in this strange little town is over, Herbert Lemon. You are finally going home."

CHAPTER 9

MIDNIGHT VISITOR

After Caliastra has gone, I flop back down in the arm-chair and stare into space.

I'm *leaving*? Going *home*? I can't take it in. How can I just leave Eerie-on-Sea? And am I really going to travel the world with a great magician?

I look at the ship's ticket in my hand—the proof that Caliastra and I are connected—then down at the two rows of gleaming brass buttons on the royal porpoise blue of my uniform. I'm a Lost-and-Founder, not a magician's apprentice. And yet, I can't help noticing that there's something about the words *magician* and *apprentice* that go together very nicely indeed.

"But . . . but you can't go!" Violet declares. "She can't just waltz in here and take you away, Herbie! We don't even know if she is who she says she is."

"But, the ticket . . ."

"That doesn't prove anything!" Violet cries. "It's only a piece of paper."

"A piece of paper can change your life," says a voice. "It just depends what's written on it."

And Erwin jumps up onto the counter.

"You're back, then, are you?" Violet says to the cat, scratching him behind the ear. "Have you seen Jenny?"

Erwin must have slipped in when I opened the door for Caliastra. Now he strolls along the countertop and peers down at the grubby yellow book. He twitches his whiskers.

"Where *is* Jenny?" I ask, suddenly realizing I haven't seen her yet. I notice the cold, empty hearth again and feel a sense of unease.

Jenny always keeps a merry blaze going in the colder months, and she often treats customers to hot chocolate or cups of herbal tea and spiced biscuits, to cheer them up before their lives are turned upside down—or flipped right-side up, or just knocked sidewise—by the books the mermonkey dispenses. It's strange not to have been greeted by her or offered a biscuit, and that Violet has been left to mind the shop all by herself.

"That's what I was trying to tell you, Herbie!" Violet

declares. "Didn't you read my note? *That's* the emergency. Jenny is missing!"

"Missing?" I ask. "Are you sure?"

"I heard her leave late last night, and she hasn't come back," Violet replies, pulling her notebook back out of her coat pocket. "Her bed hasn't been slept in. Plus, we were going out to buy books this morning, and she'd *never* miss that. And then there's the curtains not drawn, as they always are, and . . ."

"OK, OK, I get it," I interrupt, straightening my cap. Then I put on my most professional voice. "But when it comes to Lost-and-Foundering, Violet, missing people aren't as straight-forward as missing *things*. Missing things don't have legs, for example."

"Herbie"—Violet fixes me with a fierce look—"Jenny hasn't just wandered off. She'd *never* go away without telling me, and that's *that*."

There comes a meow from the counter, and I see that Erwin is pawing at the yellow book. I wonder for a moment if Caliastra was right about why she'd been dispensed *The Subtle Mask*, by Questin D'arkness. She seemed very sure about it. Violet snatches Erwin up into her arms and holds him like a hot-water bottle, furiously stroking his head.

"I'm sorry," I say. I feel bad now that I thought this was just another of Violet's attempts to start an adventure.

"It's horrible," she replies. "To get up in the morning and find myself all alone . . ."

"Wow!" says Erwin.

"I mean, all alone except for you, puss," Violet corrects herself. "But it's the first time for a long time that I've felt so . . . abandoned."

Erwin rubs his head on her chin and gives one of his best purrs.

Violet lost her parents when she was only a baby. And while she believes they'll one day find their way back to her, she and I both know that's not guaranteed. Jenny is the closest thing to a parent . . . to a *mother* . . . that Vi has ever known. And Violet is the closest thing Jenny's ever had to a daughter.

So, I agree: Jenny would never, *ever* leave Violet alone without explaining why.

"I think you'd better tell me what happened," I say.

"It was late last night," Violet explains. "I went to bed with some good books and left Jenny down here tinkering with the mermonkey. Then I heard a loud banging on the front door of the shop."

"A visitor?" I ask. "Who was it?"

"Mrs. Fossil," Vi replies. "I was curious, so I crept downstairs. I heard Mrs. Fossil talking hurriedly to Jenny, and Jenny making soothing noises back. It sounded as though Mrs. F had had a scare."

I nod. "It does often sound like Mrs. F has had a scare," I say. "She's got one of those voices. Besides, she's always especially jumpy around Ghastly Night. What did she say was the matter?"

Violet looks at her toes.

"I . . . I don't know. I crept back upstairs to bed."

"Really? You? Whatever happened to looking for adventure?"

"Herbie!" Violet looks annoyed. "You're the one who tells me to stop looking for adventures under every rock and to read books instead. And now, when I finally do as you suggest, *BOOM*—an adventure started without me!"

"But what *happened*?" I ask, getting annoyed myself. "How do you know this is an adventure and not just a misunderstanding?"

"Because soon afterward, I heard the shop door close, and I saw Jenny leave with Mrs. Fossil. I thought she was just going to walk her home. But when I got up this morning, Jenny's toolbox was still open, and there was no sign that she'd slept here. And it looked as if the whole place had been searched."

"Searched?"

"Yes, like someone had rifled and rummaged every shelf," says Vi, "looking in every book. And I haven't seen Jenny since."

"Have you gone to Mrs. Fossil's place to ask?"

"That's the first thing I did," says Vi, "but I think she was out beachcombing. That's when I came to find you, Herbie, but you weren't there, either, so I left my note. Where were you, anyway?"

Spying on breakfast is where I was, but I don't want to admit that.

"On a scale from one to ten," I say instead, "how worried about Jenny are you? Where one is not very worried at all, and ten is so worried that you might actually explode."

"I'm a seven," says Violet without hesitation. "But I might go up to an eight if we don't do something soon."

"The tide's back in now," I say. "We could try Mrs. Fossil again. I'm sure there's just a simple explanation for all this."

"Thank you, Herbie." Violet smiles gratefully at me.

"Ahem!" says Erwin from the countertop as we head for the door. We turn to find him regarding us, his head on one side. He hooks one claw into the cover of the yellow hardback book and flips it open.

"We don't have time to read now, puss," I say. "If Jenny comes back, tell her we're looking for her."

And with that—and with Erwin glaring at us icily from beneath very flat ears—we slip through the door of the Eerie Book Dispensary and head out into Dolphin Square.

CHAPTER 10

MANGLEWICK CANDLES

W hen we arrive at Mrs. Fossil's Flotsamporium, the sun is almost shining.

On the pavement outside the ramshackle shop lie buckets and baskets of sea-tumbled things for sale, while more beachcombed curios hang from lengths of salt-bleached rope. But already the change of the season is making itself felt: the ropes are tangled by the wind, and the baskets have a huddled look, as if gathering for warmth while they wait for their owner to take them inside for the winter.

Wedged upright beside the peeling shop door is a surfboard, with what looks like a shark bite taken out of it. And on the surfboard, Mrs. Fossil has painted some words:

END OF SUMMER

SALE!

I'VE FOUND THE PERFECT GIFT SO YOU DON'T HAVE TO!

I'LL TAKE A LITTLE BIT OFF ANYTHING – JUST ASK!

ALSO: HOMEMADE CAKES! TO EAT IN OR TAKE AWAY.

WARM FIRE AND CHITCHAT FOR FREE☺.

PLUS:

MY WORLD-FAMOUS MANGLEWICKS ARE READY!

COME IN AND PICK YOURS TODAY.

"They're hardly world-famous," says Violet. "I'd never even heard of a manglewick candle till a few days ago. Just as I'd never heard of the Shadowghast or any of this Ghastly Night business."

"Do they really not have manglewicks where you come from?" I ask.

"Nope," says Vi. "On Halloween, people mostly leave carved pumpkins out to scare off evil spirits—not weird homemade candlesticks that . . . argh! What's that?"

Above the gusting of the wind, a strange droning sound

cuts through the air. Then the drone is joined by a melody, leaping jauntily and dancing around in our ears.

"Oh, that's just Mrs. Fossil," I reply. "Practicing. Come on! That means she's in."

And I push open the door to the shop and step into the curious world of beachcombed treasures.

Piled high against every wall are buckets and crates and barrels and lobster pots, and basket upon basket of curiosities. And it's bonkers to think that everything here was found washed up on the beach. More containers—heaped with beach-rolled plastic, twists of driftwood, glass fishing floats, and every conceivable thing that could ever be lost at sea—crowd the floor, below a ceiling hung with fishing nets and salvaged parts of ships. And all of this is bathed in a rainbow of sunlight from the countless jars of colored sea glass that fill the wide window of Mrs. Fossil's Flotsamporium.

"Hellooo, my dears!" cries a singsong voice as Mrs. F herself looks up from her seat beside her stove, frowning with concentration. In her arms she cradles an extraordinary musical instrument of gleaming red wood, inlaid with patterns of shell. With one hand she cranks a handle, while the fingers of the other fly across wooden keys, and her foot taps a beat on the floorboards.

"Can't stop yet! Hold on . . ."

And the music tumbles on—buzzingly, mesmerizingly—as blue driftwood flames dance in the window of the stove, and my own foot starts to tap, until, with a droning flourish—like a choir of bees coming to the end of a particularly manic song—it's over.

"Phew!" gasps Mrs. F, sitting back in the ringing silence that follows and giving us a snaggletooth grin. "Still got it! Bit rusty, though. Must put in all the hours I can before the big night."

"Mrs. F, what is *that*?" Violet says, the reason for our visit briefly swept aside by curiosity about the object in the beachcomber's lap.

"Hurdy-gurdy," comes the reply, and Mrs. Fossil gives the instrument another crank and spins the wheel that makes it drone. "Played it for years, on and off." And she lifts the strap of the funny-looking thing over her head and lowers the instrument gently to the ground. "You two are just in time. Clever of you to guess my latest batch of ginger cookies is almost ready. Want a cup of tea?"

And I can't help making an enormous grin of my own. Because, sure enough, somewhere behind the smell of wood smoke, seaweedy beach treasures, and drying waxed coats, my nose picks up the warm scent of fresh baking.

"Sounds perfect, Mrs. F. Thanks!" I reply. "By the way, would you believe Violet hadn't heard of manglewick candles before? Imagine that!"

"Well, I never!" cries Mrs. F, standing up and stretching. "But I suppose it is just a funny old local tradition. Most folks outside Eerie don't much bother with it, or so I'm told. And they are lucky they don't have to, I suppose."

"What do you mean?" asks Violet?

Mrs. Fossil glances over to one corner of her shop and gives a nod at the strange objects there.

"Well, people outside Eerie don't need their protection, do they?"

In the corner are dozens of strips of gnarly driftwood, attached to the wall so that they stick out like brackets. Each piece of wood has a candle fixed at the end. And the candles all have wire twisted around them. The ends of the wire, which stick up beside the candles' wicks, are turned and bent and, well, *mangled*, in a strange way. Each wire is different from the next, but frankly—seen like this—they don't look very impressive.

"Manglewicks," I say, picking up a nearby box of matches and heading over to the corner. "Can I light one, Mrs. F? So Violet can see . . . ?"

"No! Wait, Herbie . . . !" Mrs. Fossil calls out, but it's too late. I've already struck a match and placed the flame against the wick.

The dark corner is bathed in a flare of soft light.

Now that the candle is lit, the real skill of what Mrs. Fossil has done is obvious. The little twist of wire, nothing much on its own, throws a shadow onto the wall behind—the shadow of a crooked man with horns on his head, who dances with the flicker of the flame.

Mrs. Fossil runs forward, slides to a halt in her woolly socks, and, with a puff, blows the candle out.

"Herbie, it's bad luck to light them before dusk," she gasps. "Didn't you know that?"

"Why?" says Violet. "Why is it bad luck?"

Mrs. F clutches at her dungaree straps and looks around nervously.

"Because," she replies, in a trembly voice, "a manglewick only distracts the Shadowghast *at night*, when he's on the prowl. But if you light it early, *before* the sun goes down . . ."

"Yes?"

"Well, then you'll summon him, won't you? And he'll snatch *your* shadow instead!"

I'm about to give Violet a "Yeah, right!" grin when I happen to catch sight of the candle. From the wick curls the smoke of the dead flame, and for a moment—just a tiny, fleeting moment—the smoke takes on a wispy shape.

The shape of a crooked, grinning man with horns on his head.

CHAPTER 11

SOMETHING IN THE WINDOW

A t least, that's what people say," Mrs. Fossil adds, waving the candle smoke away and grinning sheepishly. "But you know what Eerie folk are like. I expect it's just a bit of fun to mark the changing of the season, but all the same, Herbie, it's not something to take lightly. Now, let's get that kettle on."

"They're beautiful," says Violet, glancing back at the unlit manglewick candles as we follow the beachcomber to her corner kitchen, "in a weird sort of way. And that shadow was wonderfully creepy."

"Thank you, my dear," says Mrs. Fossil. "I make them every year. It gives me something to do when the tourists are gone. Each one is ready to go to a home here in Eerie, to cast a little shadow at night and keep the Shadowghast at bay."

"But what *is* the Shadowghast?" Violet asks.

"Ah, but of course!" Mrs. Fossil says as she fills a big copper kettle with water. "You haven't been here for Ghastly Night before, have you? This will be your first. Well, if you've got some time now, the doc will be around soon with his puppets and props, to rehearse. And you can see for yourself."

"Rehearse?"

"Yup," I say. "Dr. Thalassi and Mrs. F put on a Ghastly Night show of their own, down on the pier, every year. At least, they usually do . . ."

"We *always* do!" Mrs. Fossil corrects me. "Do please stay to watch. It would be good to have an audience. Now, let's get those cookies out . . ."

"But are you still performing?" Violet says, exchanging a look with me. "This year, I mean. I thought Lady Kraken had invited a big-name magician to do the Ghastly Night show. At least, that's what I've heard."

"Where did you get that idea?" Mrs. Fossil chuckles, sliding her big fat golden ginger cookies onto a cooling rack. "What famous magician would waste their time coming to Eerie-on-Sea? Ghastly Night's just a few locals gathering on the pier, with hot drinks and caramel apples, while Doc tells the story and I grind my old gurdy."

"The reason we came around," Violet says hastily, changing the subject to the business that brought us here in the first place, "is to see if you're all right, Mrs. F. After what happened last night, I mean."

"Oh, that!" Mrs. Fossil says with an embarrassed grin. "I was just being silly, I'm sure. I'll be jumping at my *own* shadow next."

"But what did happen?" Violet says. "You came around to the book dispensary, didn't you? Afterward you and Jenny went off somewhere, and she hasn't come back."

"She hasn't?" Mrs. Fossil turns her head sharply and drops the last cookie. It plops to the floor. "Are you sure?"

We both nod.

"Oh!" Mrs. Fossil clutches her dungarees again. "You . . . you haven't seen her today at all?"

"I haven't," Violet replies. "Do you know where she went? After she saw you?"

Mrs. F scoops up the dropped cookie with a spatula.

"She just walked me home. That's all," the beachcomber explains. "I had a bit of a scare, you see, while out delivering my manglewicks. Some customers like me to drop them off personally, but I left my rounds a bit late last night. I'm always a bit jumpy this time of year, and I got spooked. Jenny knows what I'm like, so when I came banging on the door of the bookshop, she let me in and gave me a cup of tea. Then she saw me safely home."

"But where is she *now*?" Violet demands. "You're the last person to see her. Surely, you know something! Why didn't she come home?"

"What scared you, Mrs. F?" I ask gently, putting a reassuring hand on Vi's arm. "What did you see?"

Mrs. Fossil sends a fearful glance over to the corner where she displays her manglewicks.

"I saw . . . well, I *thought* I saw . . . in the window of that boarded-up house down the street . . ."

"Yes?"

"I thought I saw . . . now, you mustn't laugh! But . . . I thought I saw the Shadowghast."

Just then the door of the Flotsamporium bursts open, and a tall shape fills the doorway, spilling a long, dark shadow across the shop floor.

"Agh!" Mrs. Fossil cries, throwing up her hands in surprise. The dropped cookie now flies off the end of her spatula and sticks to the ceiling. "Dr. Thalassi! You frightened the life out of me! You're early."

"Good day," says Eerie-on-Sea's medical doctor as he enters the shop and removes his astrakhan hat. "If it is a good day, that is, which I'm beginning to doubt. Have you heard? Apparently,

Lady Kraken has decided to invite *someone else* to perform the show on Ghastly Night this year. A professional! Do you know anything about this, Herbie?"

I do an awkward grin.

"It's true," I admit. "There's a magician up at the hotel. They're opening up the theater on the pier specially for her. Ghastly Night is going to be big this year. I . . . I'm sorry, Doc."

"But it's *our* show!" Mrs. Fossil cries. "We do it every year! No one tells the story quite like the doc. He does all the voices and everything."

Dr. Thalassi shrugs a cloth sack off his shoulder onto the floor, and it falls open. A jumble of sticks and props clatter out—the doc's collection of shadow puppets.

"It's an outrage!" he booms, his caterpillar eyebrows low over his Roman nose. "I've invested precious time in rehearsals—not for fun, you understand, just to keep a piece of local history alive—and then Her Ladyship repays me by getting some jumped-up little conjuror in and not even telling us! I've got a good mind to go over to the hotel and demand an explanation."

I don't think Caliastra is a jumped-up little conjuror. And I don't think the doc would either if he met her and saw one of her tricks. But I don't say anything. Mrs. Fossil and the doc clearly have enough to say about it all without me joining in, and they go on moaning about the situation as Mrs. F pours the tea and the doc sets out chairs beside the stove.

And anyway, here is something else for Violet and me to think about.

There is only one "boarded-up house down the street" that I can think of, and that's the house of a man Violet and I would like never to think about again. A man who is gone for good but who seems, nevertheless, to have left a very long shadow of his own across our lives.

A man named Sebastian Eels.

"Herbie"—Vi leans in close to whisper—"are you thinking what I'm thinking?"

"That depends," I reply. "Are you thinking how soon we can help ourselves to a cookie without being rude?"

"No, I'm not! I'm thinking how could Mrs. Fossil have seen something in the window of a boarded-up house when its *boarded-up*!"

"You think it's been un-boarded, then?"

"One window must have been, at least," Vi replies. "Maybe someone's been in Sebastian Eels's house. And maybe Jenny wondered the same thing last night. And *maybe*, after dropping Mrs. Fossil back here, she decided to investigate. And maybe something happened to her!"

"That's a lot of *maybes*, Vi," I say. "And here are a few more: maybe Mrs. F really did just get spooked by her own shadow.

And maybe Jenny really has just been delayed somewhere, and *maybe* you're still just seeing adventures where there aren't any."

"Perhaps," says Vi, with a sigh, "but there's only one way to know for sure. We should take a look at Sebastian Eels's house for ourselves."

And probably we would have done that straightaway, if something extraordinary didn't start to happen right in front of us, beside the cozy fire in the Flotsamporium, in the presence of a loaded plate of ginger cookies.

Because somehow, using only things from his bag, Dr. Thalassi has built a striped fabric booth around himself, like the kind used for puppet shows. Only, where the little stage should be, he has stretched a cotton screen. With a scratch from a match, the doc lights a kerosene lantern, and the screen begins to glow. Then, with one of his puppet sticks, he makes a shadow silhouette dance and cavort across the screen.

"We will rehearse anyway," comes the voice of the doc from inside the booth. All we can see are his tweed trousers and shiny shoes showing underneath. "I won't be able to persuade Lady Kraken to change her mind if we aren't ready with our own show."

"Come sit, Violet," Mrs. Fossil calls. "You wanted to know the story of the Shadowghast. Well, now's your chance!"

And Mrs. F sits beside the doc, straps her hurdy-gurdy around her waist once more, and cranks out an eerie drone.

I can see that Violet is about to argue. But I can also see that she's curious to see what will happen next. And besides, there really are plenty of innocent reasons why Jenny hasn't come home yet. I steer Violet to a chair and hand her a cookie.

"Who's that?" she asks after a moment, as the cutout shadow of a tall man with a fat belly and muttonchop whiskers walks across the screen in front of us, looking grand and important.

"That's old Standing Bigley," I explain from the cushion beside Violet. "He was mayor of Eerie-on-Sea a long, long time ago. He's a big part of the story of how Ghastly Night began, way back when the pier was first built."

"What are those things in his hands?"

"Money bags," I reply. "Shh! The show's about to start."

"Gather close, people of Eerie!" cries the doc then, in a loud showman's voice. The shadow of Mayor Bigley vanishes from the screen, and a model of Eerie Rock with the town on it appears above a rolling sea. "Gather close for the story of the misdeeds of old Mayor Bigley . . ."

"Boo!" cries Mrs. Fossil, pretending to be in the audience and nodding at us encouragingly.

"Boo!" I cry. "Hiss!"

". . . and the coming," the doc continues, "of the fearsome Shadowghast! And, lest that terrible spirit come again even now, hold your manglewicks high!"

"Hurray!" cries Mrs. Fossil, and Violet and I join in.

Mrs. F plays a short seafarer's jig on her hurdy-gurdy while the doc changes the scene and I sit munching the munchiest cookie I've had in ages, as the story of Ghastly Night unfolds before us in a spectacle of light and shadow.

CHAPTER 12

THE PUPPET MASTER

....

O nce upon an autumn night, on All Hallows' Eve, the fisherfolk brought a strange seafarer to Eerie-on-Sea. They had found him caught in the strong currents around Maw Rocks, though no one could say where he could have come from in such a small boat, and the stranger himself wouldn't say. But what made this stranger strange even for Eerie-on-Sea was the bronze lantern he carried with him. It was sculpted to resemble a dragon with a silver orb in its mouth, and it gave off a pungent stink of naphtha.

"Who are you?" the fisherfolk asked.

"I am the Puppet Master," replied the stranger, with a bow and a curious twinkle in his pale eyes. "And this is my magic lantern."

This happened back in the days when the mayor of Eerie-on-Sea was trying to change the town from an ancient tumbledown coastal settlement, haunted by mystery, into a jolly seaside resort of cotton candy, beach huts, and profit. The mayor—a rich man of business named Standing Bigley—had already bought up most of the seafront and kicked out the people he found there. Only the Grand Nautilus Hotel held out against him.

Mayor Bigley's master plan was to build a pleasure pier opposite the hotel and cover it with lights and amusements, beneath a new sign calling the town CHEERIE-ON-SEA. He said it would bring in tourists by the thousands. He said it would make the town rich. He didn't say it would make him richer than anyone else, but he didn't need to.

The people of Eerie were beginning to think that they needed a new mayor.

"We should put on a show," declared Mayor Bigley to his nervous investors as the pier was being finished, "to demonstrate to the people that I am right. But where can I find entertainment at such short notice? And cheap entertainment, at that!"

It was just as this question was being asked that the stranger with the lantern arrived.

"I can put on a show for you," the Puppet Master said. "And it will be a puppet show of such wonder and delight that you will happily pay me five golden coins."

"Five!" Mayor Bigley cried, nearly losing his wig. "To a poor, dirty fellow such as you? I will pay two and not a penny more. And these puppets of yours had better be good, my man, even at that price. *Five!* I've never heard of such greed!"

"Then two it is." The Puppet Master bowed and stepped back into the shadows. "And may you get what you pay for."

⚙●✤

Although the structure of the pier was at that time complete, work had barely begun on its buildings, and the grand theater due to crown it was nothing but a drawing in the architect's office. No matter—that night the Puppet Master set up a make-shift stage of planks and canvas at the end of the pier, and with a hissing taper he lit his lantern's wick.

The folk of Eerie-on-Sea gathered in the dark—carrying chairs and cushions if they had them, or rolling barrels if they didn't—and huddled together in the chilly air. All around them tumbled billows of perfumed smoke from the lantern as the Puppet Master plucked the silver orb from the dragon's mouth and released a strange light from its lens.

Afterward, no one could say quite how he'd done it. With the light came creeping shadows, which the sailor, seemingly by using little more than his hands and fingers, was able to bend and twist in the smoke and lantern light above the audience— bend and twist into wonders!

Creatures from legend, characters from old tales, monsters from prehistory— all flew and slithered and strode around the clouds of scented smoke. Eerie-on-Sea's own Malamander crept in and out of view to cries of happy fright from the audience. Pterosaurs and thunderbirds wheeled and arched in the air to gasps of wonder, and even the great storm fish Gargantis rolled across the sky, swimming through the clouds. It was the most astonishing show the people of Eerie had ever seen, and all of it was narrated by the Puppet Master himself in his strange, lilting voice.

Throughout the show, just at the edge of sight, many thought they saw an extra shadow, one not mentioned in the stories and narration—the shadow of a grinning man with horns upon his head, who flicked and flew between the other shadows, snatching at any that tried to escape the clouds, and swirling them back into the spectacle.

"Who is that?" cried a small, round-eyed child near the front.

"That," answered the Puppet Master, with a dark twinkle in his eye, "is the Shadowghast. A ghost that haunts my lantern and who keeps my shadows for me."

"Why does he snatch them?" cried a little girl from behind her dad. "When they try to escape?"

"What kind of puppet master would I be," replied the stranger, "without puppets to master? And now, good people, my show is over."

The wonderous forms collapsed back into the creeping and wretched shades from which they had arisen. The Puppet Master held up the silver orb and commanded them to return to the light. The shadows in the clouds were dragged back into the lens as if sucked by an unseen force, leaving only the hiss of the lantern, and the Puppet Master bowing in the eerie light, and everyone clapping madly. Some even threw coins.

Mayor Bigley smiled to himself the smile of a man who had just been proved right. With entertainment like this, his pier was bound to be a success. And he was bound to become the richest man for miles around.

"I don't suppose," said the mayor to the Puppet Master, just as he was about to replace the silver orb in the dragon's mouth, "that you could be persuaded to stay and put on your show once the theater is finished? The tourists will pay a *fortune* . . . I mean, they will pay *tolerably well* to see a . . . a goodish puppet show like that."

The Puppet Master raised one long eyebrow.

"Even if the showman is a 'poor, dirty fellow' like me?" he asked. "But I cannot stay. I am traveling and would like my two gold coins now, so that I may sail with the tide."

"Well, really!" declared Mayor Bigley, stamping one foot in annoyance at seeing such a profitable opportunity slip between his fingers. "And as for your fee, did we really say *two* coins? I believed I was paying for a proper puppet show, and yet all you did was make shadows with your hands. As everyone knows, a shadow is only *half* a thing and not its whole. Therefore, I shall pay you only *half* the fee."

And he dug out a single gold coin from his pocket.

"Two was the price agreed," the Puppet Master replied, narrowing his eyes. "And you will regret it if you double-cross me."

The mayor of Eerie-on-Sea snorted. Who was this little

vagabond to threaten him? There were plenty of other clowns and players around—hungry artists who would perform for next to nothing and be grateful. And no one—*no one*—waggled their finger at Standing Bigley and got away with it.

"Here is your coin, wretch," said the mayor, holding it up. "And I will give it to you in the same way you gave us your so-called puppet show!" And with this he flicked the coin up into the beam of lantern light, sending a shadow of the coin flitting across the clouds of smoke. "Catch that, if you can!"

But something strange happened. Even though the mayor caught the actual coin in his pudgy little fist, the shadow of the coin continued to tumble through the clouds above. When it finally fell silently to the deck of the pier, it began to roll—a tiny black disk of shade, and nothing more—around and around the mayor until it came to lie at the feet of the Puppet Master. The Puppet Master picked up the shadow coin and held it in his own fingers, to gasps of astonishment from those nearby.

"But . . ." Mayor Bigley gasped, too, staring at the actual gold coin in his own hand. He waved it in front of the light, but the only shadow he made was that of an empty hand, holding nothing. "But how . . . ?"

"Did I not say my lantern was magic?" said the Puppet Master, slipping the shadow coin into his pocket. "And did I not say you would get what you paid for? You will regret the day you mocked me, Mayor Bigley! The Shadowghast is always hungry for one more shadow."

And he made a motion in the lantern light as if drawing something out of the lens.

A shadow slipped across the clouds, darting here and there, always just at the edge of sight, as new clouds of smoke poured from the lantern . . .

The shadow of a grinning man with horns upon his head.

The Shadowghast!

The mayor backed away from the shadow, waving the smoke from his face, coughing.

"Stop!" he cried. "Stop, I cannot see . . . !"

Soon he was completely shrouded, visible only as a silhouette in the lantern-lit cloud.

The Shadowghast darted forward, reaching his terrible crooked hands toward Mayor Bigley. At a nod from the Puppet Master, the Shadowghast snatched Standing Bigley's cowering shadow and pulled it with a silent scream into the lantern.

"Another silly trick!" spluttered the mayor as the clouds parted and revealed him still standing there, waving the fug away. "Smoke and mirrors, that's all! Why, I've a good mind to . . ."

But he stopped speaking when the gasping started.

All around, people were pointing at the deck of the pier

behind the mayor. Mayor Bigley swung around, and to his horror he saw not the shadow of a well-fed a man of business, but . . .

Nothing.

He had no shadow at all!

Disbelieving, the mayor raised his right arm and waved his fat little hand.

Nothing waved back.

"What . . . ?" he cried. "What have you done?"

"Your greed has fed my Shadowghast." The Puppet Master grinned. "And your debt is settled. And it seems the good people of Eerie-on-Sea will have an entertainer for their pier after all. *You!* Dance, Mayor Bigley! Dance!"

And the Puppet Master waggled his finger to and fro, as if conducting music only he could hear. The mayor began to dance, leaping from one foot to the other and turning a pirouette when the puppeteer twirled his hand.

"Stop!" cried Mayor Bigley as he spun on his heel perilously close to the edge of the pier. "Release me! I command you!"

"No," replied the Puppet Master, waving his hand and making the mayor lurch back toward the stage. "I have your shadow, so it is *I* who command *you.*"

But just then, in his desperation, Mayor Bigley grabbed onto the makeshift stage and pulled the cloth and planks down. The lantern tipped, and fiery liquid spilled out over the wreckage.

The dark at the end of the pier was suddenly filled with towering light as the flames took hold. The mayor, still clutching the flaming curtain, was engulfed in fire and leaped screaming off the end of pier, dragging the lantern with him into the rolling sea.

The people of Eerie ran to the burning stage, and using their chairs or whatever came to hand, pushed the rest of the flaming ruin into the waves before the town could burn. But search the waves as they did, there was no sign of Mayor Bigley.

"And so," said the Puppet Master, visibly shocked in the silence that followed, "it seems my show really is over."

"The sea is deep here," said one of the fisherfolk. "You won't see your lantern again in a hurry, showman."

"No matter," replied the Puppet Master after a long sigh. "The lantern has a new home now, on the bottom of the ocean. And perhaps it's for the best. But never forget my show, good people, for the Shadowghast certainly won't! And it's always hungry for one more shadow."

And with this he threw the silver orb off the pier after the lantern.

Before the sun could rise next day, the stranger had sailed away from Eerie-on-Sea, never to be seen again.

But the same cannot be said of the Shadowghast. Even today, there are some who swear that on All Hallows' Eve, a disembodied shadow can sometimes be seen in the streets of Eerie—the shadow of a grinning man with horns upon his head, searching hungrily for new shadows to snatch.

✿⚫✿

"And that, my friends, is the story of Ghastly Night," says Dr. Thalassi.

Mrs. Fossil's hurdy-gurdy grinds to silence, while the doc lowers the screen and puts down his puppets. They both look at us—the doc peering from inside his striped booth—anxious to know what we thought.

"Hurray!" I cry, spraying cookie crumbs around like I don't care (which I don't) and clapping as if I enjoyed the show (which I did!). And beside me, Violet is clapping, too.

"Bravo!" she cries. "That was great. And so spooky!"

Dr. Thalassi climbs out of the canvas frame, tugs down the front of his waistcoat, and gives a deep bow of satisfaction. But Mrs. Fossil remains in her chair, her face slowly changing to a look of horror as she stares past us into the corner of the room.

I turn and look where she's looking, into the corner where the manglewicks are.

And I see it immediately.

One of the candles is alight.

And on the wall behind it leaps the quivering shadow of a grinning man, with horns upon his head.

CHAPTER 13

PADLOCKS AND
CROWBARS

T hat wasn't lit before," says Dr. Thalassi as he strides
over to the corner of the shop and blows out the candle.
"Or was it?"

"I lit it earlier," I say. "But then we blew it out, didn't we?"

"Well, it's usually considered bad luck to light a manglewick
candle before dark," Dr. Thalassi explains. "I thought you knew
that, Wendy."

But Mrs. Fossil doesn't reply.

"Of course," Doc continues, "that's nothing but a simple
superstition."

"So now I know the story of Ghastly Night," Violet says
then. "And you put that show on every year?"

"We do," Dr. Thalassi replies as he makes some adjustments to the puppet booth. "It would be a shame to let the old tradition die out. We'll have to train some younger puppet masters one day, to take over when Wendy and I are old and doddery." And he raises one caterpillar eyebrow at us suggestively.

I'm not sure what to make of this, but I can see a light in Violet's eye that tells me all I need to know about what *she* thinks.

"Shall we go again, Wendy?" the doc asks then, tweaking the crooked arms of his Shadowghast puppet. "Your playing was lively, as ever, but I fluffed some of Mayor Bigley's lines. Wendy? Are you listening?"

But it's clear the beachcomber isn't. It's only when the ginger cookie that was stuck to the ceiling finally falls onto the floor with a soft thud that Mrs. Fossil speaks again.

"I think I really did see it," she says as if taking part in some other conversation none of us can hear.

"See what, Mrs. F?" I ask.

"Last night. When I was out on my rounds." Her eyes are wide and fearful now. "When I . . . when I had my funny turn. In the window of the boarded-up house, I *do* think I saw the Shadowghast. Creeping across the room!"

"Oh, honestly!" Dr. Thalassi scoffs, his eyes twinkling with amusement. "That's preposterous!"

"But I *did*," Mrs. F insists. "And now, if Jenny Hanniver is missing . . ."

"Jenny's missing?" The doc stops laughing. "How long has she been missing?"

"We don't know for sure that she *is* missing," I say, feeling that it's time for the expert opinion of a Lost-and-Founder. "Only that we don't know where she is."

"But it's just not *like* her, Herbie," Violet insists, "to go away for so long without leaving me a note. And we were going book shopping this morning. It was all arranged. It's one of our favorite things to do together. She'd *never* miss that."

"You're right." The Doc frowns. "That is very unlike Jenny."

"We should go," says Violet, looking panicked again. "We shouldn't have delayed, Herbie! Oh, why did we stay here? Come on, we need to find her!"

And she grabs her coat and runs out of the Flotsamporium before I or anyone else can respond.

So, of course, I follow.

⚙

Sebastian Eels's house is only a few doors down from Mrs. Fossil's ramshackle place, but in terms of style it might as well be a million miles away. It's the tallest and grandest house in all of Eerie, standing four stories high and painted sulphur yellow, with a great front door of gleaming black wood. But these days, with its owner gone for good, the old place is locked up and neglected—all eight front windows boarded up.

"Wait, isn't that a bit odd?" says Vi as we stand together on the cobblestones and look up at the abandoned building. "Why board up the upstairs windows as well?"

"To keep people out," I reply.

"What, out of the *fourth* floor?" Vi nudges me. "Who's going to climb in up there, Herbie? A cat burglar?"

"Meow?" says a voice, and we look down.

Without our noticing, and as quiet as mist, Erwin has appeared and is winding himself around Violet's legs.

"Hello, puss," says Violet, scooping Erwin up. "Has Jenny come home? Is there any news?"

Erwin, as if he were just like any other cat in the world, says nothing. And yet, we can still tell from the twitch of his whiskers that Jenny has not come home.

"So, in which window was it that Mrs. Fossil saw . . . whatever it is she saw?" I say, clutching my cap as I look up at the grand town house. "All these seem firmly shuttered to me."

But when we walk around to look at the side of the house, we see that on one of the smaller windows, the boards have blown loose and are hanging down, giving a view into the dark of an upstairs room.

"That must be it," says Vi. "I wonder if we *could* get up there somehow."

"Up there?" I blink. "Vi, if I'd known we were going to do a bit of burglary, I'd've put a couple of ladders under my cap. And a crowbar!"

Even if we climbed the tree that grows low over the garden wall, there would be no way up to this particular window. Not without climbing the sheer wall.

"Did you bring Clermit?" Violet asks, glancing at my cap. "Your clockwork hermit crab? Like I asked?"

I give her one of my looks.

"Well, maybe Erwin could do it instead." Vi rumples the bookshop cat's head. "His claws are like grappling hooks."

"Na-o," Erwin meows, and he starts to wriggle in Violet's arms.

So she puts him down.

"Hey, where's he going?" I say as Erwin scoots off along the street, toward the front of the house. "There's no way in over there."

"Apart from the front door," says Vi as we follow.

"A front door," I reply as we reach it, "that's firmly bolted shut with this." And I rap my knuckle on a large steel padlock and iron bar across the main entrance of Sebastian Eels's house. "Unless you're planning to use Erwin's claw to pick the lock."

Erwin gives me a stern look of disapproval.

"I don't think we could pick that lock anyway," says Violet. "But maybe that's the point! Even though this house is locked and boarded up, all it would take to get in would be just one key. In fact, maybe that's why all the windows are boarded up.

Someone could even *live* in this house, Herbie, and if they're careful, no one in Eerie-on-Sea would even know."

"Until," I reply, completing the thought, "the wind blew down some of the planks one night, and Eerie's jumpiest resident happened to walk past while you were poking around with a flashlight, and she saw your shadow."

"Yes, *that* would give the game away," Violet agrees. "Because you can't have a spooky shadow without a not-so-spooky light to cast it. The question is, who was shining that light? And why?"

But, of course, neither of us have an answer for that.

"Prr-rrp," goes Erwin, standing up against Vi's leg and rubbing his ear on her thigh.

"What?" she says to him, but the cat—now that he has her attention—pads away up the steps and approaches the front door. At the side of the door, set in the large flagstone on the top step, is an old iron foot scraper. From among the dead leaves and paper wrappers that are caught behind it, Erwin pulls something into view.

It's a blue woolly hat, stitched with little golden stars, a bit like the stars on the ceiling of the Eerie Book Dispensary.

Violet gasps and snatches it up.

"This hat!" she cries, waving it under my nose. "It's Jenny's!"

CHAPTER 14

CHIPS FOR NONE

Personally, I would never dream of making a scene in the street, and hammering and shouting "Open up!" on the door of Eerie-on-Sea's most famous resident, but Violet isn't like me. She spends a good five minutes hammering and shouting very loudly indeed on the dead author's gleaming black door before finally giving it a good hard kick with her boot.

"There's no one there, Vi," I tell her. "At least, no one who wants us to know it."

"What if Jenny is in there?" Vi demands. "Trapped? Or worse? And if she isn't, where is she? Herbie, *where* has Jenny gone?"

But all I can do is shrug.

And then, since we can do no more at the house of Sebastian

Eels, we head off through the streets toward the Grand Nautilus Hotel. The Lost-and-Foundery—stuffed to the rafters as it is with all the misplaced things that have ever been handed in and not yet reclaimed—is my home, as it has been to all the Lost-and-Founders before me. You'll find everything there from glass eyes to eyeglasses, but you won't find Jenny Hanniver, owner of the Eerie Book Dispensary.

When we arrive, I stoke up a comforting fire in my wood-burning stove. Vi plonks herself down in my big armchair and folds her arms.

"I wonder if your so-called aunt—this Caliastra—has anything to do with all this?" she says.

"Why would you think that?" I ask with surprise.

"Well, isn't it a bit funny?" Violet replies. "That she should arrive out of the blue and take over the Ghastly Night show, just as someone is seen creeping around Sebastian Eels's house *and* Jenny vanishes into thin air?"

"Sometimes a coincidence is just a coincidence," I reply, doing my best Erwin impression. But Violet isn't impressed.

"You ought to tell her to leave you alone," Violet continues. "Caliastra, I mean. Coming here and trying to change everything!"

"I doubt Caliastra has anything to do with Jenny," I say, slamming the door of the stove louder than I mean to. "Why would she?"

Violet glares at me from beneath her mass of curls.

"I will help you find Jenny, Vi," I continue. "I promise. She's mine to lose as well, you know."

Violet softens her eyes but looks worried all the same. She chews on a fingernail and stares into the flames.

"Stay here tonight," I tell her then. "I don't think you should be alone. Then tomorrow we can ask around to see about Eels's house and who might have a key."

"But we need to do something *now*, Herbie!" I can't sit around waiting for tomorrow. Shouldn't we . . . shouldn't we *tell* someone about Jenny?"

"Tell who?" I reply. "We've already told Mrs. Fossil and the doc, and they're Jenny's friends. I bet Dr. Thalassi is already looking into it. He'll know what to do."

"But what if he doesn't?" Violet cries. "Shouldn't we get out there and search ourselves?"

"It's just . . ." I start to say, my mind drifting back to the woman with the raven hair. Now that she has been conjured into the conversation, I feel the nape of my neck tingle again at the memory of her dark, honey voice and her dazzling smile. "I thought . . . this afternoon . . . I might go along to the Theater at the End of the Pier, to see what my aunt . . . what Caliastra is up to. That's all." And then I add, when I catch the look on Violet's face, "I've always wanted to see behind the scenes of a magic show. Haven't you?"

And I try a grin.

"You believe her, don't you?" Violet replies, and the atmosphere is suddenly frosty, despite the jolly blaze in my stove. "You think that she really is your aunt. You've decided!"

"Um . . . well . . . I don't know, but . . ."

"I see!" Violet jumps up, upsetting a basket of lost hairbrushes. "Now you'll be leaving me, too. So that will be my parents gone, Jenny gone, and then my best friend—*gone!*"

"Violet, wait . . ." I start to say, but Violet doesn't wait. She runs to the window that she uses to get in and out of my cellar. It's a small window, and near the ceiling, but Violet is up and through it in a moment, and I hear her feet running off across the cobblestones.

"Wait!" I cry one last time, but now *she's* gone, leaving *me*.

Should I run after her? Probably.

"You're always running after her, aren't you, Herbie?" says the voice of Caliastra in my imagination. "Why can't she just be happy for you?"

"Because Violet always thought she would find her parents first," I reply aloud, suddenly realizing this truth. "I don't think she ever really believed I'd find family of my own."

"Well, let her go," Caliastra's honeyed voice continues. "Come see me anyway. You don't need Violet's permission."

I shake my head and rub my eyes.

The last thing I need right now is to start hearing things.

I go up to my cubbyhole and pick up Clermit automatically. I stare at his pearly shell in my hand. Then I put his winder key in the little hole and get ready to wind it . . .

But I don't.

Instead, I put the clockwork hermit crab back on the shelf, flip my sign over to CLOSED, and go back down to my cellar.

It can't hurt to pay a quick visit to the theater, can it? Just to see?

And since there's no one there to answer except me, I pull on my coat, slip out through the window, and set off at a run toward the pier.

⚙○✿

The wind whistles around the flaking Victorian railings as I make my way along the pier. The summer deck chairs are chained together and stowed, and the ice-cream stands are closed for winter. Above me, the tall neon letters that spell—during the summer months—CHEERIE-ON-SEA in bright candy colors are creaking in the wind. The letter *C* has already fallen off, as it always does this time of year, and the letter *H* looks like it won't be far behind. Then the town will return to its truer, darker identity.

But the dark won't have the pier all to itself. Even in the depths of winter, Seegol's Diner—the best fish and chips shop in town—will glow with a warm welcome at the very heart of the pier.

Seegol waves to me as I walk past, and he slides open a steamy window.

"Ah, Herbie!" he cries. "You come to eat chips alone? Or will your friend Violet be joining you?"

Inside the diner, a few locals sit and chat, and the smell of freshly fried fish and salty chips takes me by the nose.

"No time for chips, thanks," I reply, unable to quite believe what I'm saying. "Have you seen Jenny Hanniver, Mr. Seegol? She's gone missing."

"Missing?" The front of Seegol's bald head wrinkles with concern, and he scratches his stubbly chin. "She hasn't been here today, Herbie. And I am sure she hasn't been to the end of the pier, either. No one has."

"No one?" I ask. "No one's been to the theater?"

"The theater?" Seegol looks amazed at the suggestion. "The theater is all closed up, Herbie. No one's there at all."

My heart sinks.

Maybe I'm wasting my time. Maybe I should have run after Violet, after all. Perhaps, if I had, we'd be here together now, ordering lunch! If Caliastra and her troupe aren't even here yet, then I've just let my best friend run away *and* said no to fish and chips, all for nothing.

I wave goodbye to Mr. Seegol, but I don't head back to the hotel—not just yet. I should leave a note for Caliastra, to let her know I came. And *then* I'll go find Violet.

CHAPTER 15

ARCADE

The Theater at the End of the Pier is open for only one month of the year—and sometimes not even that. The rest of the time it sits empty and crooked, threatening to fall into the sea with every large wave. Its four towers are lopsided, and its golden Sinbad dome hasn't looked golden for decades. Sinbad would probably be embarrassed if he saw it now.

I came to see the Summer Show here once—a handful of third-rate tap dancers, variety performers, and an impressionist who didn't make much of an impression on me. I never came again. As I look up at the creaky old building that hulks defiantly against the elements, surrounded on three sides by the squally sea, I'm surprised that anyone comes here at all.

I'll tuck a note under the door, I decide, so that Caliastra will know I didn't forget. But that's when I notice that the door is slightly open.

I poke my head in, just in case.

"Hello?"

No answer.

The foyer of the theater is empty and covered in dust—and more than a few seagull droppings. A shabby old chandelier tinkles lightly above me as the sea wind finds its way inside. On one side there is an ornate ticket booth with a CLOSED sign across the window. And ahead, above the auditorium doors, there is a bust of old Mayor Bigley, who had this whole thing built in the first place, way back in the beginning. He looks down at me, all beady eyes and bronze whiskers, as if he doesn't approve of Lost-and-Founders. On the other side, opposite the ticket booth, are the arched glass panels of the Eerie-on-Sea amusement arcade—full of old penny machines, one-armed bandits, and ancient video games—that shares the foyer with the theater.

I cross to the dark glass of the arcade and wipe some grime off with my sleeve.

Inside, the machines and game cabinets are just shapes in the gloom.

My hand goes to the doorknob before I realize what I'm doing. In fact, my brain is still sending urgent messages to my hand, pointing out that this is (a) a bad idea, (b) actually quite spooky, and (c) not likely to help find Jenny, when I feel a sharp draft around the door.

"No wonder seagulls are getting in," I say, giving a little jump at the sound of my voice in this dusty place. "There's a window open in there."

I push the arcade door, shoving it wider against the dust and detritus on the floor, and slip inside. But the window, when I reach it, is stuck fast with age, so I decide to leave it.

"I wonder what games they've got," I say to myself, now that I'm actually in the amusement arcade itself. "I've never been here before . . ."

I pull out the little keychain flashlight I always carry and switch it on.

"Argh!"

A face leers at me in the narrow beam of the flashlight, and I almost fall over with shock.

But then I see that the face—which is cracked and peeling— isn't a living face at all but belongs to a plaster man beneath a silken turban. He's sitting in a glass box marked with the word *Zoltar*, and then, in curly lettering:

Let him speak your fortune.

"Thanks for the scare, Zoltar," I say, straightening my cap and giving the fortune-telling machine a friendly kick. "But I don't have a coin on me. Besides, you aren't even plugged in." And I look around at all the outmoded devices and games around me—Ultra-Galactic Pinball, Polybius, Whack-Octopi, and Slap the Donkey. "None of the machines are."

It's just as I'm deciding to leave that my eye falls on one particularly old arcade game.

"Space Invaders!" I cry.

Sure enough, a grimy cabinet of the classic arcade video game stands in one corner, beneath of a blanket of dust.

Even though I know nothing will happen, I can't help tapping the cracked old buttons and waggling the joystick.

BOOP!

The machine makes a sudden electrical sound, and I snatch my hands away.

On the screen, a small white square has appeared, right in the middle, flashing with a steady rhythm.

"I didn't do anything!" I call out, and hold my hands up, but there's no one here to make excuses to.

Then, before my disbelieving eyes, the small white dot types out a short message.

PRESS START

Is it talking to *me*? Feeling foolish, I reach out and press START.

Instantly the words vanish and are replaced by the classic display of a Space Invaders machine: a fleet of intergalactic aliens—fizzing in crude pixels—begin a slow, juddering descent toward four bunkers at the bottom, to the sound of a slow *DUH . . . DAH . . . DUH . . . DAH* beat. At the bottom of the screen is the little mobile laser cannon the player uses to shoot the aliens.

I bang the side of the cabinet, causing the image to crackle and dust to fall.

"Stop! I'm not actually playing . . ."

On the screen, the aliens creep closer in their low-tech approach, and the beat begins to speed up.

DUH, DAH, DUH, DAH . . .

Earth is being invaded and I'm just standing around doing nothing about it!

So, I grab the joystick and start zapping. Well, what else can I do?

PEW! PEW! PEW!

I blast a few of the baddies as they get closer, but it's clear they have the advantage. I waited too long before starting to play, and now there are just too many of them. I mash the fire button as fast as I can, but the laser blasts don't seem to be going in the right direction, and suddenly I realize that something strange and eerie is happening . . .

I let go of the controls.

On the screen, the remaining aliens are arranged in a crude shape. A shape that slides from side to side on the screen as the game rushes to its end.

"What!" I cry, trying to move my head with the crazy *DUH-DAH-DUH-DAH* beat, so that I can check that I'm really seeing what I think I'm seeing.

Then the earth is invaded and I lose. The screen fills with a terrible image: a horned head with two slanted eyes and a leering puppet-like grin.

The Shadowghast!

CHAPTER 16

THINGS OUT OF THIN AIR

The hideous face of the Shadowghast rushes at me—out from the screen!—in a roar of electronic noise. I fall back in horror as the horned man swoops down, electric-light hands snatching at me, awful mouth opening as if to consume me whole, and . . .

He collapses.

Into a riot of dust and static and the sparkle of dying pixels, the face disintegrates in the air above me and is gone. I'm left lying on the floor as the last of the twinkling motes descend around me.

But not for long.

Because I'm on my feet in a second, aren't I?

And *running*!

I burst out of the arcade, cross the foyer, and charge through the theater doors—pelting, with my hand on my cap, back down the pier as fast as a Lost-and-Founder has ever run.

And straight into something big and horribly soft that brings me to a sudden stop and sends me rolling on the boards of the pier.

I sit up to see a homburg hat land with a plop beside the stout form of Mr. Mummery, who is lying where I knocked him down. He forces himself up onto his elbow and glares at me.

"What the devil . . . ?" he splutters, grabbing his hat. "You! Well, what do you have to say for yourself?"

"Face!" I shout, pointing back at the theater. "Face Invaders! No, *Spade* Infacers! But . . . with a *face*!"

Then four hands close on my arms and elbows and I find myself being lifted roughly upright by the two black-clad men named Rictus and Tristo. Their facial features are still twisted by stage makeup into a leering grin for Rictus, and a terrible frown for Tristo.

"Herbie!"

Caliastra appears.

"Unhand him!" she commands Rictus and Tristo. "Can't you see he's had a shock?"

The hands release me. Rictus steps back and gives me an exaggerated silent plea for forgiveness, while Tristo makes a show of brushing down my uniform and straightening my cap and buttons.

"What's this about a face?" Caliastra asks, putting one hand on my shoulder and looking searchingly into my eyes. "Did something scare you, Herbie? Something in the theater?"

"I . . ." I begin. Then I'm not sure where to go from there. "There was a . . . um . . ."

But I really don't know how to describe the strange thing that just happened to me in the amusement arcade. So I decide to leave the "um" hanging there and see what happens next.

"No matter." Caliastra smiles kindly then. "The theater is a spooky old place. You probably jumped at the sight of your own shadow. But you came to see me, Herbie, and *that's* the most important thing. I'm only sorry we weren't there yet, but please do come with us now. We are going to rehearse, and *you* can be our audience."

Mr. Mummery gets to his feet and sets his hat on his head. With a final glare at me, he strides off toward the theater, with Rictus and Tristo behind him. Then I follow with Caliastra.

"Have you had a little more time to think about everything I said this morning, Herbie?" Caliastra asks. "I know it must be hard for you, after all these years of not knowing anything about your past."

"Well, I have been wondering," I admit. "If you are who you say you are, then . . ."

The next words just come tumbling out:

". . . then you could tell me about my *mum*! What color eyes she had. What she used to say about me! Or, or about my *dad*! What was he *like*? What did we *do* together? Or about my brothers and sisters. Do I even *have* any brothers and sisters? And where was I born? And what's my *real name* ? And . . . ?"

"Herbie, enough!" Caliastra comes to a stop and turns me by the shoulders to look at her. "You need to take it easy. I see now that my appearance has been more of a shock than I realized. Of course, I will tell you all those things in time. But right now, I think you need to just get used to me being here and to the change that is happening in your life. OK?"

I manage a nod.

"And I am a bit disappointed, I admit, to hear you say '*If* you are who you say you are . . .'" Caliastra turns a hurt smile on me. "I hope you don't think I'm lying."

"No!" I say quickly, wanting to fix that smile. "But, it's just that I was talking about it with Violet, and . . ."

"Ah, yes, your friend." Caliastra nods. "You know, I have a feeling she doesn't quite trust me."

"I think . . ."

"Yes?"

"I think she'll be sad if I leave."

"Oh, she'll make other friends," Caliastra replies, waving

the problem away like an annoying fly. "But you must always be careful of others being jealous, Herbie."

"Jealous?"

"Not everyone can have an opportunity like the one I'm giving you," says Caliastra. "Violet has a different destiny."

"I'm really going to be a magician's apprentice?" I ask, trying to steer the conversation as far away from Violet as I can. The idea of leaving her behind is not something I want to think about just yet. In fact, the whole idea of leaving Eerie-on-Sea, the Grand Nautilus hotel, and my Lost-and-Foundery is all so utterly incomprehensible that I'm amazed I'm even considering it. And yet, here I am, chatting with a woman—my aunt!—who seems about to make it happen.

"Of course," says Caliastra. "But no one will force you to do anything, Herbie. I just hope that once you have seen my work, you will understand what adventure awaits you."

"Lady Kraken . . ." I begin, but Caliastra waves her name away, too.

"Oh, don't worry about the old lady." She laughs. "I have everything I need to convince her that this is the best thing for you. Don't you worry."

And that's when we arrive at the flaky doors of the theater.

"Perhaps," the raven-haired magician continues, looking at me closely, "in exchange, before we leave town, you will give me a thorough tour of your famous lost-property cellar."

"You want to visit my Lost-and-Foundery?" I ask, surprised.

"But of course. I want to know everything you've been up to since . . . since the tragic event that separated us. I'm sure there must be lots of interesting things in your cellar. Things that have been lost for centuries. I'd love to see them, Herbie."

I blink at Caliastra. It's true, there *are* lots of curious old unclaimed things down there, and yes, some of them appear older even than the hotel itself, which has always seemed a mystery to me, if I'm honest. But then why shouldn't a famous travel-ing magician be curious about things such as these? *Mystery* and *magician* are surely two words that always belong together.

"OK," I say, giving the only answer I can think of.

And then Rictus and Tristo open the doors and we enter the Theater at the End of the Pier.

⚙○✿

Back inside the theater foyer, I can't help but peer over at the glass door of the amusement arcade. Everything is dark inside and just as I left it. It's clear, though, that Caliastra and her troupe have no interest in the arcade—they walk past it without a second glance.

Mr. Mummery approaches the great double doors to the auditorium, and under the bronze gaze of old Mayor Bigley, he pulls a chain of keys from his pocket.

"I trust the apparatus is set up," he says to both Rictus and Tristo. "We don't want to waste any time."

The two strange men in black answer with silent bows.

I want to ask Caliastra "What apparatus?" but I also feel another question come into my head, so I ask her that instead.

"Don't they ever speak?" I say. "Rictus and Tristo?"

"Never," she replies. "They are mime artists, Herbie. Didn't you realize that?"

"Mime artists?"

"Indeed. I met them years ago in Prague, and they have been part of my act ever since. They are entirely silent, and yet with their bodies they can say almost anything they like."

I look at the two tall, slender-built men. They turn to me and strike exaggerated poses. Then Tristo steps away but immediately bounces back, as if he has come up against an invisible barrier. Quickly he presses against the air around him with his hands as if he is suddenly surrounded by the insides of an invisible box. And the way he moves his hands is so convincing that instantly I believe that he really is trapped!

Beside him, Rictus places his hands flat on either side of his face and turns to me with an expression of grinning pantomime horror at his friend's predicament. But then he snaps his fingers as if a light bulb has appeared over his head. He has an idea!

Silently, Rictus implores Caliastra to lend him her honey-colored glass cane. She smiles indulgently and hands it over.

While Tristo continues to describe the inside of the box with panicky gestures, Rictus fits one end of the cane firmly behind its invisible lid. Then, as if the cane is a crowbar, he starts to lever it in the air, heaving with all his might. I want to shout "Be careful, it's only glass! It'll break!" and it takes all my self-control to remember that *there is no lid*—this is *all* a mime.

Then the invisible lid flies open, and Tristo—relief written all across his painted face—steps out of the box and embraces his friend, as if they are overjoyed to be reunited after such a terrible experience.

And despite everything, I find myself grinning and clapping.

"That's amazing!" I say. And it was. I've never seen mime artists perform before. "It's like they can make things out of thin air!"

Rictus and Tristo turn and, arm in arm, they bow for me.

"Save it for the show," grumbles Mr. Mummery.

And he unlocks the door to the auditorium.

CHAPTER 17

PRESTOCADABRA!

Mr. Mummery flips a switch and a few wall lights snap on, flicker for a moment as if unsure whether they can quite be bothered, and then illuminate the interior of the theater.

Two hundred faded velvet chairs huddle opposite the stage. They are stacked at a dizzyingly steep angle, one row above the rest, and I can easily imagine old Mayor Bigley ordering the architect of the place to cram in as many bums-on-seats as possible. Above this is a small gallery of cheaper seats, pushed right up beneath the gilded ceiling, whose view is surely obstructed by three giant chandeliers of dusty crystal and bat droppings. On either side of the auditorium there is an ornate private box for any fancy people who might have accidentally found themselves in Eerie-on-Sea.

The stage itself, the focus of all this empty-chair attention, is surprisingly small. But, as if to make up for this, the arch around it curls with so many golden rococo decorations that it reminds me of the scrambled egg I never got to eat at breakfast.

The stage curtains, threadbare with age, are pulled aside, revealing the empty, shrunken floorboards of the stage itself—half hidden by a line of enormous footlight reflectors, the backs of which are shaped like upright crabs.

Except wait! The stage isn't entirely empty. An object is already there, under a silver cloth in the center. The drape is disturbed, as though something has crept out from underneath. Rictus straightens it, hiding the gap.

"What's under there?" I ask.

But before Caliastra can answer, Tristo pulls down a large master switch on the backstage wall, and everything explodes into brilliant light. The entire lighting rig comes on at once, flooding the stage below with blinding illumination.

"Argh!" Mr. Mummery shoves his fists into his eyes.

"Be careful!" Caliastra shouts, also shrinking back. "Turn it off!"

Tristo quickly raises the switch back to the off position, plunging us into relative gloom once again.

"I told you before," Caliastra snaps angrily. "We don't need stage lights. They're old and dangerous to use, and besides—we have our own source of light, don't we?"

I'm left blinking purple blobs out of my eyes as Tristo waggles his fingers in apology.

"Come, Herbie," says Caliastra then, leading me back up the aisle. "Take a seat near the middle, so you have the best view. We just need a moment to set up, and then—I promise—you will see something amazing."

I slide along a row of seats until I find a good spot, and I'm surprised to see Caliastra sliding along, too, and sitting beside me.

"Aren't you going to do any magic?" I ask.

"Magic?" Caliastra smiles. "Of course not. There's no such thing as magic, Herbie."

"Oh," I say. "But I didn't mean . . . that is, you're a magician, so I thought you'd be doing some magic tricks, and . . ."

"Exactly!" Caliastra raises her slender index finger. "And just like that, Herbie, you have explained *everything* about my act."

"I have?"

"I don't do *magic*." Caliastra holds up the owl on the top of her cane, turning it so that it glints with reflected light, drawing in my gaze. "I do magic *tricks*. When you realize that, you'll have taken your first step toward becoming my apprentice."

"I . . . I will?"

Caliastra swings her cane around till it's pointing at the stage. I find my sight sliding along it to the where the mime artists are unpacking cases and setting up.

"Do you see what they are doing, Herbie?"

"Yes."

"Then watch them closely. Don't take your eyes away for a moment. Tell me what you see."

"Um, well, Rictus—or is it Tristo?—is assembling a cabinet," I say, watching the mime artists go about their work, "while the other one, Tristo—or is it Rictus?—is approaching the back of the cabinet, holding up a sparkly black cloth. I wonder what it's for . . ."

"Keep watching," comes the hypnotic voice of Caliastra. "Keep your eyes fixed on the box."

And that's when I know I'm going to see something amazing. I clutch the seat in front of me and nail my gaze to the cabinet, wondering what's about to happen. Tristo has draped the sparkly cloth over the cabinet with a flourish, and now Rictus is spinning the whole thing. The light of the sequins on the cloth sparkles in my eyes, and I find it hard to focus.

Then the cabinet stops spinning, and the cloth is whipped away.

"Keep watching, Herbie!"

The door of the cabinet swings open, and . . .

My jaw hits the floor.

With a cry of "Prestocadabra!" Caliastra steps from the cabinet. She twirls her cane in her fingers, smiling in triumph as she holds out one arm to the audience that isn't there, as if the theater seats are packed with cheering spectators.

I grab my cap with both hands. Somehow I manage to turn my bamboozled noggin to look at the seat next to me.

Of course, it's empty.

"But . . . !" I blurt out, jumping to my feet. "How did you . . . ?"

When I look back, both Rictus and Tristo are doing exaggerated belly laughs at my expense, while even Mr. Mummery manages a chuckle.

"When it comes to magic tricks, Herbie," Caliastra calls back, leaning on her cane in the center of the stage, "people are so eager to see the *magic* that they forget to look for the *trick*. You were too busy watching the stage to notice that I'd slipped away."

"But you spoke to me—you were right here!" I call back.

"Not quite," replies a voice somewhere behind me. I spin around, but the seats there are all empty, too.

"It helps," Caliastra continues, "that I can throw my voice."

I sit down heavily.

"Hey," says Caliastra, laughing, "I told you I'd be honest.

These are my secrets I'm telling you. The secrets of my success. One day they'll be the secrets of yours, as well."

I say nothing. I stare at the stage and wonder if I, too, will one day be able to do the amazing things Caliastra does.

Then I shake my head. It feels as if whatever I say, and however I feel about it, I'm being pulled irresistibly into the life of this strange magician. But as I get closer to Caliastra, I drift farther and farther away from my Lost-and-Foundery, and Eerie-on-Sea, and everything I know. And away from Violet.

"Don't look so worried, dear Herbie," the voice of the raven-haired woman says into my ear.

And Caliastra is beside me again, sitting exactly where she was before, as if she'd been there all along.

"This is your destiny." She leans in, as if I'm the most important person in the world and she is confiding in me above all others. "Your birthright. You are meant for greater things than lost property, my boy, and I can teach you everything. People are easily confused, and they'll believe anything you say, once you know how to spin the right story." Then she lowers her voice to a whisper. "It's the greatest power in the world."

I look up. Caliastra's eye are glinting, but I feel the beginnings of a frown come over mine. Using tricks to get power over people seems, well, it seems a bit . . .

"That hotel manager," the magician says quickly, with a

suggestive twitch of an eyebrow. "Mr. Mollusc. You play tricks on him already, don't you?"

"He's mean," I reply. "He deserves it."

"Exactly! But just think what you could do to him once you've learned a few of *my* secrets."

I look into Caliastra's eyes again. I like the glint much more now. Old Mollusc has made my life miserable for long enough. With my aunt's help, he won't stand a chance.

"We'll *destroy* him," the magician whispers, her face so close now that our foreheads are almost touching. She laughs at the thought, and I can't help laughing, too. "When you give me that tour of your Lost-and-Foundery, Herbie, we'll sort out Mr. Mollusc once and for all."

Caliastra puts her arms around my shoulder and squeezes.

And I feel more powerful already, as if together we could conquer the world.

Which is why it's a shame that the auditorium doors burst open just then, and Violet walks in.

CHAPTER 18

THE COILED DRAGON

N

o, it's not a *shame* that Violet walks in just then.

What am I thinking?

"Violet!" I cry, jumping up. "I . . . I was looking for you."

"Were you?" Violet replies, striding down the aisle. "This is a funny place to look, Herbie, since I've *never been here before*. It's just as well I stopped by, isn't it?"

And she gives Caliastra a cold stare.

The magician rises to her feet.

"Hello again, Violet," she says. "Why don't you join Herbie in the audience? We were just about to rehearse our show."

And she steps out of the row, offering up her seat for Violet.

"Thanks, but I can't stay," Violet replies. "My guardian, Jenny, has gone missing, so *I* don't have time to sit around watching magic tricks."

And she turns her frosty gaze onto me.

I want to say "I'm looking for Jenny, too!" or "Violet, it's not what you think!" but before I can say anything, there's a creak at the auditorium door, and someone else enters—someone wearing several coats and at least three hats, tied on her head by a piece of string.

"Mrs. Fossil!" I cry. Then I notice the look on her face. "Are you . . . are you all right?"

"No, I am not all right, Herbie," Mrs. F says. "Thanks for asking. Not all right because of *this*!" And she waves a piece of paper in the air.

"Mrs. Fossil isn't happy that her Ghastly Night show, the one she does every year with Dr. Thalassi, has been stolen," Violet explains.

Mrs. Fossil hands the paper to me. It's a poster, its corners ripped where it was torn off the pins. Caliastra's name is printed right across the top in dramatic letters, advertising her Ghastly Night show as the "greatest spectacle that Eerie-on-Sea has ever seen." The magician is depicted on the poster, waving her amber cane dramatically beside a strange lamp that is giving off clouds of colored smoke in the forms of weird and wonderful creatures.

The date of the show, of course, is tomorrow evening.

"We paid good money for those!" growls Mr. Mummery, coming over and snatching the poster from me. And I'm amazed at the sight of him. The manager has changed out of his somber gray suit and hat and is now wearing a candy-striped blazer, with a funny little straw boater hat on his head.

"Really, Mummery." Caliastra rolls her eyes. "This is hardly the moment to worry about that."

"I wouldn't have to worry," the theatrical manager replies, "if you were actually charging something for our time." And he holds up the poster, jabbing at the words FREE ADMISSION! with a chubby finger. "You didn't get where you are today by giving away *freebies*, Caliastra, and neither did I."

"Free?" I say. "You're doing the show for free?"

The magician nods solemnly.

"I want the whole town to come. It's my gift to Eerie-on-Sea to thank the place for looking after you, Herbie. It's the least I can do."

"But what about me and the doc?" Mrs. Fossil grabs at the poster. "We *always* do the show."

Mr. Mummery, still clinging to the other end of the sheet of paper, pulls back, and soon he and Mrs. F are caught up in a full-blown tug-of-war.

"Stop!" cries Caliastra. She swings her cane in a deft movement, slicing the poster in half.

"My dear Mrs. Fossil." Caliastra turns to the beachcomber. "I shall reserve the very best seats for you and the doctor. As experts on the legend of the Shadowghast, you will be our guests of honor."

Mrs. Fossil, who can never stay angry with anyone for long, gives a little smile.

"Experts?" she says, putting her hands into the pockets of her waxed coat and rocking back and forward in her rubber boots. "Well, if you put it like that. And I admit, it *would* be good to see how a professional does it. And perhaps I can even play my hurdy-gurdy a bit, as the townsfolk arrive."

"Of course," Caliastra says. Then she turns to the theatrical manager. "As for you, Mummery, I have explained all this. We must ensure that everyone in Eerie-on-Sea has a night they will never forget. Now, get back to your organ, or I'll ask Mrs. Fossil to do *all* the music."

Mr. Mummery scowls harder than ever. But he doesn't seem to be able to hold his employer's eye for long.

"But what gives you the right to put on the show!" Violet demands as opposition to the magician crumbles all around. "Just because you're famous doesn't mean you can walk in and take over. What makes *you* so special?"

"It isn't just my fame, Violet," Caliastra replies, the hint of annoyance in her voice not quite concealed. "I have studied the lore of Ghastly Night for years. And thanks to my correspondent in Eerie-on-Sea, I have something no other performer can bring to the act: I have . . . *this!*"

And with that she claps her hands in command.

Up onstage, beside the object concealed beneath the silver drape, Rictus has clearly been following our conversation closely. At the sign from the magician, he seizes the drape, sweeps it away with a dramatic gesture, and reveals what is hidden beneath.

A lantern.

A large, old, tarnished, and battered lantern, made of bronze but green with age. There is a rickety chimney rising from the top, around which a sculpted serpent—no, a *dragon*—form is coiled. The dragon's wings are curved on either side, like handles, and the head of the beast projects forward on a long neck, toward the audience. The dragon's mouth is stoppered up with a silver orb, jammed between its teeth.

Rictus and Tristo both mime mock horror and retreat from the stage as if the strange dragon lamp might come alive and chase them. Despite everything, I can't help laughing to see them clowning around.

"Ooh!" says Mrs. Fossil. "That looks old. Is it anything like the one used on the first Ghastly Night? When the Puppet Master took his revenge on old Mayor Bigley."

"*Like* it?" Caliastra looks surprised. "My dear Mrs. Fossil, this *is* it. Recovered from the sea after all these years and restored to working order by a local expert."

"That would be Dr. Thalassi, I expect," Mrs. Fossil replies. "Though, he has never said anything about it to me."

"Not the doctor, no," Caliastra replies, ushering us toward seats. "Now, if you would be good enough to sit, we will light the lantern and rehearse for tomorrow's big performance."

And she hurries to the stage.

"Who?" Violet calls, the last to sit, her hands clenched at her sides. "*Who* is this local expert?"

"I'm sure you've heard of him," the magician replies, climbing up the steps to the stage. "He was an author—quite famous before he disappeared—and a specialist in the folklore of your town, Violet. His name was Sebastian Eels."

CHAPTER 19

PHANTASMAGORIA

Violet sits down heavily beside me.

We stare at each other.

"Eels again!" Violet mouths.

Sebastian Eels, as you'll know if you've been to Eerie-on-Sea before and heard all the rumors, is more than just the owner of a boarded-up house. He's Violet Parma's sworn enemy—and the main reason she's been left without parents. To have his name come up twice in one day is a shock.

Up on the stage, Rictus brings a lighted taper to the open lantern and places the flame inside. Tristo, beside him, squeezes a bellows, and—with a crackle and a fizz—thick smoke begins to billow out from the chimney of the lantern and escape in hot gouts from around the silver orb in the bronze dragon's mouth.

"I should have known." Violet tears her eyes from the extraordinary sight and hits me with a frown. "It makes perfect sense that Caliastra and Eels would be working together."

"Except," I reply, "it doesn't! Eels is gone, Vi. Forever. Caliastra said herself he'd disappeared."

"She *said* that, yes," Violet agrees, "but his house isn't gone, is it? Or his stuff. Someone has been in there, and Jenny found out. And now Jenny is missing! It's all connected. It must be."

I open my mouth to say the one true thing that will stop Violet's suspicion of Caliastra once and for all and make it all OK.

But nothing comes out.

"Besides," Violet continues, "I've seen enough of this magician to know she's good at saying exactly what needs to be said to get her own way."

I cast a desperate glance at Caliastra, who is preparing herself on the smoky stage, and Violet catches me doing it.

"Herbie?" Violet grabs my arm. "Please don't tell me that you've fallen under her spell, too."

I manage a shrug—not a very reassuring one, but it's the best I can do right now. I'm just about to add a small grin, for good measure, when Vi and I jump in our seats as a loud musical note reverberates around the auditorium.

"Golly!" cries Mrs. Fossil beside us, pulling the flaps of her middlemost hat over her ears.

From down in the small orchestra pit, in front of the stage, Mr. Mummery's head and hat have appeared, rising up jerkily. Then his shoulders arrive, still clad in the candy-striped blazer. Before him, rising also, is a large, dusty, white object, spotted with seagull droppings. The man continues to ascend, wreathed in smoke from the lantern, while all the time a jolly fairground tune—slightly out of key and far too loud—blares out. Then he comes to a halt, and we see that the object is some kind of musical organ. Mr. Mummery is playing it, his fat fingers leaping around the keyboard, while his feet jump around the pedals.

He turns, gives his small audience a leering, over-the-shoulder smile that he clearly doesn't mean, and then finishes with a flourish and at least one wrong note.

"Golly!" says Mrs. Fossil again. "The old Wurlitzer organ! I haven't heard that since I was a little girl. Sounds a bit rough these days. That settles it, I'm definitely bringing my gurdy tomorrow night."

Now our eyes are fixed on Caliastra, who is standing before the fiery lantern, shepherding the clouds of perfumed smoke with motions of her cane as she begins to tell the tale of the first Ghastly Night in Eerie-on-Sea. Then, at just the right moment, Rictus reaches forward and plucks the silver orb from the bronze dragon's mouth, releasing the strange light of the magic lantern.

"Ooh!" gasps Mrs. Fossil. "Isn't that lovely?"

The light is bright and shifts and shimmers as if alive. I'm not sure *lovely* is the word I would use to describe it. *Supernatural* would be better.

Where the lantern light hits the clouds, they fill with a diffuse glow, as bright as Dr. Thalassi's canvas screen. Shapes creep in the billowing clouds—shadow shapes that seem almost as if they are trying to find a way out—and I wonder what's causing them. Something mechanical inside the lantern? Something on the lens?

But then Caliastra lays aside her cane and thrusts her hands into the light, changing everything.

The magician shapes and commands these creeping, cowering shadows, casting them into sharper, more vivid forms. One of them—the portly silhouette of a tall, whiskered man—strides into center stage and strikes a haughty pose.

"Old Mayor Bigley!" cries Mrs. Fossil, clapping her hands.

Then other shadows come, creating the story as Caliastra speaks it aloud. One becomes the Puppet Master, holding in his arms the mysterious lantern. Others are shaped into the people of Eerie-on-Sea, gathering on the pier to watch the first Ghastly

Night show. And all of it is seemingly formed and cast by nothing more than the dexterity of Caliastra's hands.

"That's amazing!" Violet gasps, her suspicion of the magician, even her worry about Jenny, temporarily forgotten. "How can she do that? It's so . . . so real!"

But nothing we've seen yet prepares us for what happens next.

One of the shadows flies into the air, changing and reforming, until . . .

A mermaid appears!

A curvaceous and tangle-haired siren, who swims through the cloud with a flick of her tail.

Then another shadow becomes a giant squid, its tentacles rearing high above the stage before crashing back into a sea of smoke. In its wake comes a succession of legendary creatures, dancing and cavorting and prowling among the roiling cloud, as Caliastra tells the story and Tristo works the bellows.

Finally, before our disbelieving eyes, the silhouette of a creature we thought we'd never see again creeps across the misty scene, its spines quivering, its tail swishing from side to side, its mouth hanging loose to display row upon row of terrible tooth needles.

"The malamander!" Violet and I gasp, shrinking back in our seats.

"Oh!" Mrs. Fossil's quivery voice reaches us. "Oh, the poor doc! If he saw these . . . these *wonders* . . . he'd be embarrassed for our poor little lamp show of sticks and cloth. This is *truly* magical!"

But I think back to what Caliastra said to me just a little while ago: "People are so eager to see the *magic* that they forget to look for the *trick*."

So what, I ask myself, is the trick we're missing here?

How can a magician, no matter how skilled, make shadow shapes like this using only her fingers?

I look deep into the smoke, searching for some clue—for some hint that Rictus and Tristo are helping somehow, or some sign that Mr. Mummery is pulling strings from offstage. And that's when I see it.

"What's that?" I grab Violet's arm and point into the smoke.

"Shadows," Vi replies. "It's all just shadows."

But then it's there again, a spindly, crooked shadow that doesn't seem part of the carousel of creatures conjured by Caliastra. It stoops forward, snatches a shadow that has crept to the edge of the cloud, and whirls it up into the spectacle.

Then the crooked shape shrinks back into the dark, as if it had never been there. But not before Vi and I both get a good look at it.

It is the shadow of a grinning man with horns upon his head.

CHAPTER 20

THE VOLUNTEER

D id you see that?" Violet turns to me, blinking.

All I can do is blink back.

I scan the clouds of smoke carefully, but the crooked form is no longer visible. Then I remember I haven't told Vi about the scare I had with the Space Invaders game . . .

"Vi, earlier on, in the arcade, I think I saw . . ."

But my voice is drowned out by another blast of organ music as Mr. Mummery digs his fingers into the keys of the Wurlitzer again.

Above him, Caliastra commands the shadows back into the light, before parting the clouds of smoke with expansive motions of her glass cane. The menagerie of magical creatures is gone, and Rictus deftly replaces the silver ball in the mouth of the dragon. The music dies, and the magician addresses the audience.

"Ladies and gentlemen! Now we come to the moment in our show where you, too, can play a part. We need volunteers! From the audience! Volunteers to take their place for one magical moment among the shadows of Ghastly Night. Raise your hands! We will call you up, one by one."

Then she adds, in a lower voice, because during this rehearsal there are actually only three people in the audience, "Don't worry, we'll settle for just one today, so . . ."

I put my hand up.

"Actually, Herbie," Caliastra says, "I wondered if Violet might like to volunteer."

I lower my hand. I only put it up because being onstage is probably my best chance of seeing how this trick of light and shadows is done. But, of course, now that Caliastra has started revealing her secrets to me, maybe she prefers someone who is still in the dark. Maybe that's why she's pointing her cane at Violet so definitely, and lifting her free hand as if willing her to rise.

Hesitatingly, shakily, Violet gets to her feet.

"Herbie . . . ?" She turns to me, her eyes round beneath her tangled hair.

"Me, me!" cries Mrs. Fossil, jumping to her feet just then. "I volunteer! Pick me!"

And before anyone can stop her, she starts pushing past us, filling our nostrils with the smell of old waxed coat and beachcomber's pocket, as she squeezes down the row of seats.

"I really think, Mrs. Fossil . . ." Caliastra starts to protest, looking taken aback. "That . . . that *Violet* would be . . . Oh, you're already here."

Mrs. Fossil is indeed already there, puffing up the steps to the stage, her rubber boots squeaking on the wood. Tristo steps forward, ushering her to center stage with beckoning mimes.

Violet sits back down again.

Caliastra darts a look at my friend—a look I don't quite understand—before turning to welcome Mrs. Fossil into the act. And I wonder why the magician seems reluctant to have Mrs. F volunteer. Mrs. Fossil, though excellent in many ways, is the least likely of us to spot any tricks, and she is easily the most likely to be amazed and bamboozled by everything.

But I don't have time to wonder. The show is already moving on. Tristo is working the bellows again, and Caliastra is once more gathering smoke with her cane, returning to the story of Ghastly Night in Eerie-on-Sea. The silver orb is removed from the teeth of the dragon, and eerie light spills back across the stage. The beachcomber is caught in the full beam of it, raising her hands to shield her eyes. Her tatty and over-hatted shadow stretches out behind her.

Then the smoke closes in, and Mrs. Fossil disappears.

Except, not entirely. Her shadow is now contained wholly in the clouds—standing nervously in the smoke as if trapped there.

"Golly!" comes Mrs. Fossil's echoing voice. "It's strange in here."

Then she coughs.

"And tickly . . . on the tonsils . . ."

Mrs. Fossil's hesitant shadow is joined by another, spikier one that flicks between the clouds and then rises up beside the beachcomber with a terrible grin.

"Behold!" declares Caliastra. "The Shadowghast!"

"It's all part of the trick," I say, clutching the seat in front of me. "Isn't it?"

The Shadowghast reaches out to the shadow of Mrs. Fossil and makes her jump.

"Who's that?" comes the beachcomber's voice, from inside the smoke. "Who's there? Oh!"

The Shadowghast seizes Mrs. F's shadow hands in his own. As Mr. Mummery strikes up another ghastly tune on the Wurlitzer, the horned man whirls Mrs. Fossil's shadow away in a dance. Soon the two of them are spinning like waltzers—the Shadowghast, leggy as a spider, and Mrs. Fossil, plump with too many coats, her hats coming off in all directions.

And then they are flying!

In front of our bulging eyes we see Mrs. Fossil's silhouette leave the stage to be whirled and whirled high into the smoky air—her terrifying dance partner pulling her ever upward. He spins her again and again, till—as the music reaches a climax—the Shadowghast leaps back into the lantern, dragging our friend's shadow behind him.

Then the music dies away.

Caliastra steps forward, slicing the clouds of smoke away with swoops of her cane, as the orb is placed once more in the lantern's dragon mouth. Tristo slams shut the back door of the lantern with a metallic *CLANG*, and all falls silent.

On the stage, standing alone in the center as the smoke clears, Mrs. Fossil sways from side to side in her boots, staring into space. Her hats are lying all around her, as if they really did fall from her head as she swooped into the air and flew.

"G-g-golly!" she manages to say.

I jump to my feet, my hands clapping madly. Beside me, Violet claps, too, but as if she's in a daze.

Caliastra opens her arms to acknowledge the applause, and Rictus and Tristo begin a little clown act as each tries not to trip over the other. Even Mr. Mummery gets to his feet and takes a bow, though he bumps the keys of his Wurlitzer with his bottom as he does so, causing a musical honk. Something tells me this is deliberate, though, and I clap all the more.

"So, Herbie," Caliastra calls to me. "A little proud of your aunt, I hope."

"It was amazing!" I call back. "*You* were amazing."

Caliastra beams at me, though I can't help noticing she darts the briefest of glances at Violet.

Beside me, Violet gets to her feet.

"Are you OK, Mrs. Fossil?" she calls. Then she turns to me. "Stop clapping, Herbie! Something's wrong."

Up onstage, Mrs. Fossil sways to the left, then to the right. Then, before either Rictus or Tristo can reach her, she spins on one rubber-boot heel and topples over in a dead faint.

CHAPTER 21

A BIT BAMBOOZLED

M rs. Fossil!"

Violet and I race down the aisle and up the steps to the stage. By the time we get there, Rictus has propped the beachcomber up on one elbow, and Tristo is fanning her with an imaginary sheet of cardboard.

"Oh!" Mrs. F manages to say. "Oh, my dears! What just happened?"

"You very kindly volunteered to be part of my act, Mrs. Fossil," says Caliastra, helping the beachcomber to her feet. "An important part, too. But do you see now why I thought Violet would be better? Dancing through the air, arm in arm with the

Shadowghast himself, can be a little taxing for someone of your, um, more senior years."

And the magician aims a wink in my direction.

"You'll be all right again in no time," says Mr. Mummery, entering stage left with a glass of water. "Won't you," he continues, forgetting to add a question mark and making it sound like an order instead. "We need to be careful who we call up onstage tomorrow night, Caliastra," he adds quietly to his employer. "The last thing we need is to kill off any of the local fogies and get ourselves sued."

"I promise to choose only the more vigorous members of the audience," Caliastra replies testily. "Everything will be fine, Mummery."

"But what *did* happen to her?" Violet demands. "Why is Mrs. Fossil so dizzy?"

"You'd be dizzy, too," I say, "if you'd been danced off the ground like that."

"She wasn't really danced off the ground!" Violet snaps. "Herbie, it was a *trick*, remember? We saw *shadow puppets* dancing into the air, not actual people. I just wonder what made the *actual* Mrs. Fossil so wobbly."

"It was so strange," Mrs. F explains. "And with the smoke, I found it so hard to breathe! I did feel myself being spun around and around, and something definitely touched me, but I couldn't see properly. I expect I'm just a bit bamboozled, that's all. I'll be right as rain in a jiffy."

And she drains the glass of water in one go.

"Thanks," she says, handing the empty glass back to Mr. Mummery. "I don't suppose anyone's put the kettle on? I'd love a cup of tea and a nice sit-down. And if you've got a biscuit, I won't say no."

"There, you see?" Caliastra turns to Violet. "Mrs. Fossil is fine, and no harm's done. And now, maybe you could escort the brave volunteer home, Violet? My fellow performers and I need to get back to our rehearsal."

Violet takes Mrs. F's arm and leads the beachcomber toward the doors.

"Come on, Herbie," she calls over her shoulder.

"Oh, Herbie can stay," Caliastra says in a casual voice that almost—*almost*—masks the division that has opened up between her and Violet. Violet stops and turns back to look at me.

"Herbie?" she says. And in just such a way, and with just such a look in her eyes, that memories of our amazing adventures together flash across my mind in a warm rush of friendship.

I clutch my buttons.

I try to do a grin as I glance apologetically back at my aunt.

The raven-haired magician smiles her most dazzling smile at me. Then she moves one of her hands at her side like she's conjuring a perfectly Herbie-shaped hole right there, and as if the universe is just waiting for me to fill it.

My knees start to tremble.

One of my feet steps toward the stage, but the other turns back toward Violet, near the exit. I'm just about to get my knees in a tangle and become the second person to fall over today in the Theater at the End of the Pier, when Caliastra laughs.

"I'll see you very soon, Herbie," she says with a wave of her cane. "Go! Help your friend. Make the most of your time here. We will be together again soon enough."

And just like that, I'm released.

I run after Violet.

"Herbie, there's something really not right about all this," Violet says as we head back down the pier toward the town, Mrs. Fossil walking unsteadily between us.

"It's just a magic trick, Vi," I reply. "You said so yourself."

When we reach the end of the pier, Mrs. F is almost her old self again.

"Thank you, my dears," she says. "I'll take myself home from here. No need to fuss. I just need to take the weight off my boots, that's all."

There's a poster advertising Caliastra's Ghastly Night show taped to one of the ornate lampposts beside the entrance to the pier. One corner is flapping in the wind, and Mrs. Fossil reaches out to it. But instead of tearing it off, as I expect her to do, she smooths the tape back down.

"I wish the doc had been there to see it," she says. "What an amazing show!"

And with a wave, she heads off into the winding streets of Eerie-on-Sea, back to her Flotsamporium.

"It may be just a magic trick, Herbie," Violet says, "but it has certainly changed Mrs. F. Caliastra has yet another fan, by the looks of it."

The sun emerges briefly and bathes the cobblestones in a moment of unexpected warmth. And suddenly, as I watch Mrs. Fossil go, I'm struck by a memory of seeing Caliastra and her troupe in the lobby of the hotel, when they first arrived. What was it I noticed then? Something strange about the light? And why do I feel I've just seen it again? I rub my eyes, but when I look back, the sun is gone, and Mrs. F has turned a corner and vanished.

"Herbie?"

"Let's go back to my Lost-and-Foundery," I say. "I need to tell you something."

"That settles it," Vi says when I finish telling her about the strange thing that happened to me in the amusement arcade.

We're sitting in my Lost-and-Foundery, in the warmth. Violet is curled up in my big tatty armchair—Erwin purring like an engine on her lap—while I try to look professional inside my enormous beanbag.

"Settles what?" I ask, as this is hardly the reply I was expecting after telling my Space Invaders story.

"Caliastra *is* behind all this," Violet cries angrily, causing a break in Erwin's purring. "She's doing something, Herbie. Causing all this strangeness, with her lantern and her tricks. And if she's hurt Jenny, I'll . . . I'll . . ."

"But, Vi, what if it's *not* Caliastra doing these things?" I say. "What if she's also a victim of strange events? We don't really know what's happening, do we?"

"You just don't want to see it, Herbie," Violet replies bitterly. "She's bewitched you. I wish she'd never come here."

"But . . ."

"No, Herbie!" Violet thumps the arm of the chair. "Caliastra said herself she's been in contact with Sebastian Eels. So far, all the strangest adventures we've ever had in Eerie-on-Sea have been connected with that man."

"Except"—I thump back, though only on the beanbag— "Sebastian Eels is *dead*, Vi."

"I know," Violet admits, sinking back in her chair. "But someone's been in his house. I bet that's where the Shadowghast lantern has been all these years. I wonder what else is hidden in there, what other dark secrets Caliastra has access to. What if Caliastra is taking over where Sebastian Eels left off? What if Eerie-on-Sea has a new villain to deal with?"

I respond with a *Pfft.*

Pfft is the sound you make when you want to suggest that something is ridiculous but can't think of a way to say it in actual words. Only, I'm not very good at making the *Pfft* sound and just succeed in getting a bit of dribble on my chin and making Erwin glare at me with a single ice-blue eye.

Violet gets up, putting the bookshop cat in the warmth of her seat.

She runs up to my cubbyhole. When she comes back down, she has Clermit, the clockwork shell, in her hands.

"I know you think I see adventures everywhere, Herbie," she says, "but it feels to me as if we're on a new adventure already. Doesn't it feel like that to you?"

And she tosses Clermit to me.

I catch him and hear the bright ring of the complex clockwork mechanism inside.

"You really think winding him up will help?" I ask.

Violet shrugs.

"There's definitely one thing he can help us with, at least," she says.

"What's that?"

Violet is already heading for my cellar window when she replies.

"He can help us break into Sebastian Eels's house."

CHAPTER 22

CLERMIT

··

I t's a bit later, and Vi and I are standing in the doorway of the boarded-up town house of Sebastian Eels. It's dusk, and the gloom of late October fills the air. A few people are hurrying home, not wanting to be caught out after dark. In the window of a nearby house, we glimpse one of Mrs. Fossil's manglewick candles, casting a ghastly shadow on the curtains.

A low-hanging branch—scrappy orange leaves still clinging to it—grows over the little walled garden at the side of Eels's house. Violet and I have climbed over this before. In the darkness, I hope no one will notice us climbing over it again.

"You really think Clermit can help?" I say to Vi as we crouch, a few minutes later, among the nettles and brambles of the overgrown garden. I feel the weight of the clockwork shell hidden under my cap.

"The back door is locked," says Vi, pointing to the door in the gloom. "The key is in the lock, but on the inside."

"How do you know that?"

"Because I tried to get in earlier," Violet says, her eyes flashing. "While you were busy watching magic shows and playing arcade games, *I* was trying to find Jenny."

I'm about to protest, but Violet's already speaking again.

"How did you once describe Clermit, Herbie?" she asks. "Like a windup Swiss army knife? Well, I think that's exactly what we need to get this door open."

I look at the locked door. I'm not sure how even Clermit can get the key for us. But then I look up and see the gap in the boards over the third-floor window, where they've blown loose.

"Your Clermit helped us before, Herbie," says Violet "It's time you asked him to help us again."

My Clermit?

I lift my cap on its elastic and carefully withdraw the shell from his hiding place. In the small light that remains in the sky, I see him gleaming white and iridescent on my palm.

Clermit was once in the possession of Sebastian Eels but switched sides, and even saved my life. I promised him—in so far as you can promise a miraculous windup contraption anything—that I'd get him back to his rightful owner one day. But in the meantime . . .

I fish around in my pocket, pull out Clermit's brass winder key, and fit it into the little brass-lined hole in the side of the shell.

"Ready?" I ask Violet.

She nods.

I give Clermit three good windings-up.

Tic-tic-tic-TIK, tic-tic-tic-TIK, tic-tic-tic-TIK.

At first, nothing happens.

Then, with a juddering motion—and a sound like a single annoying grain of sand being ground to dust between two delicately engineered cogs—a brass leg emerges from inside the shell.

And then another, and another.

Soon Clermit is standing upright on my hand.

"Hello there!" I grin, delighted to see the little thing working again. "How are you feeling?"

By way of an answer, a fourth appendage emerges, one that ends in a little pair of scissor claws. The scissors waggle from side to side and make a single decisive snip.

"I think that means he's OK," I say to Vi.

"We need to get into this house," Vi tells Clermit impatiently. She points to the lock.

The clockwork hermit crab sways on his tripod of brass legs, as if looking at the lock with an invisible eye. Then he looks back at me.

"Please?" I say.

In a moment, and with a whir of gears, Clermit springs from my hand. He scuttles up the front of the door and probes the lock. When this amounts to nothing, he drops down, runs to the base of the tree, and clambers up the trunk with the help of his steel blades.

"What's he doing?" Violet asks. "Herbie?"

"I think . . ." I reply. "Yes! He's going to jump."

Sure enough, we see the tree sway as the clockwork hermit crab clambers into its topmost branches. He swings himself back and forth, to gain momentum, and then leaps . . .

And hits the wall of the house with a clatter.

He starts to fall back but manages to dig two of his four sword arms into the mortar. He regains his balance and begins to climb.

"Whoa!" I say.

Jabbing into the wall with his blades, Clermit makes his mechanical way to the third-story window above us, where the boards have blown loose. For a moment, the moonlight glints on his gleaming shell. Then he slips into the house and is gone.

⚙○✿

"What's he doing?" Vi whispers after several long minutes have passed in silence and the last light of day melts from the sky.

I don't reply. I'm beginning to have a bad feeling. Clermit is one of the eerie things of Eerie-on-Sea, after all, and he's changed sides once before.

"Listen!" Vi hisses then. "I can hear something. Sounds like . . ."

"A lock being turned!" I finish. I'm just about to add that I knew all along we could count on good old Clermit, when Violet interrupts.

"But it's not *this* lock. It's coming from the street. It sounds like someone's opening the padlock on the front door of the house!"

As silently as we can, we pull ourselves back onto the branch and lean over the wall. Sure enough, a shadow is at the main entrance to Sebastian Eels's house. There's a *click*, and then a *creak*, as the big black doors open and someone goes in.

"Who was that?" I ask.

"Couldn't see," Violet replies. "Come on!"

Violet swings over the wall and drops silently into the street.

"What?" I cry, though it's pretty obvious what Violet is going to do. I feel a knot of fear in my innards as I lower myself behind her.

I'm just in time to see Violet creep up to the front door of the house, push it quietly, and slip inside.

CHAPTER 23

SECRET CHAMBER

The atmosphere inside Sebastian Eels's house is cold and unlived-in. There's a bad smell in the air as if something was left out of the fridge months ago and has developed an interesting personality of its own. Everywhere is dark, of course; though, as we stand together just inside the front door, we hear the scrape of a match and see a flare of light on the upstairs landing.

"Are you sure about this?" I manage to whisper into Violet's hair.

"The only thing I'm sure about," comes a whisper back, "is that I haven't seen Jenny since this time yesterday, Herbie."

And now I'm really scared something bad has happened to her. Come on!"

"Couldn't we just . . . ?" I begin, but apparently, we can't, because the only reply I get now is Violet groping for my hand, grabbing it, and then pulling me toward the great ornate staircase. We manage to climb it, despite the gloom, without once creaking the antique wooden steps. Something brushes against my face and I swipe it away. It's a cobweb.

I've been to this house only once before, back when Sebastian Eels was still alive. Vi and I broke in on that occasion, too—on important Lost-and-Founder business, you understand—and searched the villain's study. But we were caught in the act and had to run for our lives. As we climb the stairs now, I feel some of the fear of that day return, especially when we hear the mysterious figure entering that very same study.

As if he knew *exactly* where to go.

But as we approach the study, I see, through the open door, something that stops me in my tracks: there, gleaming white and iridescent at one end of the ornate marble mantelpiece that dominates the room, sits Clermit.

Just sitting there, as if it's where he belongs!

I grab Vi's arm and point.

Maybe we were too hasty to trust the clockwork hermit crab.

Maybe it really *is* Sebastian Eels's creature, after all. A terrifying thought jumps into my brain, setting all my alarm bells ringing.

"You don't think . . . ?" I whisper to Vi. "You don't think Eels himself could be . . . ?"

Violet glances at me fearfully, her eyes glinting in the light from the room. It looks as though the same horrible thought is troubling her, too.

"It can't be him," she mouths silently, "can it?"

Can Sebastian Eels *really* have returned from the dead?

Inside the room there is a rustling and clattering as the mysterious person hunts for something. We can hear him—and it certainly does sound like a him—muttering impatiently and cursing.

Violet puts her finger to her lips and creeps forward. Where the door hinges, there is a gap big enough for us to look farther into the room.

"Blast it all!" we hear from inside, along with the unmistakable sound of desk drawers being rifled and then slammed shut. "It's not where she said it would be."

We put our eyes to the crack.

Inside the room, we see someone's silhouette against the light of a kerosene lamp on the vast mahogany desk. And we see immediately that it isn't Sebastian Eels. The silhouette is of a short, stout man . . . with a homburg hat.

"Mr. Mummery!" I say, a bit too loudly.

Mr. Mummery, theatrical agent to the magician Caliastra, looks up sharply, as if he has heard me. Vi and I go deathly still and quiet. After a moment, the man returns to his search of the desk, but he soon gives up.

"She must have left it in the inner chamber, after all," he grumbles. "I told her, but no—madame knows best. Just as well I memorized the code, isn't it?"

And with these strange words, Mr. Mummery steps away from the desk and comes to a halt in front of the study bookshelves. He hangs his hat on a nearby hook.

"Now, let me see . . ." he says, cracking his knuckles and facing the shelves. Then, hesitantly, he presses one of the books.

The book slides in a finger's width, and from somewhere inside the shelves, we hear a soft click.

Mr. Mummery presses another and another, till soon half a dozen books are pushed in.

"And just one more . . ." he says as he jabs a final book with his pudgy forefinger.

We hear a deep, metallic *CLUNK* from somewhere in the fabric of the building. Then a stony, grinding sound as Mummery grabs the bookshelf with both hands and pulls the whole thing toward him. It swings to one side, revealing a secret doorway.

Mr. Mummery takes the kerosene lamp from the desk and steps inside.

⚙O✿

"I didn't know about that!" Vi whispers.

"Neither did I," I whisper in reply. "But I think that's kind of the point with secret chambers."

Ahead of us, through the bookshelf door, we cannot see much beyond the flicker of shadows and light. But after only a moment, we hear "Aha!" as Mr. Mummery finds whatever it is he's looking for and hurries back into view.

He has a stuffed notebook in his hands, held closed with a rubber band and filled to bursting with cuttings and loose papers. He places the notebook on the mantelpiece beside Clermit, along with the lantern, and then pushes the bookshelves closed with both hands.

For one crazy moment, I actually think about darting forward while the little man is busy, snatching the notebook, and taking my chances at a running escape. I even make a movement in the direction of the mantelpiece. It's the kind of thing I'd never have dared to do before Violet showed up in my life.

Vi puts her hand on my arm, to hold me back. Maybe that's something *she'd* never have done before meeting *me*.

And that's when Clermit makes his move.

THE COLLECTED WORKS
OF SEBASTIAN EELS

ith a slow and precise movement, Clermit the
clockwork hermit crab carefully extends one of his
appendages—the one with the little brass scissors—
and snips the rubber band that holds the notebook closed.

The book bursts open and papers spill out everywhere.

"Oh, blast it!" splutters Mr. Mummery as he finishes shutting
the secret door with a *CLUNK*. All the books that he pressed
to open it pop silently back out into place. With a grunt, the
theatrical manager bends over and begins scraping together the
spilled papers.

What he doesn't notice, though, as he scrabbles around on

the floor, is that Clermit has dragged toward him one of the papers—one that remained on the mantelpiece—and has pulled it into his shell.

"This is no way to organize anything!" Mr. Mummery moans as he shuffles the papers back into the notebook and glances nervously at his watch. With some difficulty, he slides the bulging notebook into his jacket pocket. "First thing we'll do when this is over is get all these papers properly indexed. Damn these writers and their sloppy ways. Even the dead ones!"

And with this, he extinguishes the lantern and plunges the house back into darkness.

Violet and I scoot back away from the door. In a moment, we're some way down the corridor, pressed against the wall. We can hear Mr. Mummery groping his way out onto the landing and making his cautious way downstairs.

"And when this place is legally ours," he continues, "we can finally turn the blasted lights on!"

Then we hear the front door close, followed by the scraping sound of the metal bar being replaced and the padlock snapping shut.

"That was close!" I exhale and slide down the wall till my bottom meets the floorboards. "But he might as well have caught us, for all the difference it makes."

"What do you mean?" Violet asks.

"I mean, we're *locked in*, Vi," I say. "The front door is bolted from the outside."

"There's always the back door," she replies. "The key's in the lock, remember?"

"What are we waiting for, then?"

"Herbie, we came her to find answers," Violet replies, in her taking-charge voice. "So, let's find some. Do you have your flashlight on you?"

I do, and I feel a bit silly for not having switched it on already. I pull the keychain out of my pocket and turn on the tiny beam. It illuminates a small corner of the corridor and Violet's determined face.

"Good," she says. "Now, come on."

Together we enter the study.

And see that Clermit is no longer on the mantelpiece.

"Where's he gone?" Violet whispers.

As if in answer, we hear a rattling sound. It's exactly the sound you would expect if a mechanical hermit crab were shaking a box of matches and trying to get your attention. I swing the flashlight around to the desk and, sure enough, Clermit is perched there. He taps the glass of the lamp with his little scissors.

"Good boy!" I say, coming over and grinning at the little contraption.

"He's not a dog, Herbie," Vi says as she takes the matches,

strikes one, and relights the lamp. A soft glow banishes the gloom, and the study of Sebastian Eels comes back into view.

"He is a faithful companion, though," I reply, holding out my hands so that Clermit can climb aboard.

But instead, he reaches his scissor claw inside his shell, pulls out the scrap of paper he snaffled, and stuffs it into my hands. Then he folds himself away, whirs to silence, and goes still. I pick him up and pop him back under my cap.

"What's on it?" Violet asks, coming over to look.

I spread the paper on the desk. It's very scrappy, and crumpled from Clermit's shell, but I would recognize Eels's energetic spider scrawl anywhere.

"Looks like a diagram," I say, "of the Shadowghast lantern. With notes about how to use it."

"Let me look," says Vi, tipping the lamp to get a brighter view of the sketch and scribbled notes. She taps a label on the diagram, which points to the lantern's dragon head with an arrow. "This part seems important. It's underlined twice."

He who controls the light commands the dark," I say, reading aloud the words.

"He," says Violet, "or *she.*"

I decide not to reply to that.

"Either way, it's a clue, Herbie," Vi continues, folding the paper into her coat pocket, "and we need as many of those as we can get."

"We should take that sketch to my Lost-and-Foundery," I say, stepping toward the door, eager to be gone. "For a proper look. It's risky to stay here, and we don't know for sure we can open that back door."

"True." Violet nods. Then she turns to face the bookshelves. "But obviously we can't go *yet*, Herbie."

My heart sinks.

"We can't?"

"Of course not!" Vi cries. "We have to explore the secret chamber first."

I don't argue. I know my friend well enough by now not to waste my breath.

Violet reaches out and presses one of the books in. There's a soft *click*, like we heard before.

"I just wish I'd seen *all* the books Mr. Mummery used to open it," Violet continues. "This is the only one I'm sure of. Did you notice any?"

"I'm fairly sure that was one," I reply, pointing to a second book, which has a thick bloodred spine and large lizard scales embossed on it. Inside some of the scales are white capital letters spelling out the book's title:

THE BREATH OF THE BEAST by S. E.

Vi presses this spine, too, and again we hear the *click*.

"Well, that's two." She puts her hands on her hips. "But I was counting, and Mummery pressed *seven* books. How will we know what the other five are?"

"There was one about here-ish." I wave my hand in a general way over an end of a shelf. "If that's any help."

"It's not really," says Violet, stroking her finger along the spines there. "Except, look! Here's one of Eels's own books."

Sure enough, we see a novel with a poison-green leather spine, decorated with an emaciated human figure who looks as though he's only a notch or two up from being a skeleton.

"The Sweet Smell of Despair." I read the title over Violet's shoulder. "By Sebastian Eels. Sounds charming! Let me add that to my TBRN list."

"Don't you mean TBR list?" Vi asks. "As in To Be Read?"

"To Be Read *NEVER* is what I mean, thanks, Violet," I explain. "Only a man like Sebastian Eels could have spent his life writing such horrible-sounding stories."

"Wait!" says Vi. "By S. E.! That other book—the beast one— was written by S. E. Is that Sebastian Eels, too? And if so, what about that first one . . . ?"

Violet darts over to the first book she pressed, and sure enough, there on the sickly-yellow spine is the name Sebastian Eels, beside the title *Dead, and All Bones*.

Vi jumps back to *The Sweet Smell of Despair*, presses it, and cries "Yes!" when we hear a third *click* from inside the secret doorway.

"Of course he would pick his own books." Vi's eyes flash triumphantly in the lamplight. "But his bigheadedness makes it easier for us . . ."

It takes us only a few moments to locate more of the author's titles among the works of history, mystery, and the occult that fill the shelves. Soon we have a total of six of them pressed back, each making its own clicking sound.

"We need the last one," Vi says as she grips the shelves and pulls, but to no effect. "It still won't open."

And that's when I see it.

There, on the lowest shelf, is another book by Sebastian Eels—a book I know only too well. It's the first book I was dispensed by the mermonkey when I first came to live in Eerie-on-Sea. A book that has haunted me ever since.

Violet spots it, too.

"The Cold, Dark Bottom of the Sea," I say, reading out the title. "I might have known. On my TBRN list, that book is right at the top!"

"You may hate that book, Herbie," Violet says, "but perhaps you shouldn't. After all, it's the only place I've ever seen mention of your ship, the SS *Fabulous.*"

"Except for Caliastra's ticket," I correct her. "My aunt was actually *on* the ship, remember?"

Violet raises one eyebrow at me.

"If she was claiming to be *my* aunt," she replies, "I'd want better proof than that. Maybe if you actually read the book, you'd find some answers for yourself."

"We don't have time for two mysteries," I say firmly. "Let's worry about finding Jenny first. My shipwreck can wait till later."

And I push at the spine of *The Cold, Dark Bottom of the Sea,* sliding it back till we hear . . .

CLICK!

Then comes that same stone-scraping we heard before, deep within the structure of the building, and the hidden bookshelf door is released.

We have opened Sebastian Eels's secret chamber.

CHAPTER 25

THE FORGOTTEN HAT

··

Taking up the lamp from the desk, Violet and I creep inside the secret chamber.

The room is about half the size of the study. On the walls there are wooden shelves, divided to form deep square alcoves of varying sizes. And in all of the alcoves there are treasures.

Well, maybe *treasures* isn't the obvious word for a bunch of dusty boxes, rolls of paper, notebooks, and linen-wrapped artifacts—it actually looks like some of the older and more cob-webby stuff I keep in my Lost-and-Foundery—but you can tell by the careful way everything is stored that these things were very much treasured by someone.

"There are labels," says Vi in a whisper. "On each alcove."

Sure enough, in Sebastian Eels's spider writing, we see the names of creatures we know from the legends of Eerie-on-Sea:

MALAMANDER

GARGANTIS

FARGAZER

"What's Fargazer?" I ask. "I don't know that one."

"It's an old tale," Violet replies. "Jenny told it to me once. It's really creepy and . . . Wait, look! Herbie!"

And so I look. Violet is pointing at a word that means more than any other right now:

SHADOWGHAST

"But it's empty," I say, peering into the alcove. "There's nothing there."

Sure enough, where the other alcoves contain wrapped objects and notebooks and boxes, the one marked SHADOWGHAST contains nothing at all.

"Not exactly nothing," says Vi, leaning in closer. "Look, in the dust. There are marks where something once stood."

"Looks like footprints," I squeak, feeling a sudden rush of uneasiness. "Like footprints made by four giant chicken feet!"

The marks do indeed look like they were made by bird claws. If, that is, the bird was the size of a wolf.

"Not *chicken* feet, Herbie." Vi turns to me, realization on her face. "*Dragon* feet."

"What!"

"The Shadowghast lantern, remember?" she says. "It's shaped like a dragon and stands on four clawed feet. This is where it must have been kept. All those years that people thought the lantern from the first Ghastly Night was still lost in the sea, Eels had it right here, hidden in this secret room."

"I wonder what else he's got?" I say, looking around. "I bet everything he ever collected about the Legends of Eerie-on-Sea is in here."

"And it sounds as if it's all about to go to Caliastra," Violet replies. "If she buys the house, as it sounded from Mummery like she's planning to do, she'll get everything. And something tells me that's not a good idea."

I want to protest, to say that my aunt wouldn't be up to anything really bad, but my eye catches on something. A small thing that I might have missed if the lamp hadn't flared brighter for a moment. I stoop to look closer.

"Herbie?" says Vi. "What are you looking at?"

Near the bottom of one wall, with a label I can barely read in the dark, is a particularly small alcove.

"Bring the light!" I cry. "Bring it!"

Violet leans in, holding up the kerosene lamp so that we can read the tiny, curling label above the little alcove. When I see what's written there, I can hardly breathe.

HERBERT LEMON

"But that's . . ." Violet starts to say, as if struggling to get the words out. "That's . . . *you!*"

With a trembling hand, I reach into the tiny alcove. I pull out an object and hold it up in the light of the lamp.

Violet's eyes are as wide as scallop shells as we stare at the thing in my hand.

It's a lemon.

A dried-up, slightly rubbery lemon.

"Do you think . . . ?" Vi asks, still struggling to get words out. "Do you think this is one of the actual lemons from the crate you were washed up in?"

"Maybe," I reply through a gulp. "But why would Sebastian Eels keep something like that?"

"Why, Herbie," says Vi, "would Sebastian Eels have a special 'Herbert Lemon' alcove at all?"

And I don't know the answer to that, do I? If I did, I probably wouldn't be standing there openmouthed like a fish hoping for a fly. And maybe, if I hadn't been gawping—and if Violet hadn't been gawping with me—we would have noticed that someone has just entered the study and is doing a bit of gawping of his own as he finds the door of the secret chamber open, and us inside.

"What the *blazes* are you two doing here?" demands Mr. Mummery.

He is already getting over his surprise enough to turn a furious shade of purple. One of his hands reaches out automatically and takes the homburg hat off the hook that he, Mr. Mummery, hung it on about twenty minutes before.

Violet and I exchange glances, the same thought written across our faces.

We should have noticed that Mr. Mummery had forgotten his hat.

We should have *expected* he might come back to retrieve it!

And now, because we didn't, we see as plain as day that we're about to be shut into the secret chamber ourselves.

"No!" cries Violet, starting to move.

But Mr. Mummery has already grabbed the bookshelf door and is starting to swing it shut. We're only seconds away from being entombed.

So, I do the only thing I can do in the circumstances.

I throw the shriveled lemon at Mr. Mummery.

It hits him on the nose.

"Ow!" Mummery cries, letting go of the door and clutching his face.

"Run!" I shout, though I don't really need to. Vi and I elbow the theatrical manager out of the way and rush past him. He makes a grab for us but only succeeds in knocking the kerosene lamp from Violet's hands. The lamp hits the floor with a crash of shattering glass. Light flares as blazing kerosene spills out across the rug, setting it alight.

"The door!" Violet shouts. "The front door!"

We charge out onto the landing, as the flames flicker behind us. We can hear Mr. Mummery cry in alarm and start stamping at the fire. But we're too busy rattling down the stairs to check what he's doing.

As expected, the front door is slightly open, the cold blue of night just visible around the doorway.

We run toward the door, and freedom, and pull it open, and . . .

A dark shadow falls across the doorway, blocking our way. Then another looms up, as two tall, wiry silhouettes step into the house. In the faint, crackling light of the fire upstairs, we see ghastly faces we were not expecting—the painted stage masks of Rictus and Tristo.

They rush forward to grab us.

CHAPTER 26

VOID

T his way!" Vi cries, quickly switching direction, dashing around the staircase and heading down the hallway, deeper into the house. We need to find that back door after all—the one with the key still in the lock—and we need to find it quickly!

It's really weird being chased by mime artists. There's no "Hey, get back here!" or "Just wait until I get my hands on you, Herbert Lemon!" or any of the things people usually shout when I'm running away from them. No, there's just an eerie silence and the sense of two strong men sprinting right on our heels. Even when Violet tips over a coat stand—causing the men to trip and gaining us a few precious seconds—they don't cry out.

If anything, this only makes the pair even more terrifying.

We dive into the kitchen, slam the door behind us, and lean against it.

I shine my flashlight around desperately—its light glinting off copper pots, dusty glassware, and moldy unwashed dishes. There's an almighty wallop against the door, and Vi and I are nearly shaken off our feet. Then comes another crash, and the door moves as the Rictus and Tristo force it open.

A black-clad arm reaches in and grabs my uniform front in a fistful of fabric and brass buttons.

"Erk!" I cry.

Violet snatches up a fork from a nearby counter and jabs it into the hand, which lets go and withdraws, allowing us to slam the door shut again. But we get only a moment's relief before the walloping starts once more, and I know we won't be able to hold them back for long.

Then Violet wedges the fork under the door with her foot.

When the next crash comes, there's a screeching sound as the fork gets stuck in a floor tile, and the door sets fast.

"Run!"

Together we jump away. The door is holding for now, but the mime artists are throwing their whole weight against it, and the fork is starting to bend.

There's a back way out of the kitchen, and we run into a

corridor beyond it. Here we find the back door—the one with the key in the lock, that leads into the garden—but there are boxes and things piled against it. We'll never shift them in time.

"Oh, bladderwracks!" I shout. "Now what?"

"Here!" Violet pulls my arm, and we head the opposite direction. There's a big old cellar door halfway down, and Violet heaves it open.

We are hit by a blast of cold, musty air, as we find ourselves looking into a void of darkness. I probe it urgently with my keychain flashlight, but I only manage to identify a couple of steps leading down into the fathomless black.

"We can't go down there!" I squeak.

There's a sudden shriek of metal scraping against tile as the fork finally gives way. Back in the kitchen, we hear Rictus and Tristo burst through.

"No choice!" Violet gasps, and she begins to descend into the darkness. I step after her, swinging the door closed behind us and wincing as it creaks on rusty hinges. The cold and the dark close around us as we go down, step by step, with nothing but the keychain flashlight to light our feet.

We reach the bottom step and crunch onto a gravelly surface.

There's a sound from the corridor above, and I quickly switch off the flashlight. The velvet dark engulfs us utterly.

Way above, we hear the old cellar door open creakily on its

hinge. Our night-adapted eyes see a rectangle of darkest gray in the open doorway. Two silhouettes stand there—Rictus and Tristo—staring down into the blackness, silent, listening.

I bite my sleeve to prevent a squeak of terror from bursting out, and Violet grips my other arm so hard it actually hurts.

Then—slowly, deliberately—the door at the top of the steps creaks shut and slams with a sound like the grave.

We hear the scrape of bolts sliding after it.

"Herbie," Violet's voice comes eventually, smaller and more terrified than I've ever heard it before. "Turn your flashlight back on!"

I do so, and the light springs out once more. But I can't help noticing that the beam is weaker than it should be. I give the flashlight a tap but only succeed in making it flicker.

"The battery must be running out," I say. "I'm sorry, Vi."

"Then we'd better find out where we are while we still can," Violet replies, still shaken, but as practical as ever. "This must be a cellar."

I shine the failing flashlight around, slowly, and we try to piece together our surroundings. We can see a ceiling of vaulted brickwork, dripping with white stalactites; arched alcoves filled with collapsing crates, ancient barrels, and half-empty wine racks; and a long, vaulted space that extends beyond the reach of the flashlight beam, and which offers the only possible alternative way out.

"What's that?" Violet whispers near my ear. "Over there?"

And she guides my arm so that the feeble flashlight beam picks out a table in one of the alcoves, with a few objects on top.

"Maybe there's another flashlight over there," she says. "Or some batteries."

It doesn't seem very likely to me, but I don't see what else we can do. Together we walk toward the table.

"No batteries," I say as my flashlight picks out an array of old tools, empty bottles, and cobwebby clutter. "But there is a candle!"

Sure enough, sitting alone in a blackened silver candelabra that would once have held five candles in happier circumstances, a single stub of candle with a dusty black wick offers us the tantalizing hope of light beyond the failing flashlight.

"If only," I say, "we had some way of lighting it."

Then I hear the matchbox rattle I heard earlier, in the study, and I flick the flashlight back at Violet.

"I, um, seem to have put these in my coat pocket," she says, grinning sheepishly. "Whoops!"

I don't complain. After everything Sebastian Eels has done to Violet and her family, he owes her a few matches, at the very least.

There's a scrape, a small eruption of light, and a nose-tingling whiff of sulphur dioxide as Vi strikes a match and places it against the wick. After a moment, the candle sputters to life, as if being woken from a long sleep. Violet picks up the candelabra, and the cellar of the grand town house eases into dim view around us.

"No point trying the door," I say, glancing back up the steps. "It's locked. We need to go in deeper and see what's there."

Together we enter the long, vaulted space, carrying our little circle of candlelight with us. Our shadows, flickering up the walls, follow on either side. Along each wall there are more shallow recesses, with yet more boxes and wine racks. When we reach the far brick wall, it is entirely devoid of features or doorways.

"So much for another way out," says Violet, looking at me fearfully from inside her hair. Her eyes glint in the flickering flame.

"Wait! *Flickering* flame?" I say.

"What?"

"Flickering flame!" I repeat. "Violet, the flame is flickering. That must mean there's a draft!"

And it's true: the flame of the stubby candle is leaning and dancing in one direction, causing the wax to drip.

Together we turn toward the current of air, and then we can

feel it, too—a clammy breeze against our faces. It's coming from the last recess, where there are a few old packing crates and not a lot else, except . . .

"Look!" Violet exclaims.

Half hidden behind the crates is an old, pitted metal door, open just a crack. Violet sweeps the candle high, to illuminate something carved crudely in the stone lintel above the door.

"Eerie Script!" Violet gasps.

This is the secret writing of the fisherfolk of Eerie-on-Sea, known only from a few rare examples kept by Dr. Thalassi in the museum, and officially undeciphered by anyone living. *Officially* being the most important word in that sentence.

"Do you still remember how to read it?" I ask Violet, thinking back to how she secretly cracked this code during our adventure with Gargantis.

"*N-E-T-H-E-R-W-A-Y-S*," she reads, spelling out a letter at a time as she squints up at the runes and deciphers them. "It says *Netherways*, Herbie. What's that?"

"Nothing good," I reply with a croak. "But, one way or another, it looks as if we've found our way out."

CHAPTER 27

THE NETHERWAYS

O n the other side of the door we find ourselves in a
rough, rocky passageway that leads off to the right
and to the left. Violet holds up the candle again, to
test for breeze.

"This way," she says, pointing to the right. In the gloom we
can see a brick archway with another passage leading off it, and
from somewhere beyond that comes the echoing babble of running water.

"What is this place?" Violet asks as we walk, looking up at
the dripping ceiling. "This can't be Eels's cellar anymore. We
must be under the town. But this doesn't look like sewers."

"There have always been stories about tunnels and caves

beneath Eerie-on-Sea," I reply. "Dark stories. Smugglers used them once upon a time, and others, too, before them. I once heard Dr. Thalassi refer to them as the Netherways. He made me promise to never come down here."

"Why?" Violet asks, in the way only Violet can.

"Uh, because they are *dangerous*?" I reply. "They say no one has ever been able to map the Netherways. There are loads of tales of people getting lost down here, Violet, and I'd quite like to not be one of them!"

"OK, but if there is such a vast network of tunnels, Herbie, there must be lots of ways in and out. We just have to find one, that's all."

"Well, there *is* a way in beneath the castle," I admit. "Dr. Thalassi showed me the door. He keeps it bolted, of course. He said he thought lots of the oldest buildings in Eerie-on-Sea probably have secret doors into the Netherways."

"Wait, you mean we could get into the castle from here?" Violet stops, her eyes flashing eagerly at the thought. "Or, say, into the hotel?"

"The hotel?" I blink.

"We need somewhere safe to go," Violet explains. "Imagine if there were one of these secret doors straight into your Lost-and-Foundery, Herbie! Then we could . . ."

"Can we *not* imagine that? Thanks!" I squeak. "You think I'd be able to sleep at night if there were door from my home into this horrible, dark, drippy place?"

"But . . ."

"No, Vi!" I say. "People keep their secret Netherways doors locked for a reason. We'll have to find a loose drain cover or something and get out into the streets. And the sooner we find one the better!"

We reach the archway and look down the brick-lined passage beyond. There is definitely a draft from that direction. We head down it, but soon the tunnel branches off in three ways.

Violet turns to face one direction, and then another. The candle flickers all over the place.

"I'm struggling to stay orientated," she says, clearly trying to picture the layout of the town above us. "Herbie, I don't know which way we should go."

"Well, I vote we don't pick *that* way," I say, pointing into one of the branching tunnels. It slopes steeply downward into the dark, and it seems to be where the sounds of falling water are coming from. "I vote we choose only passages that go up!"

"Let's try this one, then," Violet says decisively, waving the candelabra at one of the other two, "and hope we find a clue."

Shielding the candle flame against the draft, Vi and I set off again. But in no time the passage divides once more, and this time both ways go down.

And the candle flickers so hard that it almost goes out.

Violet and I turn to each other. I think I can see my own fear reflected in her eyes.

What if we *never* find a way out?

"Don't think it!" Violet says, choosing a direction at random. "We just have to keep going, Herbie. That's all."

And that's when we reach a bridge.

Or rather, that's when the walls of our tunnel fall away on either side, but the ground continues ahead, and we see that our path is now high above an underground river. There is no hand-rail, and the rush of water far below is terrifying.

"Look, Herbie!" Violet cries over the echoing clamor of the water. "On the other side of the bridge, the tunnel goes up again."

Sure enough, the candlelight reaches far enough ahead to illuminate steps. We begin to edge across the narrow bridge, but we stop when we hear a voice.

"What did you say?" Violet turns and asks me, confused.

"I thought it was you!" I reply.

We hear the voice again.

It's hard to pick out above the cacophony of the river, but there is definitely a human voice, saying:

"Where is it? Where can it be? Where? Where is it? Got to find it . . . but, where can it be . . . ?"

Over and over again.

We freeze mid-bridge and look forward and back, but there's no one there. Then we peer gingerly over the edge and see another narrow path far below that runs beside the river. And on that path is a person, groping along in the light of a small lantern. It's such a shock to see someone down here in this subterranean maze that I'm surprised we don't fall over the side of the bridge in fright.

"Hello!" Violet calls shakily, once we've steadied ourselves. "Who . . . who's there?"

The figure below stops and looks each way. Then—her clothes disheveled, her hair a tangle of red—she finally looks up.

"Jenny!"

The candelabra nearly falls from Violet's hand as she cries the name. Down below us, the face of the owner of the Eerie Book Dispensary is briefly visible in the flickering light from her lantern. Her face is streaked with blood and filth, and her desperate eyes stare at us. Then the darkness closes again, and the face is hidden.

"*Jenny!*"

The figure stumbles on, uninterested in us now, her muttering still audible within the sound of rushing water.

"Where is it? I must find it. I must not stop . . . not for *anyone.*

It is here, somewhere, the deepest secret. But where can it be? I must find it for the Puppet Master . . ."

And then we lose the voice as the figure vanishes into the dark below, her lantern bobbing as she follows the underground river into the bowels of the earth.

"JENNY!"

Violet clutches my arm. "Herbie, we've got to get down there!"

"Yes." I gulp. "But how?"

There is no obvious way, and we've already seen that the path ahead goes up, not down.

"There was that other passage," Violet cries, edging past me and back the way we came. "The one that went downward. Come on!"

"Violet, wait!" I shout, running after her. But she doesn't wait. And it's all I can do to keep up as she runs, shielding the candle flame and taking one side passage after another, until we come to a wide-open place where a half dozen tunnels connect.

"We didn't see this before." Violet stumbles to a halt in the middle of the cavernous room. "Or did we?"

"We didn't!" I squeak. "Vi, we really are lost now."

"But Jenny . . . !" Violet says, turning frantically to look into each passageway. "We saw *Jenny*!"

"I know," I reply. "Or . . . did we? I'm beginning to wonder if we just saw what we wanted to see, Vi. This place will drive us mad!"

"What was that?" Violet cries, spinning around at the sound of . . . *something*.

"Sounded like . . ." I whisper, drawing in closer to Violet and her candle. "Like . . . laughter?"

"I thought it was more like a sob," Vi whispers back. "Like someone sobbing in despair."

Then Violet shouts as loud as she can.

"JENNY!"

The candle flame flickers more than ever behind Violet's protective hand, and I try to shelter it, too. Around us, in the cavernous space where the half dozen ways meet, our hands cast strange and eerie shapes on the cracked bricks and stone of the walls.

Then something flickers across our vision.

Another shadow.

But not one cast by my or Violet's fingers.

It flits from one passage entrance to another, always at the edge of our sight, never there when we turn to look at it directly. And all the time comes the sound of that laughing sob.

"Do you see it?" Vi hisses, spinning one way then the other. "Herbie!"

Before I can answer, the shadow comes to a halt in full view on the cavern wall.

And we see him clearly, grinning his creepy puppet grin.

The shadow of a man with horns upon his head.

Slowly the specter reaches grasping shadow claws across the ground toward us.

Violet thrusts the candle at him, moving her shielding hand away to throw forward maximum light, risking the breeze in her desperation to dispel the ghastly apparition in front of us.

"What have you done with her?" she yells at the shadow being. "What have you done with Jenny?"

But the specter only grins more deeply as his shadow hand reaches our feet and passes *through* us. We turn in horror to see its hooked fingers closing around our own shadows, which are cowering on the wall behind . . .

About to be snatched by the Shadowghast!

Violet turns to me with a desperate, wide-eyed expression, as if—despite the awfulness of our situation—an idea has just struck her. Then she pulls the guttering candle flame toward her and, with one last look into my eyes, she blows it out.

And plunges everything into total and unending darkness.

CHAPTER 28

LIGHT AND DARK

···

W-w-w . . . ?" I stutter, my brain so boggled by terror that I'm amazed I can manage even that. "W-why?"

It's so dark now that I couldn't see the back of my beyond even if I waggled it in front of my nose. I can still hear, though.

Somewhere in the void, that babbling, chuckling noise reaches us again. Is it the echo of a sunless river? Or the wind as it whistles down a storm drain?

Or is it the noise a Shadowghast makes when it's about to snatch your soul?

I scrabble in my pocket for what's left of the light in my keychain flashlight.

"No!" Violet whispers, grabbing my arm as she senses what I'm doing. "No more light!"

"But we can't *see!*"

"Exactly!" comes Violet's voice, right in my ear. "*Think, Herbie!* If there's no light, how can there be a shadow?"

And that, right there, is a good point.

"You mean it's gone?" I gasp in relief. "The Shadowghast is *gone?*"

The babble-chuckle echoes around the cavern again, reverberating down the side passages, one by one.

"Maybe not gone," Violet admits, coming closer than I've ever heard to making a squeak of her own. "But at least, in the dark, *we* make no shadows, Herbie. And if we make no shadows, the Shadowghast can't snatch them."

Is Violet right? Is it really as easy as that to thwart the Shadowghast?

I guess we're about to find out.

"But if we can't see," I whisper back, "how can we escape?"

Violet doesn't answer. Instead she takes my hand and leads me forward into the blackness. I can sense her sweeping the candelabra in the dark ahead, using it to probe the void for obstacles. Then *CLANG!* She hits the wall. Violet begins tapping it with the silver candle holder, groping her way toward one of the tunnels.

The whispery, babbling noise echoes around us once more. I don't know if it's my imagination, but I feel I can hear a note of irritation, even anger, in it. There's a sudden icy gust of wind that blows grit right into my face.

I let go of Violet's hand as I stop to rub my eyes.

"Herbie?" Violet calls in the dark. "Herbie, where are you?"

"I'm right here," I reply.

"Yes, but *where*?" Violet's voice sounds panicky, and—I can't help noticing—slightly farther away than I was expecting. Her footsteps echo from all sides of the cavern, making it hard to determine direction. "Herbie, I can't find you!"

"Don't move!" I call back into the darkness. "I'll come to you."

And I walk a few echoing steps toward where I'm sure Violet must be, waving my arms like a zombie, but finding nothing but cold empty air. I run a few desperate steps in another direction, but still nothing!

"Herbie, why are you walking *away*?" comes Vi's voice again, much fainter and farther than it should be. "Turn around! We're getting separated!"

"Violet!" I cry. "*You* turn around! Come back!"

"Herbie?"

Violet's voice sounds so distant and cavern-far now that it's a shock to hear it.

"Herbie!"

"Vi!" I yell. *"VIOLET!"*

No answer.

And now I'm all alone.

In the dark.

But no, not *all* alone . . .

A cruel chuckle rolls around the cavern, this time with a triumphant edge. I thrust my hand into my pocket and pull out the tiny flashlight.

DO IT! comes a voice

Except, it's not a *voice*, not exactly. It's more an *absence* of voice that is speaking to me—as if the very silence of the dark roars a little quieter in my ears, to form these words.

THE LIGHT! TURN ON THE LIGHT!

My thumb is already on the flashlight's button. It would take only a tiny bit of pressure to click it on, and then I would be able to *see* . . .

THE LIGHT!

The flashlight falls from my hand, and I hear it skitter off across the flagstones.

Would I have had the willpower not turn it on? Or have I just been saved by luck and wobbly hands? I don't know the answer to that. All I know for sure is I'll never find that dropped flashlight, not now, not in the absolute dark, even if I wanted to.

So, there's nothing I can do but close my eyes, and hope.

Now, closing your eyes in the pitch-dark might sound like a bit of a bonkers thing to do. But it actually feels much better to be in complete blackness if you've *chosen* to see nothing. Really, it does. Next time you're alone in the dark, and a bit freaked out, try it and see.

I scrunch my eyes tight, fold my arms, and clamp my mouth firmly shut. Time to put Violet's it-can't-get-your-shadow-if-there's-no-light-to-cast-one theory to the test.

There's an icy swirl of air around me that tugs my uniform and plucks at my cap. It almost feels as though the darkness in the cavern is testing me, *tasting* me even, like a dog sniffs a morsel before chomping it down.

AAAAAH!

A final icy wind roars into my face—the grit it carries stinging me angrily.

YOU, the silence booms, *ARE DIFFERENT.*

"Huh?" I find myself saying, surprised despite everything. "What?"

YOU . . . ARE DIFFERENT . . .

I open one eye. Not that I can see anything, but I can't help it.

"How . . . how am I different?"

Despite the terror of the moment, I still have enough spare brain to be amazed that, basically, I'm having a conversation with some sort of ghost!

THE DEEPEST SECRET . . . roars the silence in answer, *THE SECRET THAT MY MASTER SEEKS . . .*

I say nothing.

YOU HAVE SEEN IT . . . the roaring silence continues, *BEEN TOUCHED BY IT. . . . IT HAS . . . MARKED YOU. YOUR SHADOW . . . IS DIFFERENT.*

"But . . ." I say, opening both eyes now and staring into the black. "I don't understand. Who is your master? What *is* this deepest secret?"

I'm hit by a final, furious blast of wind that forces me back so hard that I trip and fall onto the rocky floor. It's as if I'm being pushed away.

I WILL CLAIM . . . booms the echoing silence, *THE OTHER* . . .

And I feel the wind whip away—sense it spinning and twisting as it flies off down one of the passageways.

After Violet.

"Violet!" I call out, getting back on my feet. "Violet, look out!"

But she doesn't answer.

Nothing does, roaring a complete and terrifying absence of sound into my ears as the terrible shadow being that has rejected me rushes furiously after my friend.

And now I know I really am lost, in the darkness, deep in the Netherways beneath Eerie-on-Sea.

All alone.

CHAPTER 29

GUIDING STAR

How long I just stand there, my fists in my eyes, trying to stay calm, I don't know. The seconds pass like hours, and time just melts into one long moment of fear and helplessness. But eventually, somehow, I master my breathing and take my hands away from my face.

And open my eyes.

I force myself not to panic as I confront the eternal darkness once again.

I remember the words the Shadowghast said to me:

YOU ARE DIFFERENT.

What do they mean? What's so different about me that a ghost who snatches shadows doesn't want to snatch mine?

My hands are numb with cold now, so I shove them into my pockets.

I need to concentrate on finding a way out of here.

I say, at the top of my voice, "Herbert Lemon needs a plan!"

". . . AN . . . an . . . an . . ." comes the echo.

If I hoped that the reflected sound would help me locate one of the archways (and I did), then I'm disappointed. All sounds down here seem to come from everywhere at once.

I feel panic begin to rise up within me again.

But then, amazingly, I see something.

Actually *see* it.

Far ahead, somehow, there is a patch of whiteness in the gloom.

It's not *light*, as such, the patch. It's more like something that is *reflecting* a tiny amount of light, though what there is down here to reflect, I don't know. All I can do is watch in amazement—hope competing with dread—as the faint patch of whiteness approaches me with a sinewy motion.

"Sometimes the guiding light you need," comes a familiar feline voice, "is the only one you can see."

"ERWIN!" I cry out in joy and relief.

I jump forward and stoop as the bookshop cat saunters up to me. He stands to rub his head on my chin, but I grab him up into my arms.

"Erwin, thank you! Thank you for finding me!"

"Meow," Erwin replies, in a way that suggests locating misplaced Lost-and-Founders is all in a day's work for an Eerie cat. And perhaps it is.

"But how can I see you?" I ask as I put him back down. "You're not . . . you're not *glowing*, are you?"

"Prrp," says Erwin, with a hint of pride. The bookshop cat heads off in a sure-footed manner, padding down one of the passageways as though he knows where he's going. I scurry along behind him.

When we come to a corner, Erwin pauses so I can catch up. Then he sets off again, his bottom and tail waving from side to side as he proceeds to the next corner, where he pauses once more. And then, suddenly, we turn a corner and I see light—real, warm golden light!—far ahead, shining down a flight of steps.

"At last!" I cry, running toward the steps. "Thank you! Thank you, you crazy, weird, *bonkers* cat, you!"

Erwin twitches his whiskers at me. Then he scampers up the stairs—which are made of ancient stone blocks—and disappears through a square opening above. From that trapdoor, I can hear distant voices, one of them raised in alarm.

"Violet?" I call as I start up the steps myself. "Violet, is that you?"

When I reach the top, I find that I'm in a series of vaulted chambers, a little like the cellar beneath the house of Sebastian Eels, but with lower ceilings. A wooden trapdoor that would normally cover this opening is propped open on a metal brace. And all around is a terrible, bewildering mess, as if someone has ransacked the contents of this space and flung it all everywhere, higgledy-piggledy. At the corner of the room is another flight of stairs upward, and beyond that is warm electric light—and the sound of Violet talking urgently to someone.

I clamber over the clutter and run up the stairs.

"Herbie!" Violet jumps at me, overjoyed. "Herbie, you're OK!"

"I am." I gasp as Violet squeezes the breath out of me. "But I was worried about you. I thought the Shadowghast would get you for sure!"

There's a chuckle at these words, and I look over to see who it was that Violet was talking to.

"The Shadowghast would indeed be a terrifying thing to meet down in the tunnels beneath Eerie-on-Sea," says Dr. Thalassi, waggling his considerable eyebrows at me in amusement. "If, that is, it were real, and not a ghost from an old story used to scare children away from dark corners. And speaking of which—"

"But, Doc . . . !" I blurt out.

"Speaking of *which*," Dr. Thalassi insists, "I'm very disappointed to find that you two have taken it into your heads to explore the old smugglers' caves and abandoned mines beneath the town. They are a veritable labyrinth—and extremely hazardous. Many have disappeared down there over the years."

"But—" Violet blurts out, too.

"No buts, Violet!" the doc interrupts. "This is not a child's game. It's bad enough that I have to worry about Jenny Hanniver's disappearance, without mounting subterranean rescue missions for you two."

"But we *saw* Jenny!" Violet cries. "Tell him, Herbie! Didn't we see her? Down in the Netherways."

"Yes," I say. "I think. I mean, it was dark, and we didn't see much, but we definitely saw *someone* down there, Doc."

Dr. Thalassi looks at us both, furrowing his brow.

"*Netherways?*" he says. "Where did you hear that word?"

"Herbie told me about it," Violet replies, giving me a look. Dr. Thalassi still has no idea that Violet can read Eerie Script.

"Well, I wish he hadn't!" Doc glares at me. "Once you give something a mysterious name, you make it intriguing and give it a glamour that is bound to end up attracting the bright and the curious." And with these words, the doc turns his glare onto Violet. "It would be better if the word *Netherways* was forgotten for good. If I had my way, every secret door into that infernal maze would be found and bricked up for good."

"But what about Jenny?" Violet demands.

The doc shakes his head.

"I don't know," he replies, rubbing his temples. "Right now, I'm already engaged in another worrying matter. Someone has, it would appear, raided Mrs. Fossil's shop."

"What?" we both cry.

And it's then, finally, that I realize where we are.

All around us, the baskets and crates, the lobster pots and nets, the minerals and nodules of Mrs. Fossil's weird and wonderful Flotsamporium are scattered across the floor. Barrels and baskets are upended, driftwood is flung, and the ammonites, flip-flops, and recovered plastic knickknacks are jumbled together. Even the sea glass—which fills the windows of Mrs. F's beachcombing shop in hundreds upon hundreds of bottles and jars—has been tipped all over the floor in rainbow drifts that crunch underfoot.

To one side, upside down, and with a broken string, lies Mrs. Fossil's hurdy-gurdy.

Dr. Thalassi, who is wearing striped pajamas and a silk robe beneath his coat and hat, is standing in the middle of it all, looking as if he's auditioning for the part of Sherlock Holmes but has forgotten the lines.

"Who did this?" I say, surveying the mess. If there's one thing that a Lost-and-Founder doesn't like to see, it's a jumble. In a jumble, it's hard to know what is or isn't lost. "Is Mrs. Fossil OK?"

"I have no idea," the doc replies. "But the alarm was raised, and I came as quickly as I could. I found the trapdoor open in Mrs. Fossil's basement, so I suspect the intruders came in that way. It was as I was about to close it that I saw Violet appear. Well, I saw the cat Erwin appear, to be precise, with Violet just behind. I've never been more surprised in my life!"

"That's how I got out, Herbie," Violet explains. "Erwin found me and led me out. Then he went back to look for you."

"I think you are putting a little too much faith in the intelligence of this feline." Dr. Thalassi chuckles again and rubs Erwin's head slightly too roughly. Erwin, who is in Violet's arms, gives him an icy stare of annoyance, which the doctor fails to notice. "But, well done, both of you, for surviving the Netherways. Now, promise me you won't ever go down there again."

"But Jenny!" Violet protests. "We can't just leave her down there!"

"I suspect you didn't see Jenny at all," the doc replies. "It was dark, and perhaps you saw what you wanted to see. Besides, Jenny Hanniver knows all too well the dangers of the Netherways. She wouldn't do anything so foolish as to go down there herself."

Violet starts to protest again, but the doc waves away her concerns. I wonder if she has told Dr. Thalassi about our adventure in Sebastian Eels's house. Or about being chased by Mr. Mummery and nearly mimed to smithereens by Rictus and Tristo. Somehow, I don't think she has.

"Besides," Doc continues, picking up the hurdy-gurdy and gently wiping some dust off it, "now we have a second missing-person mystery to solve: Mrs. Fossil has disappeared."

CHAPTER 30

GHASTS AND GURDIES

iolet and I stare at each other. We remember how
wobbly Mrs. F was after her moment onstage this
afternoon.

"You know the legend of Ghastly Night, Doc?" Violet says
carefully. "And the Shadowghast . . . ?"

"Yes." Dr. Thalassi arches a wary eyebrow. "You know I do,
Violet."

"Well," she continues, "what is actually supposed to happen
to you if the Shadowghast snatches your shadow?"

The doc waggles his eyebrows and lets his specs fall onto his
nose as he lowers himself into a chair. The curator of the Eerie
Museum seems to have recovered his poise, now that he's back

on the familiar ground of the strange and colorful legends of Eerie-on-Sea.

"You saw the story of Ghastly Night that Mrs. Fossil and I performed," he says, tapping his fingertips together. "Once your shadow has been snatched by the Shadowghast and taken into the Shadowghast lantern, you yourself fall under the influence of the Puppet Master and become, in a sense, a living puppet. Just as old Mayor Bigley did when the Puppet Master made him dance. It's a fascinating piece of folklore, because—"

"I see," Violet interrupts, before the doc can get too far into lecture mode. "So does that mean the Puppet Master can use the Shadowghast to take control of people? Anyone they want?"

"According to the legend, yes," replies the doc. "Whoever commands the Shadowghast lantern is the Puppet Master in more ways than one. He controls it all."

"Or *she* does," says Vi, glaring at me out of her hair.

"Excuse me?" says the doc.

"I think Violet's trying to say," I explain, glaring back at her, "that she thinks my . . . that Caliastra, the magician, is up to no good."

"Whether or not she is up to no good can have little to do with the legend of Ghastly Night." Dr. Thalassi chuckles. "After all, it's just a story, and she's only a stage magician. The only question I'd ask is whether or not her shadow show is any good."

"Your show is great, Doc." Violet smiles kindly. "Really nice and fun, and I'm sure Eerie people love it. But Caliastra's show is . . . well, it's . . ."

"It's *amazing*!" I declare. "*Truly* magical, Doc. The best shadow puppet show I've ever seen!"

Then I go a bit sheepish when I see the slightly offended expression on the doc's face.

"She is a professional, though," I add, hoping to save some of the doc's feelings.

"It's all right, Herbie," Dr. Thalassi replies. "I would expect her show to be better than mine, for that very reason. Maybe I should go along tomorrow to see for myself."

"You should," says Violet. "It's quite a spectacle. She even has the original magic lantern, a big bronze thing with a dragon's head and wings. Really ancient looking—"

"What?" The doc jumps right out of his chair. "She has *the* Shadowghast lantern? Are you sure?"

"That's what she says," I reply. "It gives off this strange perfumed smoke. And the shadows she conjures are amazing! She can do anything with them, change their shape, make them dance and fly—"

"You need to go home." Dr. Thalassi suddenly looks agitated.

"I will lock up here. And tomorrow—*first thing* tomorrow—I will visit the theater myself and take a look at the lantern. It's high time I met this Caliastra."

"But what about Jenny?" Vi asks. "And Mrs. F?"

"Leave that to me," says the doc. "Oh, and, Violet, you shouldn't go back to the book dispensary tonight, not if you're going to be there on your own. Do you have somewhere you can go?"

"I can stay with Herbie," Vi replies.

"What about the trapdoor?" I ask, pointing down into the Flotsamporium basement.

"I'll leave it open," says the doc. "Just in case. But I will certainly lock the front door of the shop. Now, come along. Shoo! And take your cat with you. Good night!"

And with this we are ushered out into the blustery nighttime street.

"Herbie, what are we going to do?" Violet says. "Two people are missing now! And you saw what I saw down in the tunnels, didn't you? If there's even a chance that was Jenny, we've got to do something!"

"I know," I agree. "But what about the other thing we saw?"

"What other thing?"

"The *Shadowghast*!" I say, in a harsh whisper.

And I tell about my strange encounter with the specter— and the even stranger things it said to me.

"Deepest secret?" Violet says, after a stunned silence. "What did it mean by that?"

"The only other time I've heard those words before was when Sebastian Eels once told us that all the eeriest things in Eerie-on-Sea were connected by a 'deepest secret,'" I reply. "Just before he died. Remember?"

He also said I was connected to it myself somehow, but I don't like that part, so I don't add it.

Violet shakes her head in amazement as we hurry along.

"If I hadn't seen the weird things I've seen since I came to Eerie-on-Sea, Herbie," she replies, "I'd never have believed in legends or deepest secrets or in a shadow-snatching specter that haunts a magic lantern. But now I'm just terrified that the Shadowghast has snatched Jenny's shadow somehow. And Mrs. Fossil's!"

"Do you really suspect Caliastra?" I reply. "I mean, maybe if you spent more time with her, and heard the things she has to say, maybe . . ."

"Maybe nothing, Herbie!" Violet snaps. "Of course it's her. The only thing we don't know is why she's doing it. Why snatch Jenny's shadow and then send her down into the Netherways?"

"*If* it really was Jenny we saw down there," I say quietly.

But Violet doesn't reply.

When we reach the small window to my cellar, Violet slips

inside. But I don't follow. I'm annoyed that she is so completely against Caliastra. I just wish I could think of a reason why she's wrong.

I decide to head around to the front of the hotel and enter by the great revolving doors. I need to be seen using the proper entrance from time to time, or Mr. Mollusc will make good on his promise to block my cellar window.

But this time, as I stroll into the hotel lobby and prepare to look busy, I find myself face-to-face with disaster.

CHAPTER 31

UNDERGROUNDED

There he is!" booms Mr. Mummery, who is standing beside the large potted fern near my cubbyhole. "I demand to know what you are going to do about him, Mr. Mollusc. He's a menace. And a trespasser!"

"Herbert Lemon!" The hotel manager, who is standing beside the theatrical agent, screws up his fists like an enraged toddler and narrows his mean little eyes. "Come here this instant! What have you got to say for yourself, boy?"

"Me, sir?" I say, trying to hide my shock at seeing Mummery again behind my annoyance at being asked pointless questions by Mollusc. "I've got loads to say for myself, sir. What would you like me to say first, sir?"

"I'd like you to *explain*"—Mr. Mollusc grinds out the words, angrier than I've seen him for a long time—"what you were doing sneaking around private property. You're a Lost-and-Founder, not a Break-in-and-Burglar!"

"I wasn't burglaring!" I cry. Then I look at Mr. Mummery. "If anyone was burglaring, it was him."

But I dry up at the sight of further outrage dawning across Mr. Mummery's red face.

"You dare to accuse *me*?" he demands. "You dare to suggest that *I* was in that house illegally! It was *I* who had the key. Did *you* have a key, boy?"

Well, there's nothing I can say to this, is there? I mean, I'd like to say "But *you* were the one sneaking around in the dark, opening secret chambers, and chasing us into underground passages!" but I don't dare. And since Violet's not here right now, none of that gets said by anyone.

"You set fire to a valuable antique rug!" Mr. Mummery continues, as if sensing victory and going in for the kill. "And you even threw this . . . this . . . *thing* at my face!"

And he produces the lemon I discovered—shriveled and rubbery after years in the secret chamber in the house of Sebastian Eels—and flings it at my feet.

I pick it up.

As evidence goes, it's pretty damning.

"You've gone too far this time, Herbert Lemon," says Mr. Mollusc. "Lady Kraken will hear of this."

I droop.

"I was just looking for my friends," I mumble. "Jenny Hanniver from the book dispensary, and Mrs. Fossil, too. They have gone missing . . ."

"But why did you think they would be in that boarded-up house, Herbie?" comes a voice, and I turn to see Caliastra step out of a shadow, swinging her candy-glass cane. Behind her, leaning like statues on either side of the great ornate fireplace in the hotel lobby, Rictus and Tristo peer at me through their ghastly face paint. And between them sits the unmistakable shape of the Shadowghast lantern, covered in its silver drape.

I'm surrounded.

"I am disappointed in you," Caliastra says. She brushes a scrappy lock of hair from my forehead but doesn't smile. "I realize this is a difficult time for you, Herbie, and that I've turned your world upside down by coming here, but I do expect to be treated with respect. We are *family*, after all."

"But . . ." I say, still in mumble mode, "it's my job to find lost things."

"I'm sorry to hear you are worried about your friends, Herbie,"

Caliastra says with a hint of impatience. "Of course there'll be an innocent explanation for these disappearances. Isn't it around Halloweentime that the town shuts itself up for winter? Maybe Mrs. Hanniver and Jenny Fossick have gone away for a little holiday. And very well deserved, too, I'm sure."

"But . . ." I start to say, not knowing whether to launch into a protest or correct the names. Something moves behind the counter of my cubbyhole. It's Violet, eavesdropping in on the conversation, unspotted by all but me. "But . . . they would have *said* something."

"The fact remains," protests Mr. Mummery, "that the boy was snooping in matters that don't concern him. Caliastra and I want something done about him."

"And I," sneers Mr. Mollusc in triumph, "would like to be the one who does it."

Behind me, I sense Rictus and Tristo stand to attention. I think, when it comes to doing something about me, Mr. Mollusc will have plenty of competition.

Caliastra holds up a commanding hand.

"The boy is my responsibility now," she declares to everyone there. Then she turns to me. "Herbie, I think it's time you accepted that things have changed for you. We'll talk again, but its late now and way past your bedtime. You look exhausted!"

"Bedtime?" I'm confused by the concept. "Lady Kraken has never given me a bedtime."

Caliastra smothers my bafflement with a smile.

"But you are no longer Lady Kraken's concern," she says. "I have an appointment with her now, as it happens, to finalize your future. And I intend to give her a little demonstration of my Shadowghast lantern while I'm there. In her wheelchair, Lady Kraken will struggle to reach the theater for the show tomorrow night, so I have brought my show to her. I wouldn't want one of Eerie-on-Sea's most prominent residents to miss out."

I glance fearfully at the lantern beneath its drape. I remember the things the doc said about the Shadowghast and the puppets it creates of all those whose shadows are snatched. Lady Kraken won't stand a chance.

"You mustn't light the lantern again," I say. "Please, Caliastra, it's dangerous!"

"Dangerous?" The magician blinks at me in surprise. "What do you mean?"

"The Shadowghast!" I cry, seeing my chance. "When you let it out, it snatches people's shadows, and . . . and then . . ."

"Oh, Herbie." Caliastra stops a laugh by covering her mouth with the owl on top of her cane. "Now I *know* you have been overdoing it. The Shadowghast isn't *real*. It's just a story."

There's a ripple of laughter around the hotel lobby, and Rictus and Tristo mime a huge guffaw. Mr. Mollusc's mustache is bristling with mirth, and even Amber Griss—the hotel receptionist—suppresses a giggle.

"I thought you understood that stage magic is all about illusion, Herbie." Caliastra looks more disappointed than ever as she steers me gently toward my cubbyhole. "I see that you have more to learn than I realized. Sleep now, dear boy. We'll talk again tomorrow. And don't forget, you promised me a tour of your Lost-and-Foundery before we leave. I want to see *everything*. Now, good night!"

And she closes the counter behind me. I watch, helpless, as Caliastra leads her troupe to the hotel elevator—Tristo and Rictus carrying the Shadowghast lantern between them—to visit Lady Kraken.

"Mr. Mollusc," the magician calls as she enters the elevator, "please be so good as to ensure that my nephew does not leave the cellar again. He needs a good night's rest."

"Very well, madam," says the manager as the elevator door closes. Then he turns his sour grin in my direction. "Leave it with me."

"But, sir!" I cry. "We have to stop her. Lady Kraken is in danger."

"You heard your aunt," Mr. Mollusc snaps, crossing the

lobby to loom over me in my cubbyhole. "It's bedtime for little boys. You, Lemon, are confined to the Lost-and-Foundery until further notice. You're grounded."

"What?"

"Sweet dreams," Mr. Mollusc croons sarcastically, blowing me a kiss, "*dear boy!*"

Then he slides the metal grill down over my cubbyhole with a vicious *CLACK!* and locks it.

I'm trapped.

CHAPTER 32

NINNY BRAIN AND YELLY BELLY

....

N ot exactly trapped," says Violet a moment later, when
I join her down in my cellar. "We can still get out
through the window, remember?"

"But what's the point?" I slump down on my beanbag and lift
my Lost-and-Founder's cap. Clermit, who's been there all along,
falls out and I catch him. He extends his scissor claw, gives a
small snip of encouragement—or is he wishing me good night,
too?—and then retreats back inside his shell.

"We need to warn Lady Kraken," Violet says. "If Caliastra
makes the Shadowghast snatch her shadow, too, it will be a disaster for you. And the whole town. Come on, Herbie! Let's get out
of here."

But before we can reach the window, there's a rumbling, scraping sound from outside. Darkness falls as a heavy metal object is rolled in front of the cellar window, blocking the streetlight.

"What's happening?" says Violet, turning to me in surprise.

"The hotel garbage cans, I expect," I reply. "Old Mollusc breath has been threatening to block my cellar window for ages. He meant it when he said I'm grounded."

"But we've got to get out!" cries Violet, running to the window and flinging it open. She pushes at the metal bin there, but it won't budge. "Herbie, help me!"

I join her, but even heaving together we can't shift the stinking garbage can.

"Did you know how much waste a hotel kitchen creates?" I ask, slumping down on the floor. "Because you do now. We really are well and truly boxed in this time."

"Well, *of course* we are, Herbie!" Violet waves her arms in fury. "I've been telling you all along we can't trust Caliastra, and now, without breaking a sweat, she has us imprisoned down here, while she can go around unleashing the Shadowghast at anyone she pleases. Soon she'll control everyone!"

"Unless she doesn't realize what she's doing!" I say, jumping up. "You saw how she reacted when I told her that the Shadowghast was dangerous."

"Yes, Herbie, she laughed at you!" Violet raises her voice. "Then *everyone* laughed at you."

"OK, but for a moment—just a moment—she seemed genuinely surprised," I reply. "Maybe she really is just here to perform a magic trick and doesn't understand that she's feeding a monster."

"Herbie, how can you not see it?" Violet cries. "How can she have gotten her claws into you so deep that you can't see the truth. Caliastra *is* the monster!"

And I want to shout "No!" to that. I want to find the words to explain to Violet—to *show* her—just how it feels to be smiled at by someone who isn't merely a famous magician or a hotel guest, but someone who has spent years looking for me. Someone who knew me as a baby.

Someone who makes me feel what it must be like to have a mother.

You can't explain, says the voice of Caliastra in my imagination. *Violet will never understand. I said she would be jealous of you.*

"And anyway," Violet continues, speaking into the awkward silence that I've created by thinking all this, "what was that about you promising her a tour of your Lost-and-Foundery?"

"She just wants to see where I've been all these years." I shrug. "That's all."

"Really?" Violet looks disgusted with me. "You think a

celebrity magician—with an actual magic lantern—wants to visit a cluttered cellar full of lost property and dusty old whats-its just because she thinks you're her nephew?"

"She might," I say, gazing around the overfilled shelves, the boxes and chests and baskets of lost things that I call home.

"Herbie!" Violet grabs my uniform front and rattles me so hard my cap slips over my face. "She's tricking you. She's tricked everyone. Oh, why can't you see that if she puts on the Ghastly Night show tomorrow she will capture the shadows of everyone in Eerie-on-Sea? The whole town is in danger!"

"NO!" I shout, louder than I've ever shouted in my Lost-and-Foundery before. Violet stops, and blinks at me in surprise, so I shout it again. "NO! You are *wrong*, Violet Parma!" I yell. "I mean, yes, the town is in danger, but it's not Caliastra who's doing it. She's not the Puppet Master. She *can't* be. She's come to Eerie-on-Sea to find *me*!"

"Oh, Herbie." Violet looks at me pityingly. "That's only what she wants you to think."

"You're just *jealous*," I shout, pushing Violet away, "because no one has come to find *you*!"

Violet looks aghast, as if she has been slapped.

"It's true!" I yell. "Caliastra warned me this would happen. You can't stand that it's me who found my family first, so you're . . . you're seeing evil plots everywhere."

Violet grabs me again, but rougher this time, as if she can shake me into having different ideas.

"Caliastra is evil!" she cries. "She's made you think these horrible things about me!"

I grab Violet's coat front and shake her back.

"The *Shadowghast* is evil," I cry. "Caliastra is in danger, too. We've got to save her!"

And then we're falling, shaking each other off our feet, crashing into a box of lost walking sticks, and sprawling over the floor, each trying to get the other one to shut up.

It's the first time Violet and I have had a fight. And even while it's going on, I know how stupid it is and how ridiculous we must look. No amount of kicking or shoving is going to change what the other one is thinking. And yet, here we are anyway, rolling around like a pair of ferrets in a pillowcase.

"Numpty-headed ninny brain!" Violet cries, trying to get me in a headlock, and kind of succeeding.

"Shouty McShout Face!" I gasp, trying to pull Violet's coat over her head but getting mostly tangled in her hair.

"Dumb muppet!"

"Yelly belly!"

I'm just so glad there's no one around to see this!

But then comes a bone-jarring, monstrous *SCREECH* from

somewhere deep in the Lost-and-Foundery that makes us pause in our struggle.

"What's that?" I say.

"Fomeone'f in here!" Violet replies, muffled because of the coat.

We hear the screech again—an ear-twanging, blood-chilling noise from inside the cellar.

"Someone," I squeak, from beneath the crook of Violet's arm, "or some*thing*!"

CHAPTER 33

THE BATTLE OF THE LOST-AND-FOUNDERY

B ut what could it be?" Violet gasps as we untangle ourselves and stand up hastily. "And how did it get in here?"

The screech comes again, louder than before.

"It's coming from over there . . ."

The cellar of the Lost-and-Foundery is *L*-shaped. Most of the action takes place where we are now, in the main part, with the cozy fire and comfy chairs and the biscuits. But the strange sound is coming from around the corner—from the dark and dustier space where I hang the coats and keep the bigger things. Violet has a bed over there—made of blankets and cushions—for when she stays over.

Then the screech comes again, and our fight is quite forgotten.

"What *is* that?" Violet demands.

"Terrifying!" I squeak. "That's what!"

Violet picks up an umbrella—an antique one with a particularly sharp brass point—and then the lid of a wicker hamper, which she holds like a shield. In a moment, she's ready for battle. I look around, but all I can see to arm myself with are the hefty walking sticks we spilled on the floor or a nearby tennis racket with broken strings. It's obvious which I should pick.

"Ready?" says Violet.

"No," I reply, clutching the tennis racket in both hands.

And, so armed, we advance around the corner into the gloom.

The coats and blankets Violet sleeps on are heaped where they usually are, against a hot-water pipe. A paperback book is spread open on the floor nearby, surrounded by candy wrappers and a pair of dirty socks.

Violet glances at me sheepishly.

"Sorry," she says.

"I don't mind," I say with a shrug. "I just wish you'd use a bookmark like a normal person . . ."

"No, I mean the fight. I . . . I shouldn't be surprised you're so stubborn about Caliastra, Herbie. She hasn't made things easy for you."

I blink.

An apology?

From *Violet*?

But then I notice the word *stubborn*.

"Yes, well, I'm sorry, too," I say, in my iciest voice. "Sorry you can't be happy for me to have found my own family at last."

"Happy for you?" Violet turns on me, raising her umbrella sword and basket shield. "Happy that you can't see the truth, even when it's right under your squashy little button nose?"

"Button nose?" I shout, waving the tennis racket at her. *"Squashy?"*

CRASH!

A sound so loud that it makes us jump reverberates around the room.

"It came from there!" Violet says. "From inside!"

And she points her umbrella-sword at a large mahogany wardrobe standing against the far wall. This wardrobe, carved with a seaweed and octopus motif that I've never liked to look at, looms dark and mysterious.

"Oh, no," I say, starting to back away. "Are . . . are you sure?"

As if to answer this, there comes another crashing sound, like pieces of wood falling, and the wardrobe shakes.

"Herbie?" Violet narrows her eyes at me. "What do you use that wardrobe for?"

"Narnia business," I reply, hoping a joke will lighten the mood. It doesn't.

The wardrobe starts to tremble again.

Violet raises her wicker shield and umbrella and steps toward it. I clutch the tennis racket and somehow manage to step forward, too. But then we hear something new from inside the wardrobe— something so astonishingly eerie that it makes everything else we've heard so far seem like nothing at all. From within the antique cabinet, a muffled, slightly desperate voice speaks to us.

"Having nine lives is good," says the voice, "but only if you haven't *used up eight of them already!*"

We stare at each other. We'd know that voice anywhere.

"Erwin!" Violet cries, flinging her sword and shield to one side and scrabbling with the large iron key in the lock. She flings the wardrobe door open.

Inside there are several moth-eaten fur coats moldering on a rail. Obviously, I don't approve of making coats out of fur, but they were lost, these coats, so I still have to look after them—at least until a hundred years are up. Then I'll give the poor things a decent burial, I guess. But it's not the fur coats we're gawping at in amazement. It's the fuzzy head who stares down at us with frantic ice-blue eyes from a gap in the wooden paneling at the back of the wardrobe.

"Erwin!" cries Violet again, pushing the antique furs aside and climbing into the wardrobe. "Erwin, get down."

"I don't think he can," I reply. "He's stuck."

"Quick, Herbie," Violet replies. "Help me move these bits of wood."

And so we climb up into the wardrobe, and pull away the broken panels that form the back of the wardrobe, exposing the wall behind.

Except we don't expose the wall at all, do we? We expose, instead, something I knew was there all this time but had almost—*almost*—forgotten.

"A door!" says Violet in amazement as we pull the last strips of wood away and reveal the pitted surface of an iron door that wouldn't look out of place in an antique submarine. "Herbie, there's a *door* in the back of your Lost-and-Foundery!"

"Is there?" I reply, swinging the tennis racket at my side and trying to avoid my friend's gaze. "Fancy that!"

"You *knew* this was here," Violet declares, suddenly realizing the truth. "Herbie!"

But all I can do is offer up a lopsided grin.

"Anyway, looks like I wasn't the only one," I add, nodding at Erwin, whose head and front paws are dangling through a hole.

And what is that hole? Well, the iron door has a circular opening near the top, once covered by a metal grill, held in place by screws. Those screws have clearly rusted away, and my guess is the grill was forced out of the opening by sheer feline determination, causing the shrieking sounds we heard and that bang. The feline in question twitches his whiskers in annoyance and—finally—finishes coming through.

Cats are amazing. It's said that wherever a cat's head can go, its body can go, too, and Erwin seems determined to prove this. Before our eyes, the bookshop cat squirms and worms and wriggles and *toothpastes* himself through the hole in the door, till he plops down to land beside the broken metal grill on the wooden floor of the wardrobe. Then he quivers all over, ejecting rust particles from his bristling coat and flicking his ears in disgust at the indignity of it all.

Violet scoops him up.

"Clever cat!" she cries.

And she strokes his head furiously until his grumpiness melts away. His eyes narrow to closing, and the Lost-and-Foundery fills with purr.

And me? Well, I'm left staring fearfully through the hole in the door at the subterranean dark beyond. A steady gale of cold air rushes out at me, making me squint.

"A Netherways door!" Violet says in a wondering voice. "It must be. Herbie, how long have you known?"

"I've always known," I reply. "I've known from the day I first became Lost-and-Founder. I could hardly miss it, could I? Like I said, they say there are secret doors in the cellars of many of the oldest buildings in town, and the hotel is one of the oldest."

"But why cover it up?" asks Vi. "Weren't you curious to see what was on the other side?"

"Curious?" I goggle at Violet. "I knew what was on the other side—darkness and mystery and danger, and all just a doorknob away. I know you'll find this hard to understand, Vi, but I spent two whole days dragging that wardrobe in front of this door, and I've been doing my best not to think about it ever since."

"Well, fortunately for us, someone did think about it," Violet replies, kissing Erwin on the head and putting him on the ground. She turns to face the door with her hands on her hips. "Because this is our way out of here."

CHAPTER 34

CAT NAV

T he lock of the Netherways door is so fused with age that it takes a lot of oiling from my oilcan to get the key to turn. But turn it does with a heavy *SLUNK* of ancient metal parts. I give the hinges a good oiling, too.

Violet climbs into the wardrobe, places her hands on the metal door, and pushes with all her might. It swings squealingly open, and an even greater rush of chill air ripples the moth-eaten fur coats and invades my cozy home.

"OK, let's go!" says Vi, turning up her collar.

"Wait!" I cry. "We can't just . . . I mean, are you sure we should? After what happened last time? What if we get lost again?"

"How can we get lost when we have an expert guide with

us?" Violet replies, gesturing toward Erwin. The cat—sitting smartly in a narrow beam of moonlight that has slipped in the window past the garbage can—closes his eyes at me and purrs.

"I bet you know all the Netherways, don't you, puss?" says Vi. "You could lead us anywhere."

Erwin opens one eye and looks twitchy.

"Ne-ow," he says after a moment, as if embarrassed to admit he doesn't.

"But you know *a lot* of them?" Violet continues. "A magical cat like you."

Erwin tips his head to one side and peers up at Violet as if to say "I know a *few*, OK? And you're lucky I know those!"

"How about the bookshop?" Violet asks. "Is there a Netherways door in the cellar of the book dispensary?"

Erwin rumbles an affirmative purr as he gives one big nod of the head.

"OK, but still wait," I butt in. "Violet, the last time we took the Netherways, we saw . . . well, you *know* what we saw, and it nearly got us!"

"But it didn't," Vi says, as if it's the simplest thing in the world, "did it?"

And I can't answer this, can I? My mouth opens and closes a few times, but in the end all I can do is shrug.

Violet frowns at me. Then she smiles. Considering we were

at each other's throats a few minutes ago, it's nice to get a smile like that. She puts her hand on my shoulder.

"I get it, Herbie," she says. "I really do. You were on your own with all the eeriness of Eerie-on-Sea for such a long time. You must have been terrified when you found what this door was. I'm sure I would have been the same, if I'd washed up in this weird town and been sent to live in a strange cellar all on my own. I bet I would have blocked that Netherways door with an old wardrobe, too."

I look at Violet disbelievingly, but she has nothing but honesty in her eyes.

"But that was the *old* Herbie," she continues. "Not the brave, more adventurous *new* Herbie I see before me now—the Herbie who faced the malamander and survived Gargantis. Surely we've been on enough adventures for you to see that we're a winning team when we stick together."

I do a lopsided grin. *Brave* and *more adventurous* are definitely words I like hearing in the same sentence as *Herbie*.

"Are we a team, though?" I ask. "I mean, don't teams agree on everything? Seems to me as though you've already made up your mind about Caliastra, Vi. And I haven't!"

"I know." Violet looks as if she's making an effort not to get angry again. "I know. But whatever the truth is about the magician and why she is here, I think we can both agree that the Shadowghast is a danger to everyone. We have to stop that Ghastly Night show tomorrow, Herbie, or the whole town will be snatched. Agreed?"

She holds out her hand.

I sigh. Violet's right—we have to do *something*.

I shake her hand.

"Agreed," I say. "We're not going through that door, though, until we're good and ready. And that means finding a new flashlight, Vi. And winding Clermit up thoroughly. *And* finding gloves and scarves, and maybe some string to mark the way. And . . ."

"OK, Herbie, OK." Violet holds up her hands to stop me. "And while you're sorting that stuff out, I'm going to get something, too. . . ."

With this she heads back into the main part of my Lost-and-Foundery and starts rummaging around on my repair desk. After I have gathered our supplies she comes back, twisting a thing in her hands with the help of some pliers.

"You're not serious!" I say when I see what it is.

"Of course I am," Violet replies, finishing with a few last turns.

In her hand is a tall candle. Violet has spiraled a length of wire around it, which extends up from the top. Hastily, but surprisingly artfully, given the stubbiness of the pliers, she has twisted and folded the top part of the wire to form the shape of a creeping man.

"A manglewick candle!"

I'm impressed.

"It's not as good as one of Mrs. Fossil's," Violet admits, "but it should light our way."

And she takes a match, strikes it, and sets it to the wick. The flame flares up, and a creeping shadow dances into life on the wall of my Lost-and-Foundery.

"It's part of the legend of the Shadowghast that a manglewick candle gives you protection," Violet reminds me. "Well, if other parts of the legend are true, why not this part, too?"

"I'm still taking a flashlight, though," I say.

"Good," Violet replies. "Between us, we'll be ready for tomorrow's Ghastly Night show, whatever happens."

"It's not tomorrow's show anymore," I say, pointing at the clock. Its hands have just crept past midnight. "Technically, it's Halloween now. The Ghastly Night show is tonight."

The flame of the candle flickers in the cold breeze, as if the shadow man on the wall is delighted to hear this news.

Then, one by one—with Erwin in the lead—we step up into the wardrobe, push through the scraggy old fur coats, and emerge into the icy cold beyond.

We heave the iron door closed behind us with a *CLANG*, and I turn the key in the lock.

Once again my little home is as secure as a fortress. It's just that now I'm on the outside of it! I slip the key into my pocket and turn to face the rocky passageway we find ourselves in. Holding out the flashlight like a magic wand, I click it on and illuminate . . . nothing very much. The darkness ahead devours the flashlight, and I gulp.

So much for the newer, braver Herbie!

Then I see Violet do something surprising.

She hands me her candle, rummages in her huge coat pockets, and pulls out a stump of chalk. In the flickering light, she draws something on the pitted black iron of my Netherways door:

"That's the bell from my desk!" I cry. "Up in my cubbyhole. The one people ring when they've lost something."

"Exactly," says Vi, dropping the chalk back in her pocket. "So we will recognize this door again. And I'll mark other things, too, on the way. Just because no one has ever mapped the Netherways before, Herbie, is no reason *we* shouldn't start now."

"Prrp," says Erwin, and he sets off down the passageway. Side by side, Violet and I follow him into the dark.

CHAPTER 35

THE PROMISE

The first thing I notice about the passageway is that it starts to tilt upward. There are even a few places where rough, uneven steps have been cut into the rock floor. As we walk, we see other ways, too—tunnels that branch off left or right, with curtains of cobwebs billowing in the breeze. Some passages drop down into the depths of Eerie Rock at alarming angles, but Erwin leads us ever upward.

"It makes sense," Violet gasps, her breath catching from the climb. "The Eerie Book Dispensary is higher up than the hotel, so we have to gain some height, even underground."

The troglodytic dark seems to get darker still as we deepen into the maze. Violet and I draw closer together as we go, huddling around the candle in her hand, picking our way in the echoes and drips and silence. And always, at the edge of our little pool of flickering light, the dancing shadow cast by the manglewick keeps us strange company.

"I'm glad we have a guide," I whisper eventually, when I can stand the silence no longer. Erwin keeps just a few steps ahead of us, frequently pausing to let us catch up. "We've already turned more times than I can remember, Vi. I don't think I could find the way back now."

"That's why I've been drawing these," Violet replies, stopping for a moment to scratch a double-headed arrow onto the wall with her lump of chalk. "If we learn only one route through the Netherways, Herbie, then it should be the one joining my home with yours. Don't you think?"

I nod. That particular route could certainly prove useful in future adventures. If, that is, I stay in Eerie-on-Sea. But I don't say that part to Violet. Besides, the longer we stay in the tunnels— the longer we're steeped in the darkness and eeriness of the subterranean here-and-now—the harder it is to think of any sort of past or future at all.

"I just want to get out of here, Vi," I whisper.

We hurry on, following Erwin as he scampers ahead. And I've never been more grateful to see a cat's bottom, I can tell you! But then he stops, at a particularly twisty junction, and sniffs one way, before peering quizzically down another. His tail starts to swish with frustration, exactly as if whatever cat nav he uses to get around the Netherways is suddenly on the blink. I'm just about to say something rude to the hesitant feline, when Violet says something else instead that shuts me up completely.

"I'm scared, Herbie,"

It's not the sort of thing I'm used to hearing from Violet.

"I'm sure Erwin's just got his whiskers in a twist," I reply, hoping I'm right.

"I don't mean that," Vi says. "I mean I'm scared about what's happening, scared about Jenny—scared we may *never* find her. What if we can't stop what's happening in Eerie-on-Sea? What if Caliastra gets what she wants and takes you away, too?"

I say nothing. In the endless dark I see the two points of reflected candlelight in Violet's eyes as she stares at me.

"Herbie," she continues, "I don't *want* you to leave. I . . . I *don't want* to be left alone. Not again."

By now the silence from me must be deafening.

"But," Violet says then, holding her voice steady, "but, I promise you, if at the end of all this you are right—if Caliastra is not the villain after all, then I . . . I won't stand in your way. I'll even manage to be happy for you, Herbert Lemon, for finding your family before I found mine. I just hope you won't forget me, that's all."

I stare back at Violet. These words from her, this admission that she is scared, is so unlike anything the Violet who first came to town would have said, that I suddenly see I'm not the only one who has been changed by our friendship. We really are a team, no matter what happens next.

"And I," I reply, "I swear on my Lost-and-Founder's cap that I won't leave Eerie-on-Sea till I know you're OK, Violet Parma. And until Jenny has been found again, and Mrs. Fossil, too. And everything's been fixed. And *that* is a Herbie promise."

"Prp," comes a small sound of impatience, and we look over to see Erwin waiting beside one of the passages, exactly as if he's known where to go all along.

"Come on, Herbie," says Violet briskly, but with a smile in her voice. "The book dispensary must be close."

She makes her chalk mark on the archway, and we follow Erwin again down a particularly tumbledown brick passage.

"Have you ever seen a strange doorway in the bookshop cellar?" I ask. "That could be a Netherways door?"

"Actually, I have." replies Violet. "I've often wondered where it leads, but Jenny just told me to forget about it. Now I know why."

Then, a couple of cat-turns later, we're standing in a low natural cave, dodging between sparkling stalactites that poke our heads and shoulders and looking at the warped boards of a small, round wooden door.

"It's tiny," I say. "Like it was made for hobbits."

Erwin approaches the door and slips through a gap beneath it.

"Er, *we* can't get in like that," I say.

Violet grabs the tarnished brass door handle and twists it.

"Locked!" she declares. "Now what?"

"Looks like the key's in the other side," I say, peering through the keyhole.

"But we can't turn it from here," Vi replies. "And Erwin doesn't have enough thumbs to do that."

"No," I agree, "but I know someone who doesn't need thumbs."

And I take Clermit out from beneath my cap, give him three good windings-up, and place him on the ground.

"Please, could you open this door for us?" I say. "It's for important Lost-and-Founder business."

Clermit stands on his metal legs and snips a salute. Then he scuttles under the door. We hear a scraping, whirring sound and then a screeching of metal against metal, as if an antique mechanism that hasn't been turned for a hundred years is being turned now with a *CLUNK*. We push at the little round wooden door, and it creaks open.

"The Eerie Book Dispensary!" Violet cries, seeing crates of books beyond. "We did it, Herbie!"

"Wow!" says Erwin, who is sitting watching us archly from a barrel.

"With your help, of course, puss," Vi adds. "And, to say thank you . . ."

Violet takes the chalk from her pocket, and on the honey-colored lintel stone above the little round door, she draws a picture of Erwin the cat.

Then we duck into the cellar beneath Eerie-on-Sea's peculiar bookshop and pull the door closed behind us.

⚙𝗢✿

It's only when we get up into the bookshop proper that we realize how very late it is. The main room of the dispensary is cold and dark, and the books are asleep on their shelves. There's nothing but night in the windows, and silence from the town beyond, and that tingling sense of secrecy that comes from still being up when everyone else is in bed.

The mermonkey sits in the gloom, its hairy back to us, its

wide eyes and toothsome leer dimly reflected in the glass of the window. It'll be a relief to take our candle upstairs. But before we can do that, Erwin runs to the shop counter and jumps on it.

"Me-ow," he says in a significant way.

"What it is?" Violet asks, approaching him and holding up the candle.

Erwin reaches out a paw and shoves a yellow-jacketed book toward us. It's *The Subtle Mask*—the book the mermonkey dispensed for Caliastra—which is still sitting where she left it on the counter.

"He was fussing over that before, remember?" I say.

"Yes," Vi replies with a yawn. She picks up the book and slips it in her coat pocket. "But right now, Herbie, we need to get some sleep. We have to be at the museum early, to warn Dr. Thalassi."

"We do?" I ask.

"Have you forgotten he said he was going to go to see Caliastra first thing tomorrow?" Vi replies. "You know what he's like when he spots something historical. He'll want to examine the Shadowghast lantern, and something tells me that when he does, he'll go missing, too."

And she leads the way upstairs.

Jenny Hanniver's flat is in the attic above her shop. It's a cozy apartment of swirly throws, scented candles, and skylight windows, and its walls are lined with—yes, you've guessed it—books. The Eerie Book Dispensary has always offered a room for the night to travelers who have come from afar to consult the mermonkey, but Violet's room isn't one of those. When Jenny invited Vi to live with her, she offered a small bedroom of her own in Jenny's private flat. I wasn't there when the arrangement was made, and I don't know what was said, but Jenny Hanniver is Violet's guardian now, in all but name.

In Violet's room, I place my cap—Clermit nestling inside—on the windowsill. Violet climbs into bed, while I crawl into a large, dusty closet to fight some big cushions into something bed-like. Then Vi blows out the manglewick candle, and I'm happy to see the little creeping shadowman who has followed us through the Netherways all this way finally wink out of existence.

"Good night, Herbie."

"G'night," I reply.

It takes me a long time to get to sleep after all that's happened. But I must eventually, because a vision of Caliastra's smiling face blazes in my mind's eye, looking darker and more crafty than ever, and that can only be a dream, can't it?

CHAPTER 36

DR. THALASSI

Something tickles my nose.

I swipe it away.

Something tickles my nose again, and I swipe harder, punching myself in the face.

"Ow!"

I sit up to discover that the tickly something is probably Erwin's whiskers, since the bookshop cat is staring at me nose-to-nose, looking annoyed.

"What time is it?" comes a groggy voice from across the room, and I see Violet emerging from her duvet.

"Ne-ow," says Erwin, jumping up onto the windowsill.

"What!"

Violet leaps out of bed and throws the curtains of her dormer window wide open.

"Herbie, get up! We've overslept!"

"Have we?" I groan, emerging from the closet and trying to scratch away that uncomfortable feeling of having slept in my clothes. I look out the window at the sight of the sun playing across the surface of a thick sea mist that fills the town. Only the rooftops and chimney stacks are visible, poking up like geometric islands in a cloudy sea. Then I add, with a yawn, "Are you sure we haven't *under*slept?"

"We need to go!" Violet cries, getting hastily dressed. I turn and stare into the corner so she can't see how red I get. "We have to warn Doc, remember? Before he goes to the theater."

We pull on our coats and head into Jenny's kitchen.

"Are we going to use the Netherways to get to the museum?" I ask, dreading the answer.

"Better not," Violet replies, handing me a hastily buttered slice of bread smeared with marmalade while chomping a slice of her own. "Ish too rishky."

Well, I don't argue with that, do I? Something tells me we should only ever risk the Netherways in an emergency. Violet hands me another slice, which I fold into a marmalade sandwich. I slip it under my Lost-and-Founder's cap—beside Clermit—for later.

We leave the bookshop, Violet locking the door behind us, and run into the mist. We'd have to be pretty unlucky to bump into anyone who knows I've been grounded, and anyone else would just think I'm out and about on important Lost-and-Founder business.

When we reach the square in front of the castle, the mist is beginning to burn off in the sun. We duck into the great door-way of the old fortress. I keep a wary lookout while Violet pulls on the bell rope.

The door opens, and the doc leans out to inspect us from beneath his caterpillar eyebrows. He looks surprised. He also looks uncharacteristically untidy. Disheveled, in fact. *Disheveled* is a great word, but it's not one I'd ever expect to use in the same sentence as *Dr. Thalassi.*

"Oh, Doctor," says Violet. "I'm so glad you're here. You haven't been over to the theater yet, have you? We need to tell you something urgently."

"I'm actually quite busy." The doc frowns. "But if it's urgent, you'd better come in."

We enter the museum, passing the ancient fish-shaped bot-tle that the doc has displayed in pride of place in the foyer. He leads us through to the main hall, where the skeleton of a whale hangs over glass cabinets and display cases and all the peculiar exhibits of the Eerie Museum.

"Are you reorganizing?" Violet asks. "I've never seen so many cabinets open at once?"

Sure enough, there are signs everywhere that the doctor has gone through the displays, turning things over, opening boxes and rifling through drawers. He hasn't even raised the window shutters, and the museum looks as though it wouldn't be able to open again for weeks.

"I am auditing the entire collection," the doc replies, "looking for . . . well, it would take too long to explain. But please, go through to my study."

And he gestures toward the glass-fronted, book-lined office that overlooks the main hall of the museum.

"I wonder why he's doing this now?" I whisper to Vi, looking around at the shambles in the museum. "Seems odd to be worrying about exhibits when actual people have gone missing."

"Maybe he's on the trail of some clue," Violet whispers back.

The doc closes the door behind us, sits down in the large mahogany chair behind his desk, and runs his fingers through his crazy hair.

"Now," he says, "what's so urgent? Have you managed to find Jenny? Or Mrs. Fossil? Because I really must get back to work."

"We haven't, no," Vi replies, "but we think we know what might have happened to them. Actually, we were really worried it might have happened to you, too."

"To me?" replies the doc, raising one eyebrow in surprise.

"Yes!" Violet blurts out. "And all because of that magic lantern of Caliastra's. This is going to be hard for you to believe, Doc, but we have something really important to tell you about it."

"About the Shadowghast lantern?" The doc raises his other eyebrow. "What have you found out?"

"Well, for a start, whatever you do, don't go near it!" Violet says. "The story of the Shadowghast is true! There really is a bad spirit haunting the lantern. And we saw it take Mrs. Fossil's shadow, right before our eyes. Oh, Doc, I know this is going to sound crazy, but please believe me when I say that the Shadowghast is real, and if the Ghastly Night show goes ahead, then every last man, woman, and child in Eerie-on-Sea could be captured by the Puppet Master!"

All this comes out in a bit of a rush, and Violet is left nervously clutching the desk, clearly hoping not to be laughed at. Dr. Thalassi is a gentleman of science, after all, and not given to belief in goblins and sprites. But, amazingly, the gentleman of science merely nods and strokes his chin, as if considering the problem carefully.

"If what you say is true," he asks, "why would the Puppet Master use the Shadowghast to snatch the shadows of so many people?"

"Well . . ." Violet blinks, surprised to be taken seriously.

"We think . . . *I* think that the Puppet Master is sending people underground—people like Jenny, and probably Mrs. Fossil, too—sending them underground so they can be put to work searching for . . . *something*. Something in the Netherways beneath Eerie-on-Sea."

"Oh?" The doc narrows his eyes. "What sort of something?"

"We . . . we don't really know," Violet begins, but I speak over her.

"The deepest secret," I say. "The deepest secret of Eerie-on-Sea."

Dr. Thalassi glances at me for a moment, and then back at Violet. "And who, according to your 'theory,' is looking for this deepest secret? *Who* is the Puppet Master?"

"Caliastra, of course!" Violet blurts out, at exactly the same time that I say, "Mr. Mummery!"

The doc gives a nod, an inscrutable expression on his face.

"What?" Violet turns to me. "You think Mr. Mummery is the Puppet Master?"

"Well"—I take a deep breath—"it was Mr. Mummery we found breaking into Sebastian Eels's house and taking things from the secret chamber. And it was Mummery who reported me to Mollusc. There's something about Mr. Mummery that I've never trusted, so, um, yes, I reckon he's the one who's behind it all."

"But that doesn't make sense, Herbie!" Violet slaps the desk in frustration. "It's Caliastra who runs the whole show, and . . ."

"Stop!" commands Dr. Thalassi, holding up his hand. "I've heard enough. Violet, you are right, there *is* more to the legend of the Shadowghast than people realize."

"I am?" Violet looks stunned to be hearing this from the doc, of all people. "There *is*?"

"Indeed," the doc replies. "And I believe it's time for you to become part of it. It's time, Violet Parma, that you knew the whole truth about Ghastly Night."

"Oh!" is all that Violet can say then.

"If you'd like to come this way," the doc continues, straightening his robe and getting to his feet, "I will start by showing you something that I believe will interest you both."

And the doctor strides back out into the exhibition hall, stepping over boxes and papers, making us jog to keep up.

"You remember from the story of Ghastly Night how old Standing Bigley was the mayor of Eerie-on-Sea?" the doc calls over his shoulder.

Reaching the far wall, he unwinds a rope from a hook beside a shuttered window and lowers a cage from the ceiling. This, I know from visiting the museum before, is called a gibbet—a cage the size and shape of a person that criminals were once hung up in as a lesson to others. There are several in the museum, from the dark days of Eerie's past. Some of them even have spikes inside.

"Well, this is an actual gibbet from Bigley's time," the doc explains.

"It's nasty," says Violet, clearly confused. "But what's this got to do with anything?"

"Stop asking questions, Violet, and let me show you!" the doc snaps as he opens the side of the gibbet cage with a screech of centuries-old metal. He points to the floor of it.

"There!" he declares. "What do you think of that?"

I peer down to where he's pointing. I don't think much of it, frankly, because I can't see much at all. But then Violet gasps.

She jumps away from us, tugs the cord that raises the blinds on the nearest window, and lets the sunlight stream into the hall.

And over the doc.

And that's when we see it.

Dr. Thalassi has no shadow!

CHAPTER 37

PICKLED LEMON

Run, Herbie!" Violet yells, darting away from the doc's arm as he lunges for her.

My brain—bamboozled by the strange sight of a man with no shadow—is also flummoxed by Violet's desperate call, dunderfied by the doc's sudden aggression, and generally discombobulated by the whole bizarre moment. Before I can get a clear signal to any useful part of my body, Dr. Thalassi has grabbed me by the scruff, stuffed me inside the gibbet, and slammed the door.

"Herbie!"

Violet, seeing me captured, ducks beneath the doctor's sweeping arms and kicks him in the shins.

"Argh!" cries the gentleman of science, hoping on one leg. "Herbie, get out!"

Well, that's what I'm trying to do, isn't it? I push the door of the cage, and it creaks open a bit. But then the doc throws his whole weight against it, slamming it shut again and tearing my uniform.

There is a small iron loop on each side of the gibbet door where some kind of padlock would once have been fixed. Dr. Thalassi doesn't have a padlock, so instead—using nothing but brute force—he twists the loops with his fingers, bending them together and fastening the cage door shut.

"Violet!" I call out, cursing myself and my flumboozerfied brain for not acting sooner. "Just get away! Go!"

But Violet doesn't just get away or go. Instead, she runs here and there, dodging the doctor's increasingly aggressive attempts to catch her. She's clearly trying to get around to the cage, but what she thinks she can do to help, I don't know.

Then the doc changes everything anyway by striding back to the gibbet, grabbing the rope it dangles from, and hoisting me high into the air. Violet rushes at him, but Dr. Thalassi is a big man, and he just pushes her over with his foot. While she's clambering back to her feet, he ties the rope, and now I'm dangling as helpless as any eighteenth-century pirate, swinging in the gibbet.

"I don't want to hurt you, Violet," Dr. Thalassi says, turning to my friend. "If you knew what I know, you'd understand. And I *want* you to understand. You could be so useful to us. Come, let's go to see Caliastra together. She'll be able to explain."

"Explain?" Violet shouts, her eyes alight inside her wild hair. "Or use the lantern on me and let the Shadowghast snatch *my* shadow, too?"

"It's not what you think, Violet." The doc holds one solicitous hand out to her. "Come with me. You won't be hurt, I promise."

"Let Herbie go!" Violet cries, darting around and then leaping onto the doc's back. She wraps her arms around his throat.

But Dr. Thalassi simply throws her over his shoulder.

Violet crashes into an open display cabinet—gasping in pain and destroying a dinosaur skeleton. Violet is barely able to clamber out of the prehistoric ruin and run before the doc lunges once more. She must realize that she can't beat the bigger, stronger man, because she sprints away now, down the central aisle of exhibits, toward the museum exit.

"I'll get help, Herbie!" she calls, turning one last time. "I'll get . . . I'll get *someone*. I promise!"

And then she runs . . .

Straight into the stout form of Mr. Mummery, who has just entered the museum.

Mr. Mummery grabs Violet, but she slips out of her coat

and escapes him. Dodging the doc one last time, she leaps desperately for the door.

But Caliastra is standing there. In her shadow-black coat of shimmering patterns, and with her raven hair and blazing eyes, the magician looks terrifying. She raises her glass cane and jabs the end of it into Violet's chest with a cry of "Prestocadabra!"

Violet comes to a sudden halt, crying out, her arms flying wide.

"Well, well!" cries Caliastra. "I have caught a butterfly."

And that's when Dr. Thalassi and Mr. Mummery grab an arm each, and Violet is captured, too.

"Herbie, Herbie, Herbie . . ."

Caliastra walks toward me, giving her cane a few lazy swishes.

"If only you had stayed down in your cellar, you could have been spared all this. How did you get out, by the way?"

I say nothing. I *can't* say anything.

"Never mind," Caliastra replies. "In just a few hours the whole town will be under my control, and none of this will matter anymore."

"I defended you," I manage to blurt out. "When Violet said you were a villain, I thought you . . . I thought *we . . .*"

"But, Herbie, you thought *right,*" Caliastra says, hitting me with her dazzling smile. "You were right to think all those things you can't quite say about me. I could be all of that to you, if you let me." Then her smile goes hard and sour. "But Violet did have to spoil it, didn't she? Whispering doubts in your ears and poisoning you with her jealousy."

"I was the one who thought right," Violet says, struggling uselessly. "You *are* a villain. You've been lying to Herbie from the start."

Caliastra turns and raises her cane at Violet. If she were a real magician, I'd fear that lightning was about to erupt from the end. But instead, Caliastra blasts Violet with words.

"Everything I have told Herbie is the truth," she declares. "Or rather, a truth that deep down he wanted to hear. You are the one who has kept him from embracing that truth, Violet Parma. And now look what you've made me do? Lock your best friend in a cage!"

"Me?" Violet is outraged. "How dare you blame me!"

Caliastra turns toward the entrance of the museum hall.

"Bring the lantern!" she commands.

There is movement at the door and Rictus and Tristo appear, dressed all in black as ever, with their ghastly painted faces. They are carrying the dragon-carved Shadowghast lantern between them.

"Set it up over here," Caliastra instructs. "Thalassi, clear some of this clutter away," she adds, waving her cane at the exhibits and display stands scattered on the floor. "I don't suppose you have found anything useful, have you?"

"No, Caliastra," the doc replies. "There is no map of the Netherways in the museum—just as Jenny didn't find one in the book dispensary, or Mrs. Fossil in her shop. Do you really believe such a map exists?"

"Sebastian Eels did," Caliastra snaps in reply. "Though, even he never found it."

"We still haven't searched the Lost-and-Foundery," Mr. Mummery says. "According to his notes, Eels always wondered if the map could be there. Maybe we can squeeze some answers out of that pesky Lemon boy."

And he throws a look of hatred up at me.

"Perhaps." Caliastra glances up at me, too, tapping her cane on her teeth. "But in a few hours I will have an army of puppets at my command, and I can search the Netherways by sheer force of numbers. The deepest secret of Eerie-on-Sea will be found, one way or another."

"Have the others returned, then?" Mr. Mummery asks.

Dr. Thalassi nods and hands his half of Violet to Mummery, who has to struggle to hold her on his own. The doc crosses to a closet and opens it. Two more people emerge into the crowded museum hall, shuffling like zombies, and my eyes bug out of my head when I see who they are.

"Jenny!" gasps Violet.

"Mrs. Fossil!" I cry out.

Sure enough, the owner of the Eerie Book Dispensary and the town's one and only professional beachcomber step out into the light.

They look terrible. Jenny, in particular, looks as if she has been crawling on her hands and knees in the dark—her red hair bird-nesting around her face, which is streaked with blood and grime. Mrs. Fossil, who looks pretty scruffy at the best of times, hasn't a single hat on her head, which isn't like her at all, and is wearing only one rubber boot.

Of course, in the sunlight of morning, we see that neither of them has a shadow.

"Jenny, it's me!" Violet struggles violently. "Jenny! Mrs. Fossil!"

But neither Jenny nor Mrs. Fossil respond.

"What have you done to them?" Violet demands of Caliastra.

"It isn't easy," the magician replies, as if resenting having to admit to a weakness, "controlling so many minds at once. And these two puppets will soon be joined by hundreds more. None of them will need much intelligence to search a load of tunnels. I've shut most of their brains down."

"Jenny!" Violet cries again, this time with a sob. "Jenny, wake up!"

But Jenny Hanniver just stares blankly at the floor and says nothing.

"We'll find the deepest secret," gasps Mr. Mummery as he fights to keep Violet still. His homburg hat has fallen to the ground with the struggle. "We'll succeed where even the great Sebastian Eels failed. And there's nothing you can do about it, girl."

"Not if I stop you first, you won't!" Violet shouts, almost breaking Mummery's grip.

"Oh, but, Violet, you aren't going to stop us." Caliastra sounds amused. "You are going to *join* us. Just as soon as I light my little magic lantern."

CHAPTER 38

THE MAGICIAN'S ASSISTANT

L et me go!" Violet yells, and the doc hurries to help Mr. Mummery pin her down. Even Tristo—still acting the clown as he capers over and replaces Mummery's hat on his head—is needed to help. Rictus grins his terrible grin as he adjusts the angle on the lantern so that its dragon head points straight at Violet like a cannon.

"Don't be distressed by what you are about to see, Herbie." Caliastra smiles up at me comfortingly while the lantern is fired up and perfumed smoke begins to curl around the exhibition hall. "It's quite painless. And I will allow Violet to keep her intelligence. She will be more useful that way."

"Please," I beg, rattling the cage. "Please don't do this . . ."

"Sadly, you've left me with no choice," Caliastra replies, walking over to Violet and sweeping the hair away from her defiant eyes. "Violet has shown initiative and flare. She reminds me a lot of myself when I was a girl. She will make an excellent assistant. I am so very disappointed in you, Herbie. But you will have your uses, too, I expect, when all this is over. In the bag-carrying department, perhaps."

Now lit, the magic lantern is hissing and popping as it generates ever greater clouds of smoke. Streams of light are already finding their way around the silver orb in the dragon's mouth as Dr. Thalassi and Mr. Mummery hold Violet up in front of it, at firing-squad range.

"No!" I punch the cage. "Leave her alone! Do it to me instead! I'll be good. I promise!"

"I can't do it to you," Caliastra replies, almost as if she's talking to herself. "That's the point."

And she heads over to the lantern.

"Herbie!" Violet calls up to me, giving up her struggle and standing tall. "Just remember, whatever I do or say after this, it won't be me. OK? Remember it won't be me!"

I rattle the cage more desperately than ever and brace my legs against the door. I press with all the strength a desperate Lost-and-Founder can leverage in such a small space, and the twisted metal loops holding the door shut give a little.

But it's not enough.

And I sag back into the gibbet cage, defeated.

Smoke billows and frames the horrifying scene below.

"Step right up!" cries Mr. Mummery, in mockery of the show he and the others have been rehearsing for. "Ladies and gentlemen, prepare to be amazed!"

And Rictus plucks the silver orb from the dragon's mouth, letting the strange and magical light of the Shadowghast lantern pour onto Violet.

⚙O✿

The first thing I notice is that not only does the doc cast no shadow, neither does Mr. Mummery. Tristo, cavorting beside them, is also without shade. But I shouldn't be surprised. Caliastra must have commanded the Shadowghast to make puppets of them all. Violet's shadow alone streaks out across the floor, unprotected, waiting to be the next victim.

The light from the lantern illuminates the swirling clouds, and dark forms begin to appear. Shadows creep from the lantern and begin to move around. These must be the shadows of everyone captured already. There are so many! How many more will there be after the show tonight? How can anything stop the magician now?

Then I gasp.

I see someone I recognize!

A familiar shadow staggers from cloud to cloud, her arms held out as if looking for a way to escape. It's the shadow of Jenny Hanniver!

"Jenny!" I call. "Jenny! It's me! Herbie."

The shadow of Jenny Hanniver startles, as if hearing my voice, but doesn't know where it's coming from. I see her shadow mouth opening and closing as if she is shouting in reply, but I hear nothing. Then I see another shadow, this time of a person wearing at least three hats tied on with a piece of string.

"Mrs. Fossil!"

And my mind is boggled all over again at the sight of my friends' shadows completely detached from the bodies that usually cast them. Other shadows begin to gather around them, some in costumes that belong to the past, and the horror I feel doubles as I realize that these must be the shadows of people whose bodies have long since died.

"Mayor Bigley!" I cry as I spot the desperate shadow of the man who brought all this misery down on the town in the first place, all those years ago.

One by one, the lost souls begin to stumble out of the clouds, as if drawn to my voice.

Then comes a chuckling sound—a sound that may or may not be caused by the lantern's fire. It echoes around the hall as another shadow appears.

The shadow of a grinning man with horns upon his head.

The Shadowghast!

He swoops here and there, snatching the fleeing shadows, dancing with them in mock delight, taunting them, twisting their shapes into cruel and disturbing forms, before engulfing them, absorbing them into himself. With each shadow he devours, he grows darker, till he almost appears solid, stalking terrifyingly through the smoke as the only shadow that remains.

Then the Shadowghast stretches his crooked shadow fingers across the floor to take the shadow of Violet Parma.

"Remember, Herbie!" cries my friend. "Remember!"

The Shadowghast's arm darts forward and snatches her shadow.

"Herbie!"

The Shadowghast, grinning in triumph, whirls Violet's shadow in a crazy waltz to music only he can hear. Then, after twirling her in the air one last time, he leaps toward the lantern and back through the lens, dragging Violet's silently screaming shadow behind him.

Rictus swiftly replaces the silver orb, and darkness returns.

Violet goes limp in the arms of her captors.

"Ladies and gentlemen!" calls Mr. Mummery into the silence that follows. "The show is over!"

CHAPTER 39

CREEPY CLOWNS

R elease her!" Caliastra commands.

The two men holding Violet step away, letting her slump to the floor. She crouches there a moment before getting slowly to her feet.

"So, Violet"—Caliastra places a hand on my friend's shoulder—"how are you feeling? It's not too bad, now, is it?"

Violet sways a little and then turns to look up at the magician, and for a moment I almost dare to hope that this dark magic of the Shadowghast lantern hasn't worked. But then Violet speaks.

"I feel . . . fine. I . . . understand now. These thoughts . . . in my head . . . I see I have been wrong. I'm sorry, Cali. May I . . . may I call you Cali?"

Caliastra beams her brightest smile.

"You may. You and I are going to be close, Violet. Very close indeed. I believe you are just the assistant I require. I should have seen it from the start."

"Vi!" I call, rattling my cage. "Vi, it's me! Don't listen to her."

Violet looks at me from inside her hair, which seems wilder than ever. But instead of the light of friendship I am used to seeing there, I receive only a blast of stern disapproval, as if Violet has just noticed something annoying that needs to be dealt with. And that something annoying is me.

"Tell me, Violet," says Caliastra, stooping so that her head is level with Vi's, and indicating me with her cane. "You know Herbie better than anyone. Do you think he can escape from that cage? Or should we take more drastic measures to stop him from interfering with our plans?"

"Herbert Lemon is clever and sneaky," Violet replies, still looking at me as if I'm something on the bottom of her shoe. "He will try to break out, Cali, and he might succeed. He has a clockwork device under his cap that he will use to help him."

I gasp. It's only now—as she betrays Clermit—that I realize Violet is completely lost to me.

"Thank you," Caliastra says. "I cannot allow Herbie to keep any such clockwork device. Rictus! Tristo! See to it!"

The two mime artists motion to each other with exaggerated "After you!" gestures of politeness, followed by even more theatrical "No, after *you!*" mimes. Then Tristo, who is closest to me, finally accepts the task with modest bows of thanks to his partner, who blows kisses back to him, and I think, *This is ridiculous!* What villain in their right mind uses a pair of clowns as henchmen? And it's then—as I'm rolling my eyes and shaking my head and no longer paying attention—that Tristo strikes.

He cartwheels across the floor and propels himself straight up to grab the underside of the gibbet cage. The gibbet swings with an ominous creak. I stamp at the man's fingers where they are clutching the bars below my feet, but they are already gone. Tristo scampers up the side of the cage to stare in at me with his awful face of painted sadness. He rubs away an imaginary boo-hoo tear with one hand.

Then I notice that between his teeth he grips an evil-looking knife.

Before I can react, Tristo darts the knife blade toward my head and severs the elastic strap on my Lost-and-Founder's cap, which immediately pings off. Clermit tumbles out, and I clutch for him desperately, but he has already been snatched by the mime artist. A second later, Tristo has dropped to the floor and is cartwheeling back toward Caliastra.

Tristo stops and kneels before her, bowing his head low and presenting Clermit to the magician as a royal servant presents a crown to his queen. Rictus, beside the lantern on the other side of the hall, gives an adoring round of noiseless applause to his silent partner.

"Ah, so this is it," says Caliastra, taking Clermit into her hand and peering at him with interest. "I have heard of this device. It was part of Sebastian Eels's secret collection of Eerie artifacts, but it was stolen."

She throws an arched-eyebrow look up to me.

"I didn't steal him," I shout down. "Clermit is my friend. I promised to find out where he came from, and in return he helps me. That's all."

Caliastra laughs.

"Your friend?" she replies, waving the shell in the air. "This is just a collection of brass cogs in an old shell, Herbie. Merely one of the curiosities that helped Eels realize that all the eeriest things in this peculiar town are connected—connected by the deepest secret of Eerie-on-Sea. Truly, Sebastian Eels was a genius."

"A brilliant man," says Mr. Mummery, nodding in agreement.

"The greatest scholar this town has ever known," adds Dr. Thalassi. "Sebastian Eels is sorely missed by everyone."

"If only he had lived to see this day," Violet says sadly. "I . . . I really feel he was like a father to me."

And all I can do is goggle at this outburst of admiration for that villain Eels. And from Violet, too!

But I don't goggle so much that I fail to spot Clermit slowly reaching his brass pincer arm from his shell.

Go on, Clermit! I scream silently in my head, at the top of my mind's voice. *Give her a snip!*

But before the clockwork hermit crab can get a strike in, Caliastra sees what's happening. With a lightning motion, she tosses Clermit into the air, up, up toward the high medieval ceiling of the museum hall.

As he reaches the top of his ascent, Clermit hangs in space for a moment, his legs extended, ready for landing. But when he falls back down, Caliastra is ready. She swings her cane—catching its tip into Clermit's shell—and forces him down onto the hard floor with tremendous force.

I hear the sickening sound of a shell cracking open.

"NO . . . !" I yell, grabbing the cage.

The clockwork hermit crab scrabbles around on the floor, his clockwork clearly damaged, his shell split in two. With one brass leg he starts clawing himself across the floor toward me, dragging along the two halves of his shell. But Caliastra strolls around in front of him.

"Just a toy," she sneers. "And a broken one at that. No value to anyone now."

She stamps down, hard, with the heel of her shoe.

There's a tinkle of shattering shell, and a rattle of brass parts, and Clermit goes still.

"You're a monster!" I call down, the words catching in my throat. "I . . . I hate you!"

Caliastra looks up at me and smiles her brilliant smile.

"No, you don't, Herbie," she says. "My poor, dear boy, I can see in your eyes what I really mean to you, even now. And I am sorry, I truly am, that it has to be this way. But you'll come around to my way of thinking in the end."

"Shall I put the pieces in the trash, Cali?" Violet asks, pointing at the ruins of the clockwork hermit shell.

"No," Caliastra replies. "This whole sorry episode has been a huge waste of time. We must get to the theater and prepare. The townsfolk are expecting a spectacular show tonight, and I'm going to make sure they get it." She places a hand on Violet's shoulder again, steering her away. "And you, my new assistant, are going to be right at the heart of it."

CHAPTER 40

SHADOWLESS

O nce the magician, and her gang—now grown even bigger with the addition of Dr. Thalassi and . . . I can hardly bear to think it . . . Violet—have gone, there is nothing but silence in the hall. Except for the distant shriek of gulls over the town and the creak of rope from my gibbet.

I slump to the floor of the cage, which is just large enough to let me sit, provided I don't mind having my own knees right under my nose. I bury my face in my arms and sob at everything I've lost and how wrong I've been.

Remember, Herbie!

Violet's voice calls from my memory.

I look up.

Even when she's not here anymore, Violet's still right. I must remember her as she was and not listen to the shadowless Violet, who has just joyfully become the magician's assistant and part of a plan to turn everyone in Eerie-on-Sea into shadowless puppets. I have to hope that the Violet I know is still in there somewhere, despite the control Caliastra exerts over her through the dark power of the Shadowghast.

As I think about this, a question floats to the surface of my sea of troubles.

"How is Caliastra immune to the Shadowghast?" I say aloud. "Why doesn't it turn around and snatch her shadow, too?"

The wind whistling down the chimney in the medieval hall is my only answer.

"She must *have* something," I reply to myself, "or *know* something that keeps the ghast at bay. But what?"

Remember! Violet commands from a corner of my mind.

He who controls the light commands the dark.

Isn't that what it said on the scrap of paper we took from Eels's notebook? I rack my brain to try to recall when I've been present at the lighting of the lantern what it is that Caliastra does, but my mind is a mess.

There must be *something* that ensures that Caliastra keeps

control of the Shadowghast, though. And if I can find out what that something is, then maybe—*maybe*—I can stop her.

As maybes go, though, this is one of the less impressive ones. Any plan that includes a *maybe* like this one is probably not a plan anyone should rely on. Besides, I'm locked in a cage, and there's no maybe about that!

Tinkle.

I hear a small metallic sound and peer around the deserted museum. The great skeleton of the whale that hangs above the exhibition hall peers back at me unhelpfully. Then I hear it again.

Tink-tinkle.

I lean forward and force myself to stare down at the horrifying wreck of Clermit below me on the stone floor.

He's moving!

Sure enough, despite the shattered shell and the scattering of cogs, the main mechanism inside the clockwork hermit crab is still capable of some movement. I can see a steady beat, as of a clock's drive wheel and spring, and the glint of one metallic arm weakly extending into the sunlight.

"Clermit!" I cry. "You're alive!"

Well, I add, but only to myself, *as alive as something made of metal can ever be.* And to look at him, maybe not even *that* for much longer.

"I'm so sorry, boy!" I call down. "I don't know if I can fix you."

The little scissor pincer rises up weakly and snips a tiny snip.

"But," I add, angrily wiping a tear from my cheek, "if I can get out of here, I'll do everything I can to try."

Snip.

The scissor pincer waves at me as if calling me over. But I can't go anywhere. What can he mean? I set my mind racing for something I *can* do, and my eye falls on the rip in my uniform.

I gasp in sudden realization. There's a frayed end of thread hanging off. I tug it and it gets longer. As I keep tugging at the thread, it grows in loops in my lap, even as my uniform jacket gets shorter. Soon I have more than enough thread to reach the floor. I pluck off one of my brass buttons—it was hanging loose anyway—and tie it to the end of the thread to make a weight.

"Clermit!" I call down. "Grab hold of this!"

And I lower the thread down toward the ground. Soon I hear the ting of the button striking the stone floor. It lands a little way from Clermit, so I pull it off the floor again and start to swing it. When the button swings far enough to reach Clermit, I let the thread slip through my fingers, and I cheer as I see him wrap his pincer arm around the button and grab it.

Carefully, I pull my shattered mechanical friend up to the cage. I'm torn between being appalled by the state he's in and amazed by the beauty of his wondrous clockwork mechanism laid bare and sparkling in the sun. He is truly a work of art, surely beyond anything a human being could make. And yet, here he is!

"Come on, boy." I lift him gently into my cap, beside the marmalade sandwich that is—miraculously—still there. "I've got you."

Clermit's clockwork heart whirs and spins and dazzles me.

"Maybe," I say, wincing as I use that word again, "maybe, when I've found out who you really belong to, I can find some way to fix you, after all."

Clermit snips in reply.

Then, slowly, as if in pain, he climbs out of my cap and onto the side of the cage.

"What are you doing?"

Clermit climbs until he reaches the two sticking-out loops of metal—the pieces that are twisted together to hold the cage door closed. Clermit uses two of his working limbs to get a firm grip on these pieces of metal. Then he starts to strain.

"Wait!" I say, alarmed at the furious whirring from Clermit's mechanism and the sudden juddering of his parts. Clermit's drive wheel becomes a smoking blur of spinning metal as his spring rapidly unwinds. "Stop! You'll break yourself for good!"

There's a grinding, screeching sound, and I don't know if it's Clermit or the pieces of metal, until . . .

PANG!

Something breaks.

Clermit's spring unravels in a spiral of shiny steel, and the clockwork hermit crab falls, motionless, into my hands. He is holding one of the pieces of twisted metal in his pincer, snapped clean off.

"Ouch!" I gasp, sliding the hot metal machine into my cap.

I push at the door of the cage, and it creaks open.

"You did it!" I cry. "I'm so sorry, Clermit. But thank you!"

And, as carefully as I can, so as not to spill the precious contents of my cap, I lower myself to the underside of the cage and then drop with a thud to the floor.

I'm free!

CHAPTER 41

CATBROWS AND
BOOKMARKS

he first thing I do is gather up the burned-out and broken pieces of Clermit, shell and all, and hide them together in an antique vase in Dr. Thalassi's study. If, at the end of all this, I can save the doc—just as I hope I can save Violet and the others—I'll need his help if I'm to have any chance of fixing poor Clermit again.

Then I head back into the hall and sit in despair on an upturned display chest.

"What am I going to do?" I say aloud.

Of course, no one answers.

The big pendulum clock above the doc's office goes *BONG*, making me jump. It also reminds me that I've long-since missed lunch. Of course, what I would normally do at this stage in an adventure is go to Seegol's with Violet and work out one of her brilliant master plans over a huge bowl of chips.

But Violet is gone.

"Whatever I do," I say, sagging even further, "it looks like I'll have to do it on my own."

"You're never alone when you have a book," says a distant, muffled voice.

"But I don't have a book, do I?" I reply. "All I have is a broken clockwork companion and a marmalade sandwich under my cap."

I take the sandwich out and prepare to make a lunch of it.

"When a friend comes to help," gasps the faint voice, in a way that makes the speaker sound as if he's desperately clinging on and close to letting go, "it's rude . . . to keep him . . . *hanging around!*"

And I look up.

Through one of the bottom panes of the great Gothic window at the far end of the hall, I see a small furry white face peering in at me, pink nose pressed against the glass, an urgent look in his ice-blue eyes.

"Erwin!"

I jump up and rush to the window, which has a small section that opens on a hinge. I have to go on tiptoes to reach Erwin, where he's claw-clinging outside to the sheer castle wall.

I grab him by the scruff of the neck, lift him inside, and plop him onto the floor. He bristles his whiskers at me, and says, "E-ow!"

"I'm sorry!" I reply. "It was the only part I could grab. I didn't expect to see you there."

"N-ow?" says Erwin, as if surprised.

"But I'm so glad you are, Erwin. Violet's gone! Captured by the Shadowghast and . . . and by . . ."

Erwin raises one catbrow at me.

". . . and by Caliastra," I admit, finally getting the words out. "I think Violet was right about her all along."

"Phsss!" Erwin says, blowing what sounds like a feline raspberry and flattening his ears in disgust.

"Anyway," I say, pulling the front of my battered uniform flat and straightening my cap. "You have arrived in the nick of time. I was just about to formulate a brilliant plan."

Erwin gives me a doubtful look before padding away down the hall.

"Hey!" I call. "Where are you going?"

And then I see it.

Violet's coat, the one she slipped out of when Mr. Mummery grabbed her. It's still there, on the floor. Erwin reaches it first and disappears underneath. The coat wriggles and writhes a moment before the white cat reappears, pulling something in his pointy teeth.

"Caliastra's book!" I say, remembering that Violet brought it with her. "But surely we don't have time for that. What good is it to us now?"

Erwin looks as though he can't believe the poor quality of human he has to deal with these days. He touches the book with one paw, and he catbrows at me like crazy.

So I pick up the book.

"*The Subtle Mask*." I read the title aloud, turning the yellow volume around in my hand. "Well, Caliastra certainly wore a mask, all right. And it was subtle enough to fool me!"

I flick through the book and find that it opens onto a particular double page. I flick again, and the same thing happens. I'm just beginning to wonder what's so special about this page when a piece of folded paper—wedged in as a bookmark—falls out.

I pick it up, open it, and stare at what I see there.

And then I gasp.

I don't even flinch as my Lost-and-Founder's cap slips off my head.

Because, suddenly, in a rush, I think I understand everything.

Well, not *everything*, obviously—I'd still need a moment to calculate seven times nine, or to figure out when to use a semicolon—but as far as this whole Ghastly Night/Caliastra/ Shadowghast business is concerned, I've just had a brain flash.

And I'm still having it, a little while later, when I'm sitting in a quiet corner of Seegol's Diner—the fish and chip shop on the pier—surrounded by a smattering of late-afternoon customers. I'm not worried about being seen out of the Lost-and-Foundery, not now. And that's just as well, as already I'm attracting quite a few curious looks because of the company I'm keeping. Opposite me, in the seat Violet would usually be in if this adventure hadn't taken such a disastrous turn, sits Erwin, his head barely reaching over the tabletop, narrowing his eyes at me and licking his chops.

"Ah, Herbie!" says jolly Mr. Seegol, beaming at me as he comes over. "You have done well to get here early. I have had many reservations—yes, *many* reservations! It seems the whole town will be at tonight's Ghastly Night show, and most of them will stop here for fish and chip suppers on the way. It will be my busiest night of the year!"

Behind him, taped to the side of the island kitchen in the center of the diner, Caliastra's brilliant smile dazzles from her show poster, while the two mime artists cavort behind her, and her magical lantern throws fabulous shadow forms all around. Even Mr. Mummery can be seen, raising his straw boater hat and twinkling his eye. It's the poster that has gone up all over Eerie-on-Sea. No wonder the whole town will be at Ghastly

Night. Nothing this exciting has happened at the Theater at the End of the Pier for a long time.

"It should be fun," I say, forcing a smile.

"And you, of course, have been given the evening off," Seegol beams back, "to see the show. And I expect your friend Violet will be here to join you any moment."

"She's, um, she's helping with the production, actually," I reply, using all my willpower to keep the smile in place. "So, it's just a bowl of chips for me, please, Mr. Seegol. And a couple of fishfingers for my associate."

Seegol glances over at Erwin, not entirely approvingly. I think Erwin has a certain reputation when it comes to the fish and chip shop—and the occasional missing halibut. Erwin looks up at Seegol with half-moon smiling eyes and roars his rumbliest purr.

"Hopefully this will do nicely?" I say quickly, sliding a dazzling silver signet ring over to Mr. Seegol. It's been in my Lost-and-Foundery more than a hundred years, so—according to the rules—it's mine now. I always carry a few things like this in my pocket for fish and chip emergencies.

"Coming right up!" says Mr. Seegol, popping the ring on his pudgy little finger and holding it up to the light. "For a ring like this, Herbie, you can have doubles."

When we're alone again, I unfold the piece of paper I found

in *The Subtle Mask* and flatten it on the table. It's a flyer for another one of Caliastra's shows, from a few years ago, in a distant European city I've heard of but will probably never see. She looks a little younger, but her smile is just as dazzling. Tristo the mime artist cavorts behind her, while Mr. Mummery—with more hair than he has now—lifts his straw hat. It looks a lot like the poster for Ghastly Night. But something important is different.

"This is what you wanted us to see, isn't it?" I ask Erwin under my breath, tapping the flyer.

"Prrp."

"And why the mermonkey dispensed this book?"

"Prr-rr-rr."

"In that case," I whisper in reply, just as Mr. Seegol heads over with the chips, "I think I do have a plan, after all."

CHAPTER 42

AMAZEMENT
GUARANTEED!

I make the chips last until crowds begin to gather on the pier. By the time I scoop Erwin into my coat, turn up my lapels, and step out onto the deck, Seegol's Diner is busier than I have ever seen it.

With an hour still to go, a good amount of Eerie-on-Sea has already gathered, eager to see the "greatest show in town" for themselves, and more are coming along the pier behind, chatting and laughing. Mothers and fathers lead their caramel-apple children, elderly couples gossip arm-in-arm in the salty air, and even some of the fisherfolk are here, bringing jugs of mulled cider and congratulating one another on a night off. Many are carrying manglewick candles, gazing admiringly at the strange shadows they cast on paper shades. None of these folks show the slightest awareness of the danger they are in. They come to their doom gladly. I'm the only one here who knows that they are about to be exposed to the Shadowghast lantern and turned into puppets themselves.

"It looks pretty hopeless," I whisper to Erwin, feeling a wibble of despair in my knees. "Unless we can stop the show."

"Prrp," says Erwin, digging his claws into my chest. I think he's telling me to be brave, so I continue to approach the theater.

"Bladderwracks, it's Mummery!" I mutter, skidding to a halt. The theatrical manager is standing beside the main theater entrance, wearing his horrible striped blazer and straw boater hat. I had been hoping to slip in unseen, but there's no way I can do that with him standing there.

"Step right up!" cries Mr. Mummery to the crowd. "The best seats go early! Come and see the greatest show in town! Amazement guaranteed!"

"Maybe," I mutter, "there's a way in around the back."

Erwin pops his head out of my coat to take a look.

"A sofa cat by day," he says suggestively, "is a rooftop cat by night."

Dodging behind a group of teenagers eating chips from cones, I duck down the side of the theater. Here the pier is at its crumbliest—exposed as it is to the relentless elements that roar, surge, and crash from the four corners of Eerie Bay. No one dares walk around the end of the pier, not even in the summer. A hand-painted sign hangs across the gangway:

DANGER! KEEP OUT!
DODGY STRUCTURE!

"You could hang a sign like that on half the town," I say, and chuckle nervously as I duck under it. The rotten deck planks sag beneath me.

I put Erwin down and point up to a window above. It's the window I saw when I was exploring the amusement arcade, the one that was stuck open. I'm glad now that I couldn't close it.

Erwin flattens one ear at me and holds up a paw, showing how battered his claws are already after scaling the sheer stone wall of the castle. But before I can feel too guilty, he leaps up the walls of the peeling wooden theater anyway, and he claws himself up to the window.

I climb after him—using fingertips and boot tips on the weatherboard slats. I feel the building shake. The tide is in, and the waves are pummeling the pier. I look down and immediately wish I hadn't—the sea is heaving and gnawing at the old iron struts of the pier as if it has spotted a wobbly Lost-and-Founder barely clinging on and fancies a snack. It's a relief to reach the window and squeeze myself inside.

The amusement arcade is as dark and dusty as when I left it yesterday. Beyond the grubby glass screen in the theater lobby, I can see the people of Eerie-on-Sea making their way through to the auditorium, chatting excitedly, lit only by their manglewick candles.

I take off my Lost-and-Founder's cap—it is a bit of a give-away with its gold trim, and the elastic is broken anyway—and tuck it, and Erwin, under my coat. Then I quietly slip out and join the throng.

⚙O✿

Inside the auditorium is the hubbub and happy bustle of people finding their seats. Dr. Thalassi is there, guiding people toward the center, where—I can't help thinking—the light of the Shadowghast lantern will hit them at full beam. Jenny and Mrs. Fossil are there, too, lurking mutely in a shadowy corner. It makes me sick to think that these people—whom I've known as long as I can remember—are under the magical control of the Puppet Master and are now my enemies.

I turn my lapels up to their highest setting and slip away into the crowd.

There is a door to one side of the auditorium marked ROYAL BOX. When I'm sure no one is looking, I open it and slip inside. Then I climb a flight of rickety stairs.

If you don't know, a theater box is a little seating area to one side of an auditorium where people who think they are too special to sit with everyone else spend a lot of money to have a private view of the show. Calling such a thing a *Royal* Box is a bit of a joke in a place like Eerie-on-Sea. But from what I've heard of old Mayor Bigley, I guess he had high hopes of attracting the richest people in the land.

There are only three seats in the Royal Box. I slump into the darkest one and let Erwin out. He leaps onto my lap, where he stands with his paws on the rail, and together we peer down at the stage.

The threadbare velvet curtains are closed.

Is Violet down there behind them right now? Preparing to play her part in a dastardly plan to take over the town?

Erwin rubs his head on my chin, bringing me back to the here-and-now.

"I know, puss," I say, stroking him. "But I'm just starting to wonder if my master plan is really all that masterful. Or even a plan at all! It depends completely on Part A: a thing I've guessed, and Part B: a thing I've worked out."

"Mew?"

"The thing I've guessed?" I reply. "Well, that comes from the fact that the Shadowghast spoke to me once, down in the Netherways, and said that my shadow wasn't right. I don't know

what that means, exactly, but my guess is that maybe some people's shadows *can't* be snatched for . . . reasons. And maybe mine
is one of them?"

Erwin twitches an ear and looks doubtful.

"It's not much, I know," I continue, "but it's enough to make me
think the ghast will go after others first, giving me time to act."

Erwin replies with a small and encouraging purr.

"As for the other thing," I add, "the thing I've worked out,
well . . ."

I take out the copy of *The Subtle Mask*, place it on the seat
beside me, and pull out the theater flyer that was used as a bookmark. I unfold it again.

"If I'm right about this," I say, holding the little poster up,
"then I should finally get to see how the trick is done and how
the Shadowghast is being controlled."

Erwin tips his head to one side.

"Well, do you have a better idea?" I demand. And the bookshop cat can do nothing but twitch his whiskers at that.

"There is one thing you can do, though," I say. "If everything
else goes wrong, we could call it Plan C, if you like. *C* for cat.
Let me explain . . ."

And there, in the darkness of the Royal Box, above the stage
in the Theater at the End of the Pier, I give Erwin a very special
instruction.

CHAPTER 43

GHASTLY NIGHT

Before we know it, the auditorium is full, and the appointed hour of the show has arrived. For my plan to work, I need to get down on the stage just after the lantern is lit but before the Shadowghast has gone to work. I think! There's a passage down to the backstage area from behind the Royal Box, so I should have plenty of time to sneak on at the right moment. In the meantime, the show is about to begin.

"Ladies and gentlemen!" calls a familiar voice, and Dr. Thalassi walks out onstage, in front of the curtains, and holds up his hands for quiet. "We are greatly honored to welcome tonight a performer of rare talent to bring our Ghastly Night celebrations to life."

There's a round of excited clapping from the audience.

"As you know," the doc continues, "I, myself, have put on a very inferior version of the shadow puppet show for some years now, so it is a huge relief to hand it over to such a bright star. Please put your hands together for the great, the magnificent, the all-powerful Caliastra!"

As the audience erupts into cheering and clapping, the curtains swish creakily aside. Caliastra, looking amazing in a glittering black pantsuit, with a top hat perched to one side of her head, strides into the center of the stage and twirls her amber glass cane as she bows.

Behind her, the Shadowghast lantern sits dark and dragony in an unlit spot of the stage. Rictus and Tristo are introduced and perform a silly routine that makes the audience laugh but makes me shudder, now that I know what they are really like.

The folks of Eerie-on-Sea love it, though, and are completely captivated by what they see. I'm just beginning to think that now might be a good time to sneak down and get ready, when something happens to fix me in my seat: as the mime artists retreat, Caliastra retakes center stage and is joined by someone else.

Violet.

"What is she wearing?" I gasp.

"Wow!" agrees Erwin.

Violet is dressed in an extraordinary outfit of sequins and feathers, with sparkly tights and shiny shoes. She plays the role of magician's assistant perfectly, bringing props, swishing drapes, and striking smiling poses as Caliastra performs trick after amazing trick to further warm up the oohing and aahing audience. And if I still needed proof that Violet is not in her right mind, then this is surely it.

"We've got to rescue her," I say to Erwin.

"Me-ow."

Then I notice Rictus move around behind the magic lantern. He opens the door at the back and sets a flame in the fire chamber. The Shadowghast lantern is lit. The main act of Ghastly Night is about to begin, and Caliastra has the audience in the palm of her hand.

"I have to get down there now!" I cry, leaping to my feet.

And I don't know if it's the cry or the leap that does it, but somehow, despite the dark in the Royal Box, I catch the attention of someone down below.

Violet looks up.

She squints, as if unable to quite believe what she's seeing. Then her face goes hard.

She waves to someone at the far end of the auditorium and points up at me, even as the audience cheers Caliastra's final warm-up trick. There's a sudden shift in the lighting on the stage, and a spotlight swings around to flood the box, picking out my sherbety blond hair and the royal porpoise blue of my Lost-and-Founder's uniform for all to see. The entire audience turns in their seats to stare up at me, where I stand transfixed in the powerful light.

Oops.

"Ne-ow!" shouts Erwin, and he jumps to the door at the back

of the box. I run after him and hurry down the steps to the back-stage area. But before I get more than three paces, a silhouette fills the doorway below.

It's Tristo.

Who rushes up the stairs to grab me.

I pull Erwin back into the box by his tail, slam the door shut, and wedge a wooden chair under the doorknob. There's an explosive bang on the door, which buckles under the strain, but the chair holds.

"Heh!" says Erwin.

"Yes," I reply, "but now *we* can't get out!"

Behind me I hear the audience laugh and applaud, clearly taking the strange antics in the spotlighted Royal Box to be part of the show.

"Ladies and gentlemen!" calls Caliastra, from center stage. If she's surprised to see me, I see no sign of it on her face. "May I introduce Herbert Lemon, your very own Lost-and-Founder. Here to take part in our show tonight!"

The crowd cheers, while behind me Tristo flings himself at the door, nearly bursting it off its hinges.

I give everyone in the audience an awkward wave. I'm sure it goes nicely with my awkward grin. Then, because I can't think of what else to do, I bow and pop my Lost-and-Founder's cap back on.

The crowd cheers louder than ever.

Down on the stage, the strange perfumed smoke of the lantern is already billowing and rolling into the auditorium— guided by Caliastra with her cane—while needles of intense light are projecting from around the silver orb in the dragon's mouth.

The whole of Eerie-on-Sea sits in its sights. Rictus reaches for the silver ball, and I realize that my plan is already in tatters.

"Violet!" I shout, grabbing the railing of the Royal Box. "Vi! It's me! Wake up!"

"Ooh!" goes the audience in anticipation, enjoying this strange twist in the story of Ghastly Night.

Violet glares up at me and shakes her fist.

"RUN!" I say desperately, turning to the audience. "You're all in terrible danger! Run while you still can!"

The audience erupts in laughter.

It's at this moment that Rictus plucks the orb from the dragon's mouth, and the supernatural light of the Shadowghast lantern pours out over everyone.

The audience holds up their hands to shield their eyes, their shadows stretching out behind them. As smoke rolls in front of the cone of light, it shimmers in glowing clouds.

Then the snatched shadows that are imprisoned in the lantern start to appear, creeping one by one from the mouth of the dragon. Mrs. Fossil's shadow is one of the first, rolling around the clouds in confusion. Jenny Hanniver's comes next, reaching here and there, looking for a way out. Behind them comes Standing Bigley, and the whole host of lost souls.

I clutch the railing tighter than ever when I see Violet's shadow, small and alone, stumbling blindly around in the ever-expanding clouds, arms outstretched.

"Vi!" I shout again. "Violet!"

But the only answer I get is the splintering of wood as Tristo finally breaks down the door behind me.

And what do I do? Faced, as I am, with the complete failure of my plan, before it has even begun?

Well, I jump, don't I?

I mean, what else *can* I do?

I step up onto the railing of the Royal Box, high above the audience below, and leap out into space.

CHAPTER 44

BUTTONS AND CINDERS

....

But I'm not here to be the fall guy.

Instead of tumbling to a dramatic but ridiculous death, I manage—by sheer desperation—to grab onto one of the ancient theater curtains. My fingers catch in the moth-eaten holes, and there's a great rending sound as my weight causes the holes to widen. I find myself ripping slowly down toward the stage, in a cloud of velvet dust and sackcloth shreds.

"A-aa-h!" goes the audience. Someone even shouts, "Go, Herbie!"

They think this is part of the show!

I pull myself to my feet and tip my cap at the audience. On

the stage, the smoke is thicker than ever and filled with eerie lantern light and strange shadow shapes. But I can still be seen in my blue uniform and shiny brass buttons. I wave, and hundreds of hands wave back.

And suddenly I wonder—now that I have taken the audience's attention away from Caliastra, maybe . . . ?

"Ladies and gentlemen!" I cry. "Everyone, on your feet!"

And, despite some obvious confusion, many in the audience begin to stand, chuckling among themselves. I'm just about to tell them all to leave the auditorium, when a voice from the audience calls, "Look out! She's behind you!"

Before I can react, there's a wallop on the back of my head, and I fall on my face. Clouds of smoke roll over me, and the audience roars with laughter and sits back down.

I look around urgently, coughing in the perfumed clouds, and see Violet, holding a plank of wood. She is shadowless and full of rage.

"It's too late!" she yells at me through the smoke. "You cannot stop us now!"

She swings the plank again, and I only just manage to roll out of the way before it smashes down onto the boards where I was just lying.

"Vi!" I cry, struggling to my feet once more. "It's me! I'm here with Erwin! I said I wouldn't leave you, remember? I promised!"

"Oh, no, you didn't!" calls a singsong voice from the audience, to more laughter. Whatever else you can say about this strange situation, at least the people of Eerie-on-Sea are enjoying the pantomime.

"I should have known you would get out," Violet shouts, bunching her fists. "I told Cali you were sneaky. Now I'll have to stop you myself . . ."

So, I run. I take off back into the spinning clouds of light and smoke, away from a fight I never want to have again. In a moment, I am lost in the glowing smoke, though I imagine my silhouette must be clear for the audience to see. From somewhere in the mist, I hear Caliastra's powerful voice reclaiming control.

"And now, ladies and gentlemen," she cries, "the moment you've all been waiting for . . ."

And that's when I see her.

Violet.

Or rather Violet's *shadow*! Stumbling and crawling from cloud to ashy cloud, near the lantern.

But before I can reach her, Caliastra finishes her declaration with the words "Behold, the SHADOWGHAST!"

The audience gasps in wonder as a new shadow pours from the lantern like thick oily smoke and skitters around the auditorium with a cackle of echoing menace.

The shadow of a grinning man with horns upon his head.

The Shadowghast is here!

To cries of delighted horror from the audience, the dark spirit of the lantern leaps and darts, here and there, seizing the shadows that are still blindly trying to escape. Mrs. Fossil's shadow, with a silent scream, is snatched and devoured in a moment, then Jenny's. It recaptures shadow after shadow, and as each one is absorbed, the ghast grows darker and more solid, and grows stronger with it.

Soon Violet's shadow is one of the few remaining. I run toward it, just as the Shadowghast dives—his snatching claws reaching out to add Violet's shade to its own.

"No!" I cry, jumping between them.

The Shadowghast recoils, thwarted, and tries to skitter around behind me, so I spin around. Again, the shadow specter pulls back. I'm daring to hope I'm correct that my shadow is somehow distasteful to this strange being. Behind me, Violet's shadow is cowering, reaching out to me, as if it can sense I'm there.

THIS SHADOW IS MINE.

The terrible roar of the silent voice booms through my head, just as it did down in the Netherways.

STAND ASIDE!

"*None* of these shadows are yours!" I shout back. "You've stolen every one."

The Shadowghast makes a final lunge, trying to pass right through me to reach Violet's shade, but he recoils again, quivering as he tumbles back.

YOUR SHADOW . . . he roars, *NOT RIGHT* . . .

Then the Shadowghast shoots away, out into the auditorium after easier prey. But I know he'll be back to claim Violet when he's even stronger.

"Violet, take my hand," I say, reaching out to her shadow.

But, of course, my hand touches nothing.

"Maybe . . . ?" I say. "Maybe . . . this?"

And I try again, this time using the *shadow* of my hand, and *yes!* my shadow hand finds Violet's shadow hand, and the two clasp each other. And it's really eerie, this feeling of our two shadows touching, but I have no time to wonder about it.

I pull Violet's shadow along, deeper into the clouds, until . . .

"There you are!" says a voice, and Violet herself, assistant to the great Caliastra, steps out of a smoke bank and swings her very solid fist at my very squashy nose. I duck, but when I stand up again, Vi's other fist is already closing in like a missile, and it's all I can do to catch it in my hand.

"You will never stop us!" cries shadowless Violet, trying to pull her fist free.

I bring my other hand up—the hand that is holding hands with Violet's shadow—and clasp Vi's fist with that, too.

Shadowless Violet kicks me in the stomach. She yanks her fist free as I hit the deck. But when I look up, I see that Violet is shaking her hand, as if trying to detach something from it.

It's her own shadow, which is stuck to her now, clinging on.

"Get it off me!" Violet cries, trying to brush her shadow off with her other hand.

But now that Vi's shadow has finally found its rightful body, it starts oozing up Violet's arms in a tide, then over her shoulders, feathers, sequins, and all. Violet fixes me with one last look of fury before the shadow washes over her head and fades away, as if being absorbed back into her body.

Then Violet's shadow reappears, shooting out across the stage floor, attached to Violet's feet just as a shadow should be, and the audience gives a great cheer!

"Herbie?"

"Vi?" I gasp in reply. "Vi, is it you? *Really* you, I mean."

"Did Cali . . . ?" Violet starts to say, clutching her head. "Did Caliastra make me her puppet? Did the Shadowghast snatch my shadow? I can't remember . . ."

Then she looks down.

"*What* am I wearing?"

"No time for that!" I shout. "Look!"

And I spin her around to face out into the auditorium. Through gaps in the smoke, we can see people gazing at the glowing clouds above them in amazement and fear as the Shadowghast dives here and there, snatching and devouring their shadows with glee.

"We've got to stop it," Violet cries. "Those people won't even know what's happened to them. Caliastra will capture them all!"

"But it's *not* Caliastra," I say. "No, don't look at me like that, Vi. It's *true*! It isn't Caliastra who is doing all this. It never was."

"Who would have thought," says a voice like dark honey in the smoky air behind us, "that finding an assistant would be so much trouble."

We spin around as Caliastra strides through the smoke, swishing her cane.

"Wait!" I say to the magician, rummaging in my pocket till I can pull out my flashlight. I point it at her like a magic wand. "I can explain!"

Caliastra throws her head back and laughs.

"Is that supposed to stop me, Herbert Lemon?" she cries, raising her cane to point back at me.

So I flick the flashlight on and shout the magic word.

"Prestocadabra!"

The flashlight is pretty feeble, but it's just strong enough for Violet to see.

Her eyes go as wide as scallop shells.

"No shadow!" she gasps.

"What do you mean?" demands Caliastra, doubt and confusion in her face for once. "What are you staring at?"

"It's true," Violet says, amazed. "Look for yourself. You have no shadow!"

"None of them do," I say to Vi. "Not Mummery, not Tristo, not Caliastra. They've all had their shadows snatched by the Shadowghast."

"But, then, who's the Puppet Master?" Violet asks. "Who commands the Shadowghast lantern? And, wait, what about . . . ?"

"Exactly," I say.

And we turn toward the magic lantern behind us, where it stands wreathed in perfumed smoke, projecting its eldritch light. Leaning against it is Rictus, rolling the silver orb from one hand to the other, chuckling through his horrific face-paint grin.

"So," he says, speaking for the very first time since we met him. "You've finally figured it out."

Violet startles visibly and clutches my arm.

"That voice!" she gasps. "It sounds like . . . but it *can't* be!"

"Ha!" says the grinning mime artist. "Oh, yes, it can."

He lifts his arm and drags his sleeve over his face, smearing much of the paint off. The grinning mask of the mime artist Rictus is rubbed away. In its place is revealed another face, grubby but recognizable. It's a face we never thought we'd see again.

"Eels!" Violct whispers in disbelief. "Sebastian Eels!"

CHAPTER 45

WHERE THERE'S SMOKE...

Sebastian Eels, wreathed in the smoke of the Shadowghast lantern, and clutching the silver orb, points at me and Vi and shouts a command.

"Seize them!"

Caliastra grabs at us and gets a handful of Violet's hair. Violet swings a kick, and the magician cries in pain but holds on. Tristo, summoned back down from the Royal Box, comes cartwheeling through the smoke and grabs me by the arms. Dr. Thalassi, Mrs. Fossil, and Jenny Hanniver all clamber onto the stage and close in around us.

"People of Eerie-on-Sea!" Eels calls, addressing the audience. "Silence!"

In a moment, every single person in the audience stops cheering, and an unnatural quiet falls over the auditorium. The people of Eerie-on-Sea are enslaved, captured by the Shadowghast and the will of the man who controls it.

"Shadow spirit!" calls Sebastian Eels, into the smoke above us. "You have done well. Come! Come to your master!"

The Shadowghast flitters around the smoke, darting from cloud to cloud, his fire-crackle chuckle the only sound we can hear.

"I said, *come!*" Eels yells, raising the silver orb above his head. "Kneel before me!"

There is a rush of wind, and the smoke clouds billow.

Sebastian Eels looks slightly confused. But then a look of satisfaction crosses his paint-smeared face as the clouds part and the Shadowghast steps out and stalks across the stage toward Eels.

"Should it . . . ?" Violet whispers to me. "Should it look quite so . . . solid?"

And I'm wondering this, too. The ghast has absorbed so many shadows, and grown so dark, that it is moving like a thing of flesh and blood, approaching Sebastian Eels not like the beaten dog he seems to think it is, but like a being of great power. Sebastian Eels seems to notice this, too, and takes a step back, alarm in his eyes.

"What's wrong?" Violet cries to the panicky author. "Overfed your little pet?"

"Stop!" Sebastian Eels shouts. "Stay back!"

"YOU SAID COME," roars the Shadowghast, in a terrifying voice we can all hear now. "SO, I COME."

And the Shadowghast reaches out toward Sebastian Eels with monstrous, snatching hands.

"I order you to stop!" the man yells, holding up the silver orb that stoppers the lantern. I see for the first time that it is engraved with strange symbols and marks. "I hold the orb! I am the Puppet Master! I command you. I have always commanded you!"

The Shadowghast, looming over the man—his crooked fingers almost touching Eels's face—comes to a reluctant halt and quivers with frustrated menace.

"I HAVE WAITED," the Shadowghast says, slowly and carefully, his hands pressing into some invisible barrier around Sebastian Eels. "WAITED FOR A THOUSAND YEARS . . . FOR THE STRENGTH . . . TO TAKE . . . THE ORB FOR MYSELF. TO CONTROL . . . MY OWN DESTINY. I NEED BUT A SINGLE SHADOW MORE . . ."

And with wicked speed, the hand of the Shadowghast darts out and snatches the shadow of Sebastian Eels from where it is cowering behind him. The creature rolls Eels's shadow into a ball, opens his frightful mouth, and devours it in a single horrify-ing, gulping motion.

Then the Shadowghast's great black hand closes over the silver orb, as the shadowless Sebastian Eels falls on his knees before him.

"AND NOW," the Shadowghast roars, "*I* AM THE PUPPET MASTER. *I* COMMAND *ALL*."

Around us, the people on the stage, and the folks of Eerie-on-Sea in the audience—everyone except me and Violet—fall and cower before their terrible new ruler.

"NO ONE CAN STOP ME NOW."

"Yes, they can!" I squeak. Then I shout, at the top of my lungs, "Plan C, Erwin! *C* for cat! Do it now!"

From the wings at the side of the stage, I see Erwin make his leap. He lands on the master switch that controls the lighting rig above the stage, and he pulls it down.

There is an explosion of light as all the theater's stage lamps turn on at once—just as they did during Caliastra's first rehearsal. They flood the stage with intense, brilliant light that blazes down from directly above.

"Arrgh!" everyone cries, throwing up their arms to shield their eyes.

The Shadowghast roars and slumps down onto the stage as if the sudden light is pressing down on him with great force.

Shadows—the shadows he has been absorbing—are pushed out of him in all directions, forced out by the ferocious illumination. They tumble on all sides and start seeking out their proper bodies again. And as they leave, the Shadowghast grows weaker and fainter. The silver orb trembles and then falls straight through the Shadowghast's spectral fingers, crashing onto the stage.

Violet dives forward and scoops it up.

"Be gone!" she commands the ghast, as he flails in the blazing light and snatches half-heartedly at the departing shadows. "I have the orb now, so I, er, I guess I'm in charge. I command you, Shadowghast, to *get back in your lantern!*"

With a roar of wind, the Shadowghast is whipped off the ground and sucked toward the fizzing lens of the magic lantern. He makes a last, desperate scrabble against the opening, but he is sucked inside with a *POP!*

Violet jumps forward and jams the orb into the dragon's mouth. I run around the back and slam the lantern door shut, smothering the flame within.

The Shadowghast lantern shakes violently, as if something inside is trying to break out.

But then it falls still.

The Shadowghast is gone.

And we're all left blinking in the blazing light of the stage.

Until someone in the audience starts to clap.

Then someone else joins in.

Soon there is a smattering of hesitant applause from the audience—the people of Eerie-on-Sea—who seem stunned, but apparently also convinced that the show is now over. I'm delighted to see that behind them—cast by the brilliant light from the stage—their shadows are all back where they should be, clapping too.

So, I take a bow.

Well, it's only polite, isn't it? After all, surely this *really is* the most extraordinary Ghastly Night show anyone in Eerie-on-Sea has ever seen. I take Violet's hand and we bow again, together this time.

The clapping becomes a roar.

"Bravo! Bravo, Herbie! Bravo, Violet!"

Caliastra, looking dazed and confused, takes a bow—one that is probably more automatic than anything else. At this, the audience goes absolutely crazy. Even the fishermen jump to their feet and wallop their huge hands together at the bizarre spectacle of it all.

"Jenny!" Violet cries, throwing her arms around her guardian. "Jenny, I've found you!"

"Violet!" Jenny Hanniver gasps in reply, her shadow reassuringly at her feet again. "It's like I've been lost in the eeriest dream."

"Golly!" says Mrs. Fossil, nervously blinking at the audience. She does a lopsided curtsy and almost falls over. Dr. Thalassi reaches out and catches her just in time.

"Steady there, Wendy," he says, pulling her upright again. "Steady!"

And this strange but triumphant moment would probably have ended in a big group hug, and slap on the back for everyone, if what happens next doesn't happen.

But it does.

There is an almighty explosion.

All the stage lights go out at once. The old theater lighting rig, overloaded, has finally given up in the most spectacular way imaginable. Sparks rain down all around, and a flame flashes into life on the shredded theater curtains. A blaze quickly takes hold, casting an alarming new light over everything.

"Fire!" Dr. Thalassi shouts. "Form a line! Everybody out! Women and children first!"

The audience begins to move toward the exit as Tristo grabs a fire extinguisher and begins tackling the blaze.

"Where's Eels?" Violet says.

I look around. How could we have forgotten to keep tabs on the villain behind all this mayhem?

"I don't know," I reply. "I saw him crawling away behind the lantern, and then . . . I don't know!"

"We need to get out of here." Violet pulls at my sleeve as the flames on the curtain turn into a roar.

"But the lantern?" I say, pointing to it, gleaming in the firelight.

There's another crash, and a burning beam falls thunderously across the stage, landing between us and the lamp, knocking Vi and me to the boards.

As I struggle up onto my elbows and stare in horror at the blaze, it's clear that this fire is already beyond Tristo and his extinguisher.

Then I see something behind the flames. It's a shape—no, *a shadow*—darting desperately here and there across the back of the stage.

Is it Sebastian Eels?

Or the Shadowghast?

Or is it the shadow of Mayor Bigley, freed at last from the clutches of the ghast, frantically seeking a body that can never now be found?

"Herbie!" Violet cries, pulling me up. "Run!"

And so we run, as more rigging falls, and the air is filled with inferno, and the Theater at the End of the Pier is engulfed in fire.

CHAPTER 46

ASHES AND AFTERMATH

The night the theater burned will go down in legend, I reckon. Already, as I think back over it from the safety of the morning after, my memories of the disaster have taken on a strange and dreamlike quality:

The people of Eerie-on-Sea fleeing the burning building.

Mr. Seegol's startled, firelit face as he rushes to help.

Dr. Thalassi organizing a human chain to bring water—in bucket after desperate bucket—from the sea.

Violet—her dark hair wild against the blaze, her sequins sooty and one shiny shoe gone—taking a terrified child by the hand and promising to find his parents.

Erwin, orange in the reflected firelight, leaping from the

blaze. And the welcome pain of his claws as he clambered up to sit on my shoulders, barely a singed whisker out of place.

The cheers of gratitude when the heavy skies over Eerie Bay—as if in answer to the pain of the town—broke in torrential downpour, beating down onto the fire in a million drops of sparkling rain, streaking clean the sooty faces of the townsfolk who fought to save the pier.

"And it is saved, too," says Violet, "or so the doc says. He sent a message. The fire is finally out."

"Surely not the theater, though," I reply. "It looked like a goner to me."

"Well, from what I've heard," replies a dark-honey voice, "some of the building still stands, Herbie, amazing though that sounds."

And Caliastra smiles her magical smile. It's not quite as dazzling a smile as before—its owner is still getting over the shock of what has happened to her, and to all of us—but it is lit with a genuine warmth.

"True, the stage itself is all gone," she continues, "but the theater of Eerie-on-Sea will open again one day, I'm sure. And maybe I'll perform there. In my right mind, I mean."

And she rubs her left hand, which is slightly burned from her own efforts to help tackle the blaze.

"And Eels?" I ask—hating that I have to bring up the name

of that man, but knowing we can't avoid the subject forever.

"No sign," says Caliastra abruptly. "Vanished. In a puff of smoke."

"He might have actually gone up in flames," says Violet darkly, "with the Shadowghast lantern and the rest of it. But . . ."

". . . but twice before we thought that he was gone for good," I finish the thought for her, "and look how that ended up! Somehow I don't think we've seen the last of Sebastian Eels."

"How did you realize, Herbie, that *I* wasn't the villain?" Caliastra asks. "How did you know that Rictus was an imposter?"

I pat the yellow-jacketed book beside me on the table.

"Because of this," I explain. "*The Subtle Mask*, by Questin D'Arkness. Or rather, because of what was inside it."

And I take out the flyer that was used as a bookmark by some long-forgotten reader and hold it up.

"There's only one mime artist shown," I explain. "Tristo. I guessed that meant that Rictus was new to your act. And as soon as I thought that, the rest came to me in a flash. I remembered that whenever we saw the lantern—*every* time—it was Rictus who was the one taking that silver orb in and out, and controlling the light, not you."

"*Whoever controls the light commands the dark,*" Violet recites. "I can't believe we didn't see it earlier."

"Well, in a way, we *did* see it," I add. "Or I did, back when you and your troupe first arrived at the hotel, Cali—may I call you Cali?"

"Of course."

"Well, back then, I noticed something funny when the sun shone on you all. It was so surprising that I didn't understand it at the time. But I know now what it was: only one of you cast a shadow."

"Rictus," Caliastra says grimly. "Sebastian Eels in disguise. It was very observant of you to have noticed something like that, Herbie. But then, I expect that comes from all your Lost-and-Foundering. Your curiosity and intelligence have saved us all."

I do a grin. I decide not to admit that I never *wanted* Caliastra to be the villain, which surely helped, too. I glance at Vi and see that she won't say anything either. It turned out that we were both wrong, in a way, about who the real Puppet Master was; though, for once, Violet was a bit wronger than me, and that's a rare feeling I'm determined to enjoy.

"Well, I was certain it *was* you," Violet admits, turning to Caliastra, chin raised. "With your scary raven hair and wicked-witch eyebrows, I'm still a bit disappointed it's not!"

Caliastra and Violet lock eyes for a moment. Then they both break out in laughter.

⚙

We are sitting, the three of us, at the best table in the dining room of the Grand Nautilus Hotel. It's late for breakfast—no one got much sleep last night—but Caliastra has invited us, and already I can smell bacon from the kitchen, and sizzling hash browns, and see a trolley of freshly baked pastries being prepared. There is a fourth place set at the table, but it is empty.

"So, how did it happen?" asks Violet then, posing a question to Caliastra I know she's been itching to ask. "How did you meet Eels and get your shadow snatched in the first place?"

"It was just as I said," Caliastra replies. "That part, at least, was the truth. I have always been interested in the legend of Ghastly Night, and I really did correspond with Eels to find out more. He was considered the greatest authority on the legends of Eerie-on-Sea, after all, so who else would I write to? Sadly, he was very rude and unhelpful, and I gave up trying years ago. But then, one day this last summer, he wrote to me out of the blue and invited me to visit, to discuss a possible reenactment of the show. It was when he said that he had located the original Shadowghast lantern that I canceled my engagements and came straight here. The last clear memory I have is of going to his boarded-up house one night—with Mummery and Tristo—and watching him light the lantern and remove the silver orb from the dragon's mouth. After that . . . everything is clouded."

"What's it like," I ask, "having your shadow snatched and being controlled by the Puppet Master?"

Caliastra starts to reply. Then she starts again. Eventually, she shakes her head.

"It's so hard to describe. It's like you're yourself, and yet, there are these other ideas—thoughts that simply cannot be ignored—that crowd into your mind, and change how you see everything, and . . ."

"It's like a dream," Violet says, "that only makes sense when you are dreaming it, but that you find, when you wake up, was really a horrible nightmare all along."

"And the things you said to me," I ask Caliastra, fiddling with my fork, "about being my . . . my family . . . about . . . making me your assistant . . . and giving me a home?"

It's the subject no one has dared bring up yet. And now that I have, I'm fiddling so hard with my fork that it's about to bend.

Caliastra puts her hand on my arm.

"Herbie," she says with a sad smile, "I'd never heard of you, in all my life, until Eels put those thoughts into my head. I was never on the *Fabulous,* and that ticket was a forgery. As far as I'm concerned, there never was any such ship as the SS *Fabulous.* I'm so, so sorry."

"But why?" Violet asks. "Why would Eels do that?"

"There was something." Caliastra puts her hands to her head and rubs her temples. "It all seems so faint and muddled now, but it wasn't just because Eels knew that Herbie's shadow was safe from the Shadowghast. Eels deliberately wanted to turn you against each other, to stop you from working together. He was determined to poison your friendship."

"He didn't succeed," Violet declares, punching me on the arm. "Not even for a second!"

I rub my arm, but I choose not to point out that this isn't quite true.

Besides, I still have a deeper mystery to consider.

Why didn't the Shadowghast like my shadow?

Why am I different?

Sebastian Eels told me once that the mystery of my past is bound up with the deepest secret of Ecrie-on-Sea. Could the Shadowghast's reaction be a sort of proof of that? That there's something eerie about *me*?

"All I know," Caliastra says, interrupting my thoughts, "is that if you hadn't stopped him, Herbie, Eels would have made puppets of everyone in Eerie and sent them down into the Netherways. I dread to think how many would have died down there. You have saved the town."

Violet nods in agreement.

"What about Jenny?" I ask, blushing. "And Mrs. Fossil? They really were sent down there! How are they doing now?"

"The doc says they'll be fine," Violet replies. "They need to rest, that's all. But Jenny is itching to tidy her bookshelves, and when I checked on Mrs. Fossil on the way here, she was fussing over her broken hurdy-gurdy and worrying about scones. Everyone who was touched by the dark enchantment of the Shadowghast lantern seems already to be seeing the whole episode as nothing more than a fading dream."

"It's amazing," the magician declares then, shaking her head. "I have spent all my life pursuing magic, from royal palaces to capital cities, and I had to come to this tiny town on the edge of nowhere to find the real thing."

I say nothing. I can tell that Caliastra is about to leave forever. And I know that part of me, despite everything, still doesn't want her to. Not, perhaps, because of who she really is. More because of who she might have been—and the aching hole in my life this represents.

I feel my eyes prickle as I restraighten my fork.

CHAPTER 47

A SURPRISING OFFER

W hen's this breakfast going to start, then?" I demand to know. My stomach backs me up with a deep gurgle you could probably hear up on the sixth floor.

"As soon as our last guest arrives," Caliastra says with a grin. "I promise."

Then she adds, as we hear a distant *PING!* from out in the hotel lobby, "Ah! Unless I am mistaken, this is her arriving now."

And through the dining room door trundles Lady Kraken, whirring along in her bronze-and-wicker wheelchair, accompanied by Mr. Mollusc.

"Good morning!" the lady cackles, her turtle head bobbing from side to side. She is dressed in a fabulously swirling silk housecoat, and her hair—what's left of it—is wrapped in a soggy towel held together by a vicious-looking hat pin. "I hope you don't mind my state of undress. I had a night of weird dreams and strange notions and find I can't quite be bothered this morning. Can't quite be bothered at all."

"Good morning, Lady Kraken." Caliastra gets briefly to her feet. "We understand. Please join us. There is one thing left to discuss before I leave town."

"Ah, yes." Lady Kraken narrows her eyes at me and cracks her knuckles. "The business of the boy."

I gulp. Lady K parks herself at the head of the table, while Mr. Mollusc beams at me with wicked delight.

"It may be," Lady K launches straight into it, turning on Caliastra, "that after you came up to my rooms the other night to demonstrate your curious magical lantern, I gave you the impression that I was happy to let Herbert Lemon go. But, it turns out, this morning I am not so certain. That is to say, I am *not* inclined to give up my Lost-and-Founder. Not without much firmer proof of your connection than you have shown me so far, Mrs. Magician. And that, I suspect, is my final word on the matter. Dunderbrains don't grow on trees, you know!"

"What?" cries the Mollusc as he shakes out a napkin for Her Ladyship. "I thought the little so-and-so . . . I mean, I understood the boy was leaving us. I was *told* that Lemon was going . . ."

"Stop flapping and give me that!" Lady Kraken seizes the napkin. "That is what we are here to discuss . . ."

"Lady Kraken," says Caliastra decisively, "I withdraw my claim on Herbie. I withdraw it entirely. I . . . I was the victim of a . . . a trick. One might almost say a *magic* trick. I am not Herbie's family, and I'm sorry I ever said I was. I have no rights over him whatsoever."

"Indeed!" Lady Kraken fixes the magician with a yellow eye of annoyance. "Then we really do have nothing further to discuss."

"Except," Caliastra adds, nervously straightening her own napkin. "Lady Kraken, in place of the claim, I would like instead to make an offer. To Herbie." Then she turns to me to add, "And I would like him to consider it very carefully."

"Oh?" Lady Kraken's mouth curls up as if she has just chewed a wasp dipped in lemon juice. "What sort of . . . *offer?*"

"Herbie," Caliastra says, placing her hand on mine, "even though I have no claim over you, and have no right to ask anything, I would like to offer you something that, maybe, you have always wanted."

"Um . . ." I manage to say, my eyes goggling out of my head. "Really?"

Caliastra nods, as if reassuring herself.

"I would like to offer you that new life after all . . . I mean, that place at my side . . . I *mean*, the position of magician's assistant. What I'm trying to say is . . . Herbert Lemon, I would like to offer you a home."

And I can say nothing. It's all I can do to push my cap up out of my eyes so that I can stare in disbelief at the woman with the raven hair as she hits me with her most dazzling smile, full beam.

"Somehow," she explains, "despite the fog and uncertainty of the last few days, I have noticed your resourcefulness, your loyalty, and your amazing spirit. I'm not surprised to hear you are the greatest Lost-and-Founder the Grand Nautilus Hotel has ever had. If I ever *did* have a nephew, or . . . or a son, I would wish him to be just like you."

I blink in reply. It's the best I can do right now.

"Of course, I know it wouldn't be a home like most people have," Caliastra continues. "We would travel much of the year. But I can promise you constant adventure, applause, and acclaim wherever we go, and a glamorous life of luxury, bright lights, and illusion. And one day, once I have taught you everything I know, you would—as my son and heir—take over from me and—I have not the *slightest* doubt—become one of the greatest magicians of the age."

"Well!" declares Lady Kraken into the stunned silence that follows. "This is quite a turnabout, isn't it? Looks like you've got it made, boy. If, that is, you want it made. Hmm?"

She turns her wrinkled face to me, waiting for my answer.

And me? Well, I have to pick my jaw up off my plate, don't I? Because, *what*?

And yet, isn't this exactly what I've always wanted, deep down? Even though I love my Lost-and-Foundery, and my life here in Eerie-on-Sea. To find a real home? The chance to be part of a real family, however strange, and not just be a shipwrecked boy adopted by a town.

The chance to be someone's *son*?

I look down at the scuffed brass buttons and royal porpoise blue of my uniform. Visions of two possible futures swirl around in my head—one of riches and fame and applause, the other of lost property and a hotel basement.

Is it really down to me to decide which one will become real?

I look at Violet.

She's staring at me from inside her hair with eyes like headlamps. From her lap, Erwin is staring, too.

Then, quite suddenly, I find that the answer I've been looking for these last few days is already there, in a quiet corner of my mind, where it has waited all along for me to find it.

And that answer is quite simple: one of these futures is real *already*.

"Thank you," I say, giving Caliastra's hand a Herbie squeeze. "That is a truly, *truly* magical offer, and I will never forget it. But I can't leave Eerie-on-Sea, not when I have people here who need me, and mysteries still to solve, and a best friend I've made promises to, *and* huge hotel breakfasts to eat, though what's taking so long I don't know. I'm sorry, but my future is here."

Caliastra looks at me.

Then she smiles.

It's a different, sadder smile than before, but a smile nonetheless.

"You don't need to say sorry, Herbie," she says. "Something tells me you will be amazing at whatever you do in life. Eerie-on-Sea is lucky to have you. And now, I think, it really is time for that breakfast."

"Finally!" Lady Kraken declares. Then she turns to Mr. Mollusc. "Bring my egg, Godfrey. And kippers! Bring me kippers! This is a day to celebrate."

Mr. Godfrey Mollusc, blinking in shocked disbelief, doesn't seem to have heard the order.

"You're not going?" he says to me. "But . . . the riches! . . . And the being famous!"

"Herbie's already famous," says Violet. "After all, he was the star of this year's Ghastly Night show."

"We both were," I correct her. Then, winking at Mr. Mollusc, I add, "The only riches we need is the gold of freshly baked croissants, thank you very much. And lots of them."

And I hold my and Violet's plates out.

Somehow I manage to keep a straight face as Mr. Mollusc has no choice but to load up our plates with flaky, still-a-bit-warm, scrumptiously buttery pastries.

And that seems a good place to leave things for now. Because *happy* and *ending* are surely the two words that go together best of all.

ABOUT THE AUTHOR

THOMAS TAYLOR is an award-winning author-illustrator for children. His work includes picture books, graphic novels, and the previous novels in this series, *Malamander* and *Gargantis*. He lives with his family on the south coast of England, where he can often be found combing the beach for ancient or lost things.